THE WAY TO THE SEA

•

VICTORIA CONNELLY

Cover design by Design for Writers
Author photo © Roy Connelly

ISBN: 978-1-910522-21-9
Published by Cuthland Press.

To Chris Moore and Tracey Barclay with love and thanks

CHAPTER ONE

The seventh stair had a terrible squeak. Catherine had been aware of it for some time, but never more so than on the night she was going to leave her husband. She'd prepared everything meticulously. Bags were packed. Her car's petrol tank was full. All she had to do was the actual leaving.

She'd spent most of the night lying awake, listening for his snores to deepen, telling her that it was safe to move. It was something she'd learned over the years and she could tell he was soundly asleep now. She got out of bed, dressing quickly in the clothes she'd laid neatly in the bottom of the wardrobe. Then she tiptoed into the room next door where a small bedside lamp glowed warmly.

'Elizabeth?' she called gently, inching forwards, before sitting on the edge of the bed, her weight stirring its occupant whose large blue eyes opened. 'It's time,' Catherine told her and Elizabeth nodded, covering her mouth as she yawned and pushed the duvet away from herself.

'Remember what I said and dress quickly now,' Catherine said. 'We need to leave right away.'

She watched as her daughter pulled on the clothes which Catherine had left ready on the chest of drawers. Catherine then grabbed a brush from the dressing table and quickly tied her daughter's hair into a ponytail.

'Not too tight?' she asked.

Elizabeth shook her head.

'Okay, grab your things.'

Elizabeth opened her wardrobe and pulled out a small yellow suitcase.

'You're sure that's all because we can't come back for anything?' Catherine asked.

The girl nodded and they left the bedroom together, leaving the lamp switched on so as not to arouse suspicion if a certain somebody happened to get up before morning.

They reached the top of the stairs and Catherine looked down at her daughter before flashing her fingers open. Five and then two to make seven.

Elizabeth nodded in understanding and went down the stairs first, Catherine following behind. One, two, three, four, five, six...

Elizabeth's tiny feet skirted the squeak on the seventh stair and Catherine followed, her larger feet stepping over it in the half-light from the hall lamp she'd left on.

As they passed the open kitchen door, Elizabeth looked inside and Catherine read her mind.

'We'll have some breakfast later,' she whispered, thinking that she'd like to get at least a hundred miles away before they treated themselves to their first meal of the day.

They passed the living room next and its door stood slightly ajar. For a moment, Catherine was tempted to take one last look around because, although she held very little love for the house that had become her prison, there were still little pieces of her trapped within its walls like the purple velvet armchair she'd saved up for and bought secondhand. There was a part of her that wished she could take it, but she quickly reminded herself that it smelt as if it had been dipped in whisky and there were still tiny fragments of broken glass lying in wait for an unsuspecting sitter. Then there was the small shelf full of her books collected over the years. She loved them dearly, but they were heavy and burdensome and she'd been determined to travel light into the future. And that future began by getting through the front door. She'd placed her own two small suitcases in her car earlier that day, thinking it best to avoid anything that might slow them down when leaving the house.

Catherine smiled at Elizabeth now that the moment had actually arrived, but a look of pure terror filled her daughter's face.

'What is it?'

Elizabeth glanced up the stairs and Catherine frowned. 'Have you forgotten something?'

Elizabeth nodded.

'Is it important?'

Again the little girl nodded and Catherine realised what it was: Jemima the ragdoll. At eight years old, Elizabeth still loved a soft toy and this rag doll was particularly precious to her.

'Hurry!' she whispered to Elizabeth, watching as the little girl retraced her way back to her bedroom.

Those few moments on her own by the front door made Catherine realise how nervous she was. Her mouth was quite dry and she could feel her heart hammering.

'It's going to be all right,' she told herself. 'You're nearly there.'

Only she wasn't. She was still here with her daughter upstairs and the front door holding her prisoner. What was taking her so long? Catherine walked to the bottom of the stairs, seeing her daughter emerging from the half-light. Quickly,

Catherine flashed her fingers at her daughter. Five and then two to make seven. Elizabeth nodded and made her way downstairs, Jemima tucked under her right arm as she clutched the banister rail with her left hand.

Squeak!

The stair creaked underneath the girl's weight, causing her to freeze half-way down. Catherine's mouth dropped open. Her daughter was trapped on the seventh stair. What had happened? Had she miscounted? A horrible silence filled the house and, in that moment, Catherine heard a noise from the main bedroom. She swallowed hard, staring up at her daughter. She couldn't tell what the noise was. Perhaps her husband had stirred in his sleep, flinging out an arm and knocking his bedside table. That sometimes happened. Yes. Please let it be that, she prayed.

They waited a moment longer and then she stretched an arm out towards Elizabeth and beckoned her to move. As the girl lifted her weight from the step, it let out a dreadful moan-groan which caused her to gasp.

'Come on!' Catherine said, holding out her arms towards her as she made it safely to the hallway. Glancing up into the dark chasm, Catherine turned quickly towards the front door, unlocking it before picking up her daughter's suitcase. If they didn't have everything they needed, they'd simply have to buy it.

She opened the door and ushered Elizabeth ahead of her into the cold night before following herself, closing the door as quietly as she could. She reached into her pocket for her keys, cursing the beep and the flash of lights as she unlocked the car. But that couldn't be helped.

Elizabeth knew exactly what to do – opening the back door to put her suitcase inside before getting in herself and doing up her seatbelt, hugging Jemima close to her. Catherine got in and, a moment later, she pulled out into the quiet suburban road. There was nobody else around, but that wasn't surprising at three in the morning. A lone cat crossing the road just ahead of them was the only sign of life. Nobody had seen her leave and for that she was truly grateful.

Leaving the suburbs, the countryside opened up and she pressed harder on the accelerator, driving across the vast expanse of the Cambridgeshire Fenlands. It was eerie at the best of times, but was even more so cloaked in mist in the middle of the night. Catherine wasn't sorry to leave the bleak landscape behind. She'd never had any love for it. The flatness and the bitter winds that came in from the North Sea had always made her soul shiver as well as her body. She was looking forward to living somewhere else.

When she'd finally made the decision to leave, a part of her had rejoiced at the choices that lay ahead of her. She could go anywhere. Well, anywhere she could find work and anywhere she deemed far enough away from him. It had been an old school friend who'd helped her out and suggested Dorset. When Catherine had reached out to Allie and told her friend that she needed to escape, Allie had got to work right away, seeking out local employment and coming up with something very interesting indeed.

Although I'm not sure you'll like it, Allie had texted her just a few weeks ago.

Why not? Catherine had texted back.

The owner. He's a bit odd.

How do you mean?

He's known locally as Mr Fossil because he's obsessed with them and his house is stuffed full of them. Apparently, there's a dinosaur in his bedroom!

Catherine had laughed at that. To her, it sounded delightful and she was in no position to be choosy.

I can deal with odd, she texted back. *Just not cruel.*

Understood, Allie had texted back.

When Allie had told her that the job came with accommodation, Catherine hadn't needed to know anything else. It was such a relief to have somewhere to go. Now, however, she feared that Dorset wasn't far away enough. Four hours. You could leave in the morning and be there in time for lunch. Was that too close? Was she making it too easy to be found? Perhaps she should have gone further west into Cornwall or deepest Wales, or headed north to Scotland. Orkney, maybe, or Shetland – somewhere you had to catch a boat to or get on a plane to reach. Suddenly, Dorset seemed very tame and accessible. But it was too late to pull out now. She'd written to Mr Charles Thorner and had accepted the position of housekeeper and administrative assistant.

She thought about her new role as she drove. She hadn't had a job for so long. Not since Elizabeth had been born. Her husband had insisted she'd be a stay-at-home mother and she'd welcomed the role at first. Of course, it had meant that money had always been tight, but the time spent with her daughter had been such a joy. But she had lost almost a decade of experience in the workplace, having given up her job as administrator at a local solicitors. Luckily, Mr Thorner of Dorset didn't seem to be worried about the gap on her CV. Perhaps she'd been his only applicant and he needed her as much as she needed the job. But it was a job she knew she could do. After all, she'd worked in administration before and been good at it, and hadn't she spent the last decade keeping house? Her husband had made sure that her standards had always been the highest. And, if she'd ever let them slip, she'd been given just enough bruises to remind her never to let it happen again.

Self-consciously, she pulled down her left sleeve where the latest circle of bruises enclosed her thin wrist in a blue and purple bracelet. Elizabeth hadn't noticed those ones yet. Her eyes were so horribly observant and they had seen far too much for her young age. It had been one of the many reasons Catherine had known she had to leave. She couldn't put Elizabeth through any more trauma.

After a couple of hours, they stopped at a service station where they had something warm to eat and drink. Catherine was amazed by how busy the place was so early in the morning. All these people travelling to different places. Maybe they were escaping too, she thought. Maybe they were heading to new lives. But what were they escaping from? Would they be missed? Catherine had no family and there wasn't anyone else to miss her. He had made sure of that. When she'd left her job, she'd essentially been cut off from the outside world. She knew now that that was the real reason he'd told her to give up her position. It had given him more control of her, hadn't it? The only friends she'd had had been at work. She knew a few of her neighbours, but not very well. And she'd once joined a yoga class, but he'd told her that it wasn't a very good idea. She could do that at home and save the money, couldn't she?

He'd made sure that she wasn't in touch with people on social media either, telling her to cancel her accounts. What did she need them for, anyway? Weren't they enough as a family unit? Why did she need anyone else?

When he'd taken her mobile away from her, she'd felt utterly helpless and she'd protested, telling him he couldn't do that to her. He'd told her otherwise. With his fists. She'd not dared to confront him again after that, but she had managed to defy him. She'd waited patiently for the right time. He'd been away overnight at a conference and she'd gone into town where she'd bought the cheapest of phones. She wasn't the most technically minded, but the young man in the store had guided her through it and she'd managed to log on to her Facebook account, getting in touch with her old school friend and asking her for help. And that was why she was sitting in the service station in the early hours of a Tuesday morning.

She closed her eyes, suddenly feeling very tired despite the large coffee she'd drunk. It was strange to be sitting here. Nobody knew she was there. Nobody would miss her now that she was gone. Would any of the neighbours even notice? She didn't think so. The only person in the world who truly cared about her was the little soul sitting opposite her now. And Allie. Catherine might not have been in touch with Allie for years, but she'd proved her true worth.

Catherine smiled as she thought of her friend. She was excited to see her again. Excited, but nervous too. School friendships were tricky things. What bound you together as teenagers might not last into adulthood. After all, it had been fourteen years since their sixth form days together. But she couldn't worry about that now.

'Are you ready to go?' Catherine asked her daughter. Elizabeth nodded, quickly finishing her drink and then the two of them returned to their car.

It was a little after eight in the morning when they reached Dorset, crossing the border from Hampshire and following the road that stretched across the county, hugging the coastline. It had been rather magical to drive through the night, watching as daylight had greeted them and revealed their new world. Dorset, she soon realised, was a hilly place and, every now and then, tantalising glimpses of the sea could be seen between the hills.

'Look!' Catherine cried as they rounded a bend and saw a wide expanse of blue. 'Isn't it exciting to see the sea?' She looked in the rear-view mirror. Elizabeth was staring wide-eyed out of the window, clutching Jemima to her chest. She wondered what was going through her daughter's mind.

'We can go paddling when the weather's good. Won't that be fun?' Catherine continued. Finally, Elizabeth nodded. 'And we can search for seashells and fossils and all sorts of treasures. Allie says it's one of the best places in the country to find fossils.'

Elizabeth gazed out at the new landscape and Catherine focused on the road until they reached a town called Bridport which she'd made a mental note to remember because there was a turn coming up after the town that she didn't want to miss.

'Elizabeth?' she began, thinking now would be a good time to run an idea she'd had by her daughter. 'I've been thinking – this new start of ours is a bit special, isn't it? I think we need to celebrate it.'

Elizabeth looked at her in wonder.

'How about we change our names? Just slightly so we don't forget who we really are. What do you think? Wouldn't that be fun?'

Her daughter frowned.

'You know we have names that lend themselves well to change,' Catherine went on undeterred. 'Did you know that Catherine can be shortened to Cathy or Cath or Kitty? Or even Cate? What do you think? Do you like any of those?'

Elizabeth nodded.

'Which one?' Catherine asked, watching as Elizabeth got her notebook and pencil out of her pocket and wrote something down. A moment later, she held it up and Catherine glanced in the mirror.

'Oh, I'm so glad that's the one you like,' Catherine said, 'because that's my favourite too. So, Cate it is, then. Now, how about you? Let's think what you could be. There are even more choices with your name. There's Ellie and Eliza, Beth, Betty and Betsy. What do you think? Do you like any of those?'

She watched as her daughter's face furrowed in thought and

she saw her writing each of the names down in her notebook, her pencil hovering over each of them in turn as it was given its fair chance. Finally, she circled one and held it up.

'Eliza? Really? I thought you'd like Beth.'

Elizabeth shook her head.

'No? Okay, so we're Cate and Eliza from this moment on. You'll remember now, won't you? They're a link to who we really are, but a change too.'

Eliza nodded and Cate smiled. She'd spent a while wondering whether to change their names completely, but had feared what might happen if Elizabeth were to get lost and not remember her mother's new name.

'I think we should probably have a new last name too, but I can't think of one I like. I don't want to use our old one. What do you think?' Cate asked as she slowed to turn right. They drove past a church that seemed to glow gold in the early morning light and a row of thatched cottages greeted them.

She slowed the car down as they drove over a wide stone bridge which crossed a beautiful river and Eliza's eyes doubled in size as she pointed to it.

'What?' Cate asked.

Eliza continued to point only behind them now as they'd crossed the bridge.

'Bridge? You think we should be called Bridge?'

Eliza shook her head and did a wiggly motion with her hands.

'Ah, river?'

Eliza smiled and nodded.

'Cate River. Eliza River. Hmmmm, *Rivers* sounds better, I think. Cate Rivers. Eliza Rivers. How about that? Do you like it?'

Eliza was smiling and Cate laughed, looking back at the bridge and the river in the rear-view mirror which now seemed like a portal into their new lives. She sighed in contentment. Now that she was safely here in Dorset, she could feel some of the tension that had been holding her body prisoner slipping away and, although a little voice was telling her that it was much too soon to relax, she couldn't help allowing herself the pleasure of a smile.

This was good, she thought. They'd done it. They'd escaped.

CHAPTER TWO

'I suppose we'd better take a look at the directions again,' Cate said as she pulled up on the side of the road by an old gate that was sagging and covered in moss. She reached for her handbag and took out the instructions she'd been sent by Mr Thorner and which she'd managed to keep hidden inside a packet of pocket-sized tissues.

Hollow House, Church Lane, Winscombe.

Well, she'd just entered the village of Winscombe and had passed the church so she must be getting close.

Hollow House, she read again. It wasn't the most welcoming of addresses, she thought, but she was in no position to be picky. She had been offered a job and living quarters and that was good enough for her. The only trouble was finding the place as it didn't have a number. Mr Thorner had sent her brief directions which she looked at again.

Pass the church on your right and continue down the lane to the first bend. Cross the river.

Well, they'd done that, she thought.

Then turn up the drive on the right after the big field but

*before the lane ends at a farm. Do <u>not</u> drive any further down the
lane or your car will get stuck.*

She put the note down and drove on until she realised she'd
missed the drive. But curiosity got the better of her and she
didn't stop, instead heading to where the lane ended and a very
muddy track began.

'Ah!' she said as her wheels were instantly engulfed. She
hadn't expected it to happen so quickly, but it had obviously
rained the night before and the track was a river of squelchy
mud. Trying not to panic, she put the car into reverse and
attempted to move backwards slowly, only nothing happened.
She applied a little more pressure to the accelerator, hearing her
wheels spinning.

She turned the engine off and sat for a moment.

'I think we're stuck,' she told Eliza before opening her car
door and getting out. Instantly, her trainers were engulfed in
thick brown Dorset mud. She groaned. Great. That's all she
needed.

It was then that she heard a voice and turned to see an
elderly man approaching. He was short and stocky and was
dressed head to foot in green, with large wellington boots and a
cap. Unlike her, he was dressed for the environment.

'You don't want to drive down here,' he said, lifting his cap
and scratching his head.

'Yes, I've kind of worked that out for myself now,' Cate said
with a hopeless smile.

'Where are you going?'

'Well, I'm trying to reverse.'

'Not doing very well, are you?'

'No,' she said.

He shook his head and gave a chuckle. 'Cars come down
here when they shouldn't. It's not made for cars, see.'

Cate chewed her lower lip, suddenly feeling very stupid. What on earth had she been thinking?

It was then that two big burly men came out from a barn.

'Ah!' the old man said and waved them towards him in a gesture that indicated they were about to give Cate a helping hand. She quickly got back in the car and, with the help of the men who gave her a friendly push, the car was freed.

'Thank you!' Cate waved a hand out of the window, but the three men were walking away. They'd seen it all before, she thought, feeling mortified that the first impression she'd made on her new community had been such a ridiculous one.

Cate found her way back to the drive she should have taken in the first place. She glanced down at herself. She probably already looked pale and exhausted from driving through the night, but now she was covered in mud too. The drive was lined with tall oak trees, dressed in their autumn amber. It was very beautiful and she smiled as they got their first sighting of the property.

She wasn't sure what kind of place she'd been expecting, but it hadn't been this. It was a large house and, with its Gothic windows and tall pointed gables, it looked more like a church than a home. She guessed it to be Victorian and could see that it was built of brick and flint and had a large vine scrambling across its façade which was really in need of some drastic pruning.

Suddenly, she couldn't help feeling a little overwhelmed that she'd agreed to take care of such a place. It was so much bigger than their little terraced home. Could she really do it alongside the administrative work she'd said she could handle as well as her commitment to home schooling Eliza?

'What do you think?' she asked, looking at Eliza in the back. Her daughter's eyes were large and Cate couldn't tell if it was from fear or amazement. 'Shall we get out and take a closer look?'

Cate checked her watch. It was only half past eight and she hoped it wasn't too early. There hadn't really been a formal arrangement about what time she'd arrive. Mr Thorner had simply told her that he could well be out and she would find a key to the front door underneath a large concrete ammonite to the left of the porch. Cate had had to look up what an ammonite was and had found a few photographs online of stony snail-like creatures from prehistoric times. They were, she read, one of the most common fossils to be found on the Jurassic Coast and she was looking forward to searching for them with Eliza. But, first, she had to search for the one by the porch.

It didn't take long to find the glorious beast cast in concrete and, lifting it up, she retrieved the front door key along with a handwritten note.

Low tide. Out now. Make yourself at home. CT.

She went back to the car.

'Want to see inside?' she said to Eliza who nodded eagerly. 'Let's take our things in, shall we?'

They grabbed their suitcases and made their way to the large front door which had a panel of stained glass at its centre in glorious reds, blues and greens. Cate took a moment to appreciate it, thinking of the shabby front door she'd left behind in Cambridgeshire. This, she hoped, was a new beginning: a door into their future. She unlocked it and they both stepped inside, dropping their suitcases and marvelling at the large hallway that greeted them. The floor was made of terracotta tiles and the ceiling seemed so high above them with its large lantern-style light hung from an ornate plaster rose. It was all very grand and rather foreboding.

Cate led the way, venturing through a door on the left which was ajar. It was a dining room with a long dark wooden table at its centre, but it didn't seem as if it was ever used for eating as it was covered in boxes. She inched forwards, Eliza following behind her, and peered inside the boxes. Each one contained a fossil – some large, some small, but all of them fascinating. She recognised the ammonites, but she wasn't sure what the others were – some looked like plants from another planet and others were strange elongated beasts or fishlike creatures. Looking up, she noticed that the walls were lined with cabinets stuffed full of fossils.

'It's like a museum,' she said, marvelling at the contents. 'No wonder he's known as Mr Fossil.'

Eliza nodded, peering closely.

Cate wasn't sure how much time the two of them spent gazing into those curious cabinets but, finally, they left the room, walking across the hallway to the one opposite. This was the living room and Cate saw a large yellow squashy sofa and two big armchairs positioned around a beautiful fireplace. There was a basket full of logs to the right and a stack of newspapers and kindling to the left. And a massive ammonite. Cate bent to touch it, her fingers marvelling at the ancient ridges. This, she thought, was definitely not made of concrete like the one outside. This creature was the real thing.

She looked around the rest of the room, noting the sash window which looked out onto the garden and the rows of dusty books on dusty shelves which lined most of the room.

'I can see why he needs a cleaner,' she told Eliza. 'This place is a mess!'

Eliza reached out a hand and used a single finger to draw a line through the dust on one of the shelves. She pulled a face and blew on her grey finger. She then pointed to something.

'It's a cat bed!' Cate declared. 'Or a small dog's bed. What do you think?'

Eliza looked around the room again as if the bed's owner

might materialise at any moment and Cate watched as she bent down to pick up a rather sodden cuddly toy that might have once been a teddy bear, but was now missing a leg and both ears.

'There must be a dog here,' Cate said and Eliza beamed a smile. She'd always wanted a pet. Every child should have one, Cate believed but, like everything else, *he'd* put a stop to it.

They left the room, slowly moving through the rest of the house. Each room seemed even more crowded and dustier than the one before but one thing they all had in common was that there were fossils in each of them. Cate couldn't help smiling when she saw that there was even some kind of Jurassic creature trying to crawl out of its rock on the kitchen dresser, and she wasn't a bit surprised to find a large dinosaur head next to a small television in a snug at the back of the house. Fossils, she realised, took precedence in this house.

They ventured upstairs where they found one large bedroom which Cate guessed to be the master. It was a double-aspect room and had a large, unmade bed at its centre. Tottering piles of books stood on the floor at intervals and there were also, of course, shelves filled with fossils. But no dinosaur, she was relieved to discover. That must have just been a rumour her friend Allie had heard.

Along the landing, they discovered a smaller room with flocked wallpaper and a pretty double bed with pink and white bedding. A small en suite had Cate guessing that this was to be hers. Or theirs. She hadn't told Mr Thorner about Eliza yet and couldn't assume that there was a separate room for her daughter.

'We'll bring the cases up here,' she said, leaving the room. It was then that she spotted another door further along the landing. She walked towards it, noting the peeling wallpaper along the way. But when she reached the door, she discovered that it was locked. There'd been one room downstairs which had been locked too. An office, perhaps.

They were just going downstairs when Cate heard a car. Making her way to the nearest window, she saw a green Land Rover bumping up the driveway towards the house.

'Eliza – why don't you wait in the living room for a moment while I introduce myself to Mr Thorner?'

She watched as her daughter made herself scarce and then Cate ran her hands through her hair and opened the front door, watching anxiously as the driver of the Land Rover got out. Her first impression was not a good one. Like his house, Cate couldn't help thinking that Charles Thorner looked a little run-down and in need of attention when it came to his overall appearance. He was tall and his dark hair was wavy and a little bit too long, his beard a little bit too unkempt and his clothes were frayed at the edges, the pockets of his trousers were torn and his green jacket was streaked with grey mud. He was also wearing a frown which, judging by the deeply etched forehead, might well be a permanent fixture.

Cate swallowed hard. There was no turning back now. She was going to have to get along with this man.

'Mr Thorner?' she said as she crossed the driveway towards him, her voice managing to sound bright and cheerful in spite of her nerves.

'Yes. Are you my new–'

'Cate Rivers.'

His frown deepened. '*Rivers*? Not Pol–'

'I don't use that name anymore,' she interrupted him quickly. Even hearing the name was painful to her now.

Mr Thorner nodded and extended a hand towards her. Like his jacket, it was streaked grey.

'Charles Thorner,' he said.

'It's good to meet you.'

'Your journey wasn't too arduous, I hope?'

'Not at all. Just a little tiring.'

'And you've made yourself at home? You've found your room?'

'With the pink and white bedding?'

'That's the one.'

'It's lovely.'

He nodded and then turned back to his car. She stood for a moment, waiting for him to say something else, but he didn't. Instead, he opened the back of the Land Rover and a little chestnut and white terrier hopped out and ran over to Cate, barking loudly.

'Don't mind Rigs. He just likes to be heard,' Charles said.

Cate bent down towards the animal and his barks quickly stopped. He gave her proffered hand a quick sniff and instantly rolled on his back. Cate smiled and gave his furry belly a rub.

As she stood back up, Rigs righted himself and wandered off.

'Can I help with anything?' Cate asked, turning her attention back to Charles who was still fiddling in the back of the Land Rover.

'No!'

Cate blinked. It had been a very definite no and a not too polite one.

A moment later, he removed a massive backpack from the car, in which an assortment of tools were poking out at right angles and wrong angles. She guessed he must have seen her surprise.

'Tools of the trade,' he explained.

She nodded. 'Any good finds today?'

'Just a few little bits and pieces.'

'Do you go out every day?'

'When I can, especially over winter.'

'Why's that?' she asked, genuinely interested.

'The worse the weather, the better for finding fossils. Erosion. Stormy weather causes landslips and the high tides eat away at the land, revealing them.'

He chucked the heavy backpack over his shoulder and walked towards the house. Cate ran ahead and opened the door for him and watched as he dumped his things on the floor. Rigs ran inside, shooting down the hallway towards the kitchen at the back of the house.

'Well,' Cate said, clutching her hands together and suddenly feeling awkward and wondering when it would be best to mention Eliza.'Do you want to interview me or anything?'

'Not really.'

'Okay.'

'Should I?' he asked, suddenly looking concerned. 'I mean, you've told me you can do the job.'

'I can.'

'Good. Because you'd be wasting both our times if you can't.'

They looked at each other and Cate wondered if he was testing her, challenging her with his odd behaviour. Perhaps he was sussing out what she could handle.

She tilted her chin in the air. 'I've already seen plenty of chores to keep me busy.'

'I'm sure you have,' he said. 'I don't pretend to keep a well-run house. But it is organised and I should let you know that I don't like meddling for meddling's sake. So don't be moving things around. I need to know where everything is.'

'Of course.'

They held each other's gaze again but, this time, Cate was feeling more confident. At least she was until Eliza stepped into the hallway.

'Who's this?' Charles asked, his permanent frown had deepened further.

'Come here, darling,' Cate said, putting a protective arm around her daughter and swallowing hard. It would be better to get this little issue sorted out straightaway, she told herself.

'This is my daughter, Eliza. Eliza – this is Charles Thorner – my new boss.'

Charles held a hand up in the air as if to stop her jumping to such a conclusion.

'You said nothing about a child.'

'I know. I was going to–'

'I can't have a child around the place.'

Cate could feel Eliza shrinking up against her and bent to whisper to her. 'Why don't you take a look around the garden while I talk to Mr Thorner?'

Eliza nodded and Cate watched as she quickly left the house. She then turned back to Charles.

'She won't be a nuisance. I promise you.'

'Children are *always* a nuisance. They shout and they shriek and they constantly chatter and ask questions. I can't have that sort of noise when I'm working.'

'She won't make a noise. She's very quiet,' Cate said, beginning to panic now.

'Children are never quiet.'

'*She* is.'

He shook his head. 'You should have told me.'

'I know, I'm sorry.'

'You've tricked me.'

'But she won't be a problem. I can guarantee it.'

'I work from home,' he told her. 'I like peace and quiet.'

There was a dreadful pause when he simply stared at her and then he sighed. 'I'm sorry. This simply isn't going to work.'

Cate watched in horror as he walked towards the door and opened it.

'What are you doing?'

'I'm inviting you to save us both a headache and leave now.'

'But–'

'I have to have quiet here.' He gestured to the door.

Cate could feel her heart hammering not for the first time that day. She had to do something. The thought of having to leave was too awful because she didn't have anywhere to go. She had been pinning all her hopes and dreams on this job and this new start for them. She couldn't let that go now.

'She doesn't speak!' Cate cried, feeling her face flushing hot.

Charles frowned. 'What do you mean?'

'Eliza, my daughter, she doesn't speak.'

Charles looked confused. 'Why not? Was she born that way?'

'No,' Cate said, her mouth suddenly very dry. 'She... something happened.' She stopped and Charles seemed to realise that this was something she wasn't happy to discuss.

'How do you...' he paused, looking awkward, 'communicate with her?'

'We manage very well,' Cate told him. 'She writes down anything important.'

'But school? Surely–'

'I home educate her.'

Again Charles frowned. 'But how will that work here?'

'Don't worry. It won't get in the way of my duties for you.' She watched as he thrust his hands in his pockets and she wished she knew what he was thinking. 'I'm a hard worker,' she continued, 'and Eliza can help too. You won't hear her. She won't disturb you. Neither of us will. You won't know we're here.'

Cate took a deep breath, feeling calmer now. She'd made

her pitch. There was nothing more she could do save for begging.

Charles looked down at his boots as if seeing them for the first time and then looked directly at Cate.

'You've surprised me with this and I'm not sure what to make of it all.' He paused. 'Maybe we could see how we get along for a week.'

'You mean like a probation period?'

'If you like.'

Cate shook her head. 'I don't like.'

'Excuse me?'

'Well, a week – it's barely worth my petrol getting here.'

He looked surprised by her frankness. 'Right. Of course.'

'One month,' she suggested, sounding far more confident than she felt. 'If you're not happy with us in a month's time, we'll leave. No hard feelings.' She stepped forward, her hand extended. 'And I'd feel happier shaking on it.'

Charles looked a little taken aback, but he reached his grey-streaked hand out and shook hers.

'One month,' he said.

'Good,' Cate said and, with that, she left the house to tell Eliza that they were staying.

CHAPTER THREE

Charles Thorner stood in the centre of his hallway feeling completely dumbfounded. Well, he thought, that's what happened when you hired someone you'd never even met before. He hadn't really given much thought to the reality of having a stranger living in his home. He'd just assumed that they'd be quiet and compliant and – well – not at all like Cate Rivers. And what was that about her name change? She'd been Catherine Pollard when she'd first got in touch and she'd said nothing about a child. It was all so different from how he'd imagined it would be and he couldn't help but fear that trouble was just around the corner. Still he'd given his word that they would try things for a month. Things couldn't get too out of control in that short space of time, could they? Besides, she'd been the only applicant so what choice did he have if he wanted help around the place?

Picking up his backpack, he walked towards a room at the back of the house and reached into his pocket for a key. He would have to give Cate very clear instructions about this room, he thought, because this was the inner sanctum, the centre of his world, the place that came to mind whenever he thought of home.

Unlocking the door now, he entered the large, cold room and placed his bag on the floor. This was his workshop. He remembered the first time he'd seen the room when he'd viewed the house. The light, the space, the fact that it was at the far end of the house. He'd liked that last detail. Working from home could prove a strange experience and Charles had wanted to feel that his work space and his living space were separate entities, and that little length of corridor he walked down every day provided him with the feeling that he was going to work and getting into the mindset needed for it. Not that there was really any division between this room and the rest of the house for there were fossils everywhere, and he found it virtually impossible to switch off from his work because it was his whole life.

Especially now, he thought.

He closed his eyes. The dark images from the past could still halt him and haunt him. But he wasn't going to give in to them today. Instead, he opened his bag and took out the pieces he'd found on the beach that morning. A few small ammonites and a nice piece of crinoid stem. Nothing much, but they could be sold in his online shop.

Nothing much, he thought, checking himself with a smile. He remembered the days as a small boy when such finds would cause as much excitement as if he'd struck gold. That's where it had all begun: with childhood holidays. Buckets and spades. Well, to begin with. The young Charles had soon swapped those for a pair of goggles and a geological hammer. His father had humoured him, thinking that his son's interest would pass, but it had only grown. He'd started buying books about geology and fossils, reading sections out at the breakfast table.

'Isn't this amazing, Dad?' he'd say as he read about how old the universe was believed to be.

His dad had not thought it was amazing. He'd thought it heretical.

Charles had immersed himself in this new prehistoric world. He'd become obsessed by the words he learned. He'd already known of the Jurassic period, made famous because of the dinosaurs that lived during that time, but the fact that there were also periods he'd never heard of with names like Cambrian, Devonian, Ordovician and Silurian fascinated him as did the plants and the creatures that could be found in each one of them.

Charles remembered that period of his life so fondly. Even at that young age, he'd been gathering the knowledge and the tools that he would need in order to do the job he was doing now.

For a few years, Charles and his father had exchanged carefully chosen gifts at Christmas. Charles would buy his father books about evolution and geology and his father would buy Charles books about religion and theology. Each was careful to respect the other's beliefs although Charles's father never encouraged his son in his studies. His mother had been only slightly more indulgent, listening to him as he read from his books and looking at any specimens he found.

He'd studied geography and the sciences at A Level before taking a degree in geology. His father hadn't been happy with his choices and Charles had tried to understand. Perhaps, he'd thought, it was like the child of a scientist becoming a monk. Only at the other extreme, of course.

Being brought up in landlocked Wiltshire was a torture to Charles and he would count down the days to his next trip to the coast, knowing that he would live there one day. It seemed to take an age to happen but, finally, he moved into a small terrace in Lyme Regis. He felt like he'd arrived. He could hardly afford the rent, but he spent every daylight hour out on the beach, ever hopeful of a big find. It didn't come immediately, but he finally uncovered a plesiosaur – one of the most exciting creatures from the Jurassic age to be found on that coastline. Part of its right paddle was missing and Charles invested many hours preparing the impressive remains, but the money he got for it was enough for a deposit on a house.

Hollow House.

The place had come up for sale at auction and was going for a song. The elderly owner had recently died and his children were in a hurry to get it sold and divide the money up. Luckily for Charles, he'd been the only bidder. Or maybe he should have taken that as a sign. Still, he'd loved the old place even though it had been in a dilapidated state when he'd bought it and, truth be told, it didn't look much better now, but he'd poured thousands of pounds into it, repairing the roof, stabilising the walls and updating the heating and wiring. There hadn't been any money left for luxuries like fine furniture. Most of his things had been bought secondhand. But he was proud of the place, feeling a strange kind of kinship with it as he'd slowly restored its rooms.

Then he'd met Sophie and he'd been anxious about showing Hollow House to her, but she'd fallen in love with its quirks just as he had and had happily made a home there with him. And when their son arrived, life seemed complete.

Charles walked further into his workshop now and picked up one of the grey rocks he'd recovered from the beach last week. He had yet to break into it, but it had all the signs of hiding something special. Maybe Cate Rivers was like that too, he thought. Maybe he shouldn't judge her just yet.

He placed the stone carefully on his work table and walked over to the window. He'd seen Cate leave the house and tried to spot her now in the garden but couldn't. Had he been too abrupt with her? He wouldn't be a bit surprised. Abrupt. Suspicious. Even mean, perhaps. It seemed to be his default setting these days.

The truth was, he'd been living alone for too long.

Out in the garden, Cate was looking for Eliza. She was still trembling slightly after her confrontation with Charles Thorner. But she had stood her ground at least. She was proud of herself for doing that. But what else could she have done? She really had no choice. They couldn't turn around and go home. They had no home. And camping out in their car wouldn't be any fun at this time of year. She could, she supposed, get in touch with Allie, but Cate really didn't want to burden her friend when she'd already done such a good deed for her. No, they had to stay. This had to work.

Rounding the house, Cate spotted her daughter.

'There you are!' she cried, gathering Eliza up in her arms and hugging her close. 'I thought I'd lost you.' She took a step back, cupping her face. 'Are you okay?'

Eliza nodded.

'Just been looking around?'

She nodded again and then pointed.

'What is it? Show me.'

Eliza took her mother's hand and led her along a small brick pathway. There were brambles and nettles in this part of the garden, but there had clearly been some kind of formal garden in the not too distant past because Cate saw rose bushes and the tall dead stems of hollyhocks. At some point, it had been loved and well-tended.

Eliza pointed and Cate gasped. The sea! What a wonderful sight it was with the great sweep of lawn leading down towards it. Of course, it was at least a mile away, but how lovely to be able to see it at all.

'How would you like to see this view every day for a while?' Cate asked.

Eliza turned to face her, her blue eyes wide and expectant.

'We're staying,' she added with a smile. 'For at least a month, isn't that good news?'

Eliza frowned and Cate guessed what she was thinking.

'I know. I thought it would be for longer, and it probably will be, but Mr Thorner – Charles – has suggested that we all see if we like living together first. Isn't that a good idea?'

Eliza was still frowning.

'And we can have all sorts of adventures in that time too, can't we? A whole month! We can visit the sea as often as we like and go fossil hunting. Remember we talked about that? Just imagine the treasures we could find!'

Eliza was looking happier now and Cate began to relax a little so they returned to the house. There was no sign of Charles, and Cate didn't particularly want to talk to him again just yet. She'd get settled in the room he'd allocated them. He hadn't offered a room for Eliza and she didn't expect that he would, but that was fine. They would be cosy and safe together, wouldn't they?

Climbing the stairs, they found their way back to their room. It was a bit odd that Charles hadn't formally shown it to them. Indeed, it would have been nice if he'd offered a house tour, but maybe he wasn't the kind. Anyway, it didn't matter as she'd already had a good look around. She glanced at the bedroom.

Like the rest of the rooms in the house, it had a high ceiling and wallpaper that had seen better days. Still, the pattern of pink and yellow flowers on a cream background was pretty and feminine. The large brass bed stood up against the wall and there was a dark wooden wardrobe opposite – the sort you could lose children to another realm inside, she thought with a smile.

Cate opened the wardrobe now and was pleased to see some hangers there. Together, they unpacked their clothes. They didn't have much between them so it didn't take long. There was an old wooden chest of drawers next to the window and they put some bits and pieces in there too. Eliza had a few books and Cate watched with fondness as she placed them neatly on the chest of drawers together with her pencil case. She then walked over to the bed and placed Jemima against the pillows.

Cate didn't have many photographs of her daughter, but there was one she couldn't live without and that was of Eliza just after she'd started school. Her hair had been slightly longer then and worn in plaits. Cate had placed this photo in its frame carefully in her handbag when packing to leave and she took it out now and put it on the small bedside cabinet.

'There,' she said, 'we're at home now, aren't we?'

Eliza nodded.

It was then that something occurred to Cate. As they'd looked around the rooms of Hollow House, she hadn't seen a single photograph. There was absolutely nothing to link Charles Thorner with any other human being in the world. Could that be right? Perhaps one of the locked rooms housed all the pictures. That would be it. Nobody could live without photographs, could they?

Eliza was looking out of the great sash window and Cate joined her there.

'I think we're going to be very happy here, don't you?' Cate said, placing a hand on Eliza's shoulder.

Eliza didn't answer. Not that she would in words at least but, when she turned to face Cate, the soft expression of serenity on her face let Cate know that they'd made the right decision in coming to Hollow House.

CHAPTER FOUR

Allie Kendal had always been fascinated by the sea. Well, maybe not the sea itself, but the treasures it washed up on the beach each day. It had started with day trips as a child with her family. Simple bucket and spade adventures. But, whereas her brother had been happy to make sandcastles, Allie had wanted to fill her little red bucket with pebbles, shells and sea glass. And she had – much to the annoyance of her mother.

'You can't take all of that home!' she'd cried. 'Pick three of your favourite pieces and put the rest back.'

Allie's eyes had filled with tears as her little fingers had sorted through her beloved pieces. Discarding the pretty shells and smooth pebbles had felt like a betrayal.

Even now, she could never just walk along a beach without filling her pockets, but at least she could tell herself that it was an important part of her work these days. Who knew what beautiful jewellery she could create with a little bit of sea glass? Maybe she could turn what the sea had given her into a necklace someone would buy for a loved one – a piece that would be treasured for years to come, worn with pride and love. She adored that.

Allie made most of her jewellery in a workshop which was just a fancy name for a garden shed that had been painted in pastel colours and fitted with a carpet to make it as snug as possible. It was pretty basic and she longed for a larger, slightly more luxurious place in which to work. But she made do. The most important thing was that she had secured a lease on a little shop tucked away in a side street in Lyme Regis. Gifts from the Sea was her pride and joy and, although it didn't get as much footfall as a shop front on the main street of Lyme, the rent was a lot cheaper. And she adored it. Even on the dark and less touristy days of autumn and winter, she took such pride in what she thought of as her little piece of heaven. Not only did she sell her own jewellery there but also the work of other artists. There were so many talented people from painters and potters to weavers and knitters, and her shop was always chock-full of treasures. The only stipulation Allie made was that the pieces had to chime of the sea.

She smiled, tying her dark hair back into a casual ponytail, and then picking up one of the newest additions to her shop family – a collection of felt octopuses. Or was it octopi? She wasn't sure and did it really matter? She had placed the orange creations on the dresser. Well, *in* the dresser really. She'd opened two of the front drawers and they were sitting half in, half out like the naughty neptunes they were. She hoped her customers would love the scene she'd created. She did a little tour around her shop, gazing at the paintings, picking up an item here and rearranging another there, taking pride in every single carefully crafted piece.

It wasn't an easy way to earn a living, she had to admit. A lot of her sales were seasonal and the winter months relied heavily on her website. She'd had to learn about online marketing and had accounts on all the social media sites. She'd become pretty good at photographing her stock in appealing ways, placing a sea glass necklace over a piece of driftwood or taking a newly knitted pair of mittens home so she could photograph them in the cosy atmosphere of her living room. Everything had to be presented beautifully these days. Consumers were used to perfection and you got left behind if you fell short of that. Luckily, Allie loved the challenge and the feedback she got from her pictures was always positive.

It was as she was standing at the big pine table she used as both a home for her till and as a mini workshop that she thought about her friend, Catherine. She should have arrived in Dorset by now. Allie didn't want to intrude with a phone call and trusted that Catherine would reach out to her when she was ready.

Picking up a silver chain she was going to use for her next design, Allie had to admit that there was a part of her that wanted to drive straight over to Hollow House and make sure Catherine was okay. She'd seen the house once when she'd made a delivery to Sophie Thorner. Sophie had ordered several pieces of jewellery as Christmas presents and Allie had taken them up to the house as she lived in the village and it was easier than posting them. She'd never forget that first glimpse of the place. It was a stunning building, but Allie couldn't help feeling that it could easily house a whole village of ghosts. It had that creepy Victorian Gothic look about it. But it was beautiful nevertheless with its arched windows and wisteria scrambling up the front. Still, Allie wouldn't swap it for her cosy cottage in a million years.

It was sad about Sophie, Allie thought. People still talked about her leaving although it was always done in whispers. Allie often thought about her, wondering where she'd gone and if she was okay, and feeling so sad that Sophie had been unable to stay. She'd have to tell Catherine about it all at some point. It was only fair that she knew and she doubted very much if Charles Thorner would tell her anything about it. Poor man. He'd shut himself away in that bleak old house after it had happened. Not that he'd ever been the life and soul of the community, but at least he'd taken part in things before then. She remembered that he used to organise fossil hunting trips for the local school children – taking them down to the beach and showing them what to look for. He was wonderful with the kids and they all adored him which was why what had happened was all the harder to bear.

Allie picked up a piece of emerald-green sea glass and held it up to the light. The green glass wasn't rare, but this was a good size and would make a beautiful focal point for the necklace she had in mind.

As she worked, her mind journeyed back to her school days when she had known Catherine. She'd been one of those friends you always wanted to have around you because of their energy. She was so much fun. Whether it was on the hockey pitch or in the world's most boring maths lesson, Catherine always had a smile on her face and hope in her heart. With her, anything was possible, and that's why it was so hard for Allie to comprehend her friend reaching out to her recently in desperation. She'd always had everything together.

Allie smiled as she remembered one time when they'd been running late for a French lesson. Their teacher, Madame Bresson, was a fearsome brute and was particularly keen on punctuality. Allie was terrified and seriously wondered if they should spend the lesson hiding in the girls' toilets rather than being late, but Catherine took her hand and said, 'Just leave it to me.'

They'd entered the classroom and Madame Bresson, who'd

clearly started the lesson, fixed them with her glassy, unforgiving stare.

'And just *where* have you two been?' she demanded.

Allie was shaking with nerves, feeling like the Cowardly Lion when brought before the Wizard of Oz. But Catherine seemed totally unfazed.

'We had to clear up in the art room,' she said. 'Mr Preston sends his apologies.'

Allie swallowed hard. It wasn't a total lie, she thought. They *had* been asked to tidy up, but only after Allie had clumsily knocked over a pot of red paint, turning the art room into an instant crime scene.

'Oh, he does, does he?' Madame Bresson didn't seem convinced.

'Yes. He said be sure to convey his *sincerest* apologies because he knows how important punctuality is to you and he said how he admired that very much.'

Allie stared at Catherine, thinking she'd gone too far and that Madame Bresson would never believe her, but a strange thing happened and Madame Bresson's stony face slowly broke into a smile. Allie hadn't been able to believe it.

'Sit down, girls,' she'd said and they'd taken their places at the back of the room.

'Always appeal to a person's vanity!' Catherine had whispered.

Allie remembered that with affection. Dear Catherine had always taken care of her, which was why Allie had been so pleased to be able to help her friend when she'd got in touch. Catherine the Great, she'd nicknamed her. Only, when she'd got those texts from Catherine a few weeks ago, she hadn't sounded so in control of her life as she'd used to be.

Allie continued to work on her necklace. A couple of customers came in around mid-morning and one of her favourite artists dropped off a few new oil paintings of Lyme Bay.

It was after lunchtime when she received a text from Catherine.

Okay if I pop over?

Please do! Allie texted back. *I'm in the shop all day.*

Allie texted the address.

See you later, Catherine replied.

Suddenly, Allie felt nervous which was very silly really because this was her dear old friend. Still, she couldn't help wondering how much she'd changed in the years since she'd last seen her and, indeed, if Catherine would find she had changed too. Maybe they'd have nothing in common anymore except the fact that they were now both living in Dorset after spending their formative years in Cambridgeshire. Maybe they'd have to start from scratch or maybe they'd decide that their friendship was a thing of the past.

It was hard to concentrate now and Allie found herself constantly looking out of the window for her friend's arrival. At one point, a woman with long blonde hair stopped to look in the shop and Allie caught her breath, wondering if it was Catherine, but the woman moved on.

It was around three in the afternoon when the shop door opened and Catherine walked in. She was holding the hand of a young girl and Allie sprang to her feet, rushing across to hug her.

'Catherine!' she cried. 'It's been *such* a long time!'

'Allie!' Catherine hugged her back

'Oh, my god! How are you? And this must be your daughter!' Allie looked at the pretty young girl who was the spitting image of her mother.

'This is Eliza. Eliza – this is Allie, my old school friend I've been telling you about.'

'Pleased to meet you, Eliza,' Allie said, smiling at the girl who gave the very faintest of smiles. 'Gosh, how long has it been?'

'Since we were in secondary school, I guess,' Catherine said.

'No, no.' Allie shook her head. 'Didn't we meet up after that? Wasn't there some get-together for Philippa's eighteenth birthday – remember?'

'Oh, that's right. At the pub where they had all those balloons.'

'You couldn't *move* for balloons!' Allie said, laughing at the memory. 'The whole room was pink and gold. Did you keep in touch?'

'No.'

'With anyone else?'

Catherine shook her head. 'I've only just reconnected with you.'

Allie nodded. 'Social media makes it so easy now. I'm in touch with most of our old friends. I don't see them a lot, but it's nice to hear all the latest gossip and spy on their holiday photos, isn't it?'

'I guess.'

'You're not on any of the platforms anymore, are you?' Allie asked and, when she shook her head again, she added, 'Why not?'

Catherine shrugged and looked a bit vague and it was then that Allie noticed how very pale and gaunt she looked.

'Shall I put the kettle on?'

Catherine smiled. 'That would be lovely.'

A few minutes later, the two of them were sat behind Allie's table, sipping their tea as Eliza looked around the shop, mesmerised by all the pretty things.

'So, how are you settling in at Hollow House?' Allie asked.

'Okay, I guess. We've got everything we need. And there's a dog so Eliza's delighted.'

'And Charles? How are you finding him?'

Catherine sipped her tea before answering. 'He can be a bit...'

'Strange?'

'I was going to say abrupt, but strange is good too,' Catherine said. 'He said I could start work properly tomorrow and that I might want to get settled in first.'

'Well, that's good of him.'

'Yes. It is. And I wanted to come and see you.'

'I've been dying to see you too,' Allie confessed. 'I'm so glad you got in touch.'

'Me too. And I can't thank you enough.'

'You don't have to thank me.'

'But I do. I really do.'

Allie saw a look pass across her friend's face and could only imagine what she'd been through. She only knew the bare bones of the story, but anyone who had to leave their husband in the middle of the night with their young daughter must surely have a good reason. But now wasn't the time to ask questions. Instead, she reached her hand out and squeezed her friend's.

'Catherine, listen – I don't mean to pry but, well, if there's anything you need to talk about – at any time, you know I'm here, don't you? And if there's anything you need. Anything at all.'

Catherine didn't answer at first. Her eyes wore a kind of glazed expression. But then she looked up and smiled. 'Thank you,' she said. 'Actually, there's something I should tell you. I'm called Cate now. Cate Rivers.'

'Cate? Really? That's so cute.'

'It was time for a change, you know?'

Allie nodded, pretending to understand something as drastic as changing your name.

'Remember I used to call you Catherine the Great?'

Cate gave a little smile.

'It'll have to be Cate the Great now, I guess,' Allie said.

'Or Cate the *not* so Great.'

Allie frowned. 'Don't say that! You've always been my idol. You know that, don't you?'

'Well, I don't feel like an idol.'

Allie reached across and squeezed her hand again.

'I'm sorry,' Cate said. 'I'm just in a funny mood. The move and everything.'

'Of course.'

They sipped their tea together and Allie tried her very best not to stare at Cate, but it was strange to have her back in her life after so many years. They had so much to catch up on – if, indeed, Cate was going to confide in her at all. Perhaps she could be the one to make inroads.

'Can you believe my Jack's twelve now?'

'Is he?'

'At secondary school already. He's taller than me too. Not that that takes much doing!' She laughed. 'You'll have to come over some time. Come and have lunch or dinner – both of you. I'd love you to meet him.'

Cate nodded in a vague, non-committal sort of a way.

'How old is Eliza?' Allie continued.

'Eight.'

'She's a lovely girl,' Allie said, watching as Eliza's fingers delved into a small basket of blue beads on the dresser.

Cate nodded. 'You've probably noticed that she's quiet.'

'She's just taking everything in, I expect.'

Cate shook her head. 'No, it's more than that. She doesn't talk.'

'Doesn't talk?'

'No.'

Allie looked across at the young girl again. 'From birth?'

'No. It's...' Cate paused, 'a recent thing.'

'Gosh, Cate – how do you cope?'

'Surprisingly well,' she said. 'It's amazing how quickly you learn to adapt.'

'And do you think she'll ever speak again?'

Cate sighed and it sounded as if months or even years of pent-up emotion came out in that sigh. 'Who can say?'

Allie bit her lip. There was so much she wanted to ask, but she didn't want to scare her friend away especially when she was confessing like this in bits and pieces.

'Okay if I look around the shop?'

'Of course!' Allie said and watched as Cate got up and joined her daughter.

Allie did her best to concentrate on her work, but she kept glancing up to watch Cate instead. It was hard not to. Catherine. Her dear friend. So changed. Would Allie have recognised her in the street, she wondered? She hoped she would, but she really couldn't be sure.

She listened as Cate talked gently to her daughter, pointing out things of interest. It was lovely to watch and Allie was fascinated by how Cate seemed to understand a whole range of facial expressions and tiny gestures that Eliza made. But she couldn't help wondering why the young girl didn't speak if she hadn't been born with the condition. It seemed that it was a psychological disorder rather than a physical one and Allie could only imagine what had caused that. Selective mutism, wasn't that what it was called?

She watched the child, trying to imagine how she would react if her son suddenly stopped talking. Well, he would soon be a teenager so perhaps it would happen naturally. She shook her head, admonishing herself. She shouldn't joke about such things. Cate's poor daughter had suffered goodness only knew what.

'This is beautiful,' Cate said, turning around from a display of jewellery. She was holding an amber pendant which hung on a silver chain, catching the light which set it on fire. 'You're so clever to make such lovely creations.'

Allie smiled. 'I'm so glad you like it. I buy the amber from a supplier. I'm afraid we're not lucky enough to have amber wash up on our coastline here. This is from the Baltic.'

'Well, it's lovely.'

Allie watched as Cate touched the golden pendant, brushing it with gentle fingers.

'Take it,' Allie said.

'Oh, I couldn't!'

'Of course you can! It's my welcome to Dorset gift to you. Take it or I'll be mortally offended!'

'But I should really buy it from you – to thank you for all you've done for me.'

'Rubbish! It was only a few texts.'

'A few texts which could have saved my...' Cate's voice petered out and Allie wondered what she'd been going to say.

'Take the necklace,' Allie told her, getting up and crossing the room towards her. 'Let me help you.' She took the necklace from its stand and lifted Cate's long hair out of the way before she could protest further, and fastened the catch a moment later. 'You know, some people believe that amber has protective qualities and say it absorbs negative energy.'

Cate frowned as she quickly stroked her hair back into place. 'And do you believe that?'

Allie shrugged. 'I believe that it's beautiful to wear.'

Cate smiled at that and placed her right hand over the

pendant. 'I'll treasure it always.' She leaned forward and gave Allie a warm hug. 'Thank you.'

'You're welcome.'

'Well, we'd better think about getting back.'

'Come and see me soon, won't you?'

'We will.'

'I'm in Winscombe and just down the road from you so no excuses!'

Cate waved a hand.

'It was so good to see you again. And to meet you, Eliza.'

Eliza turned and gave the faintest of smiles and Allie watched as they left the shop, Cate taking her daughter's hand as they crossed the road.

Allie sighed, feeling the sudden sting of tears. She hadn't reacted at the time but, as she'd lifted Cate's hair to place the necklace on her, she'd seen a dark ribbon of bruises on her friend's pale skin.

CHAPTER FIVE

Cate was up early the next morning. Today was the start of her new job. And her new life. She took a deep breath. She could do this, she told herself. She'd carefully arranged a timetable that meant she could tutor Eliza from home while organising the housekeeping jobs and the administrative things she had to do for Charles. He hadn't told her much about that side of things yet and she was anxious to know what it would entail.

After washing and dressing, Cate woke Eliza up and got her ready for the day. It was a new life for her daughter too, she had to remember that and, although she'd been home tutored for a little while now, it had never been in tandem with Cate working.

It was going to be strange living in somebody else's house. Simple jobs like making breakfast took extra time as she found her way around the kitchen, working out where the bowls and plates and cutlery were kept, to say nothing of using an Aga for the first time. But Cate was so very grateful to have this place. It might be a little cold and her boss might be a little abrupt, but at least she felt safe here.

Cate was also grateful that Eliza loved to read and could lose herself in a book for a good long time without supervision. That made things a lot easier for Cate as she organised the day ahead. After they'd had breakfast together, they cleared everything away so that Eliza could work at the kitchen table. It was by far the warmest room in the house and she'd be neatly tucked away here while Cate tackled the rest of the downstairs rooms.

'Remember where we were with this book?' Cate said as she laid Eliza's things out for the day ahead.

Eliza nodded.

'Good. I want you to read the next chapter by yourself and then I've marked a page in this maths book, okay?'

Eliza pulled a face and Cate couldn't help but commiserate. She'd hated maths at school too.

'Well, you can't just read stories and draw all day, can you?' Cate told her, knowing of her daughter's love affair with her felt tip pens and crayons.

Eliza grabbed her pencil and wrote something in her notebook, showing her mother a moment later.

'*Why not?*' Cate read out. 'Erm, because you need numbers in life too. Look, just do your best, all right? I'll be in the living room if you need me.'

Eliza nodded and opened her book.

Cate watched her for a moment, hoping that this set-up was going to work and that Charles wouldn't object to it. She'd heard him leaving the house just before they'd got up, making the most of the shorter daylight hours now that it was autumn. Surely he wouldn't begrudge a corner of his kitchen to Eliza? She certainly wouldn't be making a noise and she really wasn't taking up much room.

Feeling happy that Eliza knew what she was doing and could be trusted on her own, Cate set about making a start on the housework. She raided the hallway cupboard, pulling out an ancient vacuum cleaner that didn't look as if it was used much because it was right at the back and everything else seemed to be piled on top of it. Cate carefully excavated it, moving the ironing board and boxes that were stacked in front of it. There was also a mop and bucket and a basket filled with cleaning products that probably hadn't seen the light of day for months if not years. She took a deep breath and pulled them all out. There was no point going into this half-heartedly, she decided.

She was going to start in the living room. After all, that was the room one was meant to feel relaxed in and how could one possibly relax amongst so much filth?

She started with the carpet, moving the sofa and chairs as she went and marvelling at the dust balls she discovered underneath them. It looked as if they hadn't been moved in years. Then, using the pipe attachment, she moved the cushions and seat pads and vacuumed underneath them, coughing as the air filled with dust. Perhaps she should be wearing a mask. And goggles.

Next she moved to the bookcases. In any normal house, bookcases could be dusted, but these shelves were way beyond the ministrations of a duster and so Cate decided to use the pipe again.

That was more like it, she thought a moment later as she sucked up the dust with ease. This was going to make life a lot easier.

At least, that's what she thought until...

'Oh, no!' Cate cried.

Something had been sucked up the tube that probably shouldn't have been and it was now rattling inside the belly of the vacuum. Quickly, Cate switched it off and unplugged it from the wall, getting down on her knees to try and see what had been gobbled up by the hungry machine, but it was no good. She couldn't see anything through the plastic cylinder because it was so full. But she guessed that there was a fossil in there. She wondered how to open the vacuum up, but couldn't work it out.

She sighed. What a great start. How was she going to explain this to Charles? He'd probably fire her on the spot and boot her and Eliza out. She looked around the room in panic. Well, there was plenty more she could be getting on with. Perhaps if she did a good enough job of tidying the room without using the vacuum, he'd be more likely to forgive her. Yes, that's what she'd do. So she got to work. Luckily, she'd already vacuumed the floor and underneath the furniture, but now she took the two rugs outside and, finding a broom, gave them a good beating over the washing line. The dust that came off them turned the air grey and made her cough. This job really should have come with a health warning, she thought. Still, she only had to do this big job once and then it would be simple maintenance to keep it all looking nice.

Once she was satisfied that she'd bashed as much of the dust out of the rugs as a human was capable of bashing, she took them back inside and got to work with the feather duster. Hollow House was one of those homes that seemed to have cobwebs in every corner. Fortunately so far, they hadn't had any encounters of the eight-legged kind because that wouldn't have been met with joy by either Cate or Eliza.

Cobwebs tackled, Cate went to work with the duster. Or rather dusters. She got through a fair few as she moved around the room, but the end result was very satisfying. She'd probably lost a couple of pounds too, she thought with a smile. It really was the very best of workouts.

Putting the cleaning equipment away apart from the vacuum cleaner which needed to be searched for the missing fossil, she went through to the kitchen. Eliza was still sat at the table, her maths book in front of her. She was frowning.

'How are you getting on?' Cate asked, pulling the chair out and sitting down next to her.

Eliza slid her exercise book towards Cate, a deep frown etched across her forehead.

'Ah,' Cate said as she saw the page. Eliza's had written the date and the subject very neatly across the top of her blank page and had written the number one in the margin. And then nothing more. Cate sighed. 'Let's have some lunch, shall we? And we'll tackle the maths together after that.'

Cate made a simple lunch of a cheese and tomato omelette followed by a delicious apple tart she'd bought them when they'd visited Lyme Regis. It was just after they'd cleared their lunch things away that she heard Charles's Land Rover pulling up on the driveway.

'Oh, dear,' she said. 'I have to see Charles about something, sweetie. Are you okay working through your history book for a while? I'll come and check in on you as soon as I've seen Charles and we can go through that maths page together then.'

Eliza nodded and Cate made her way to the living room so as not to pounce on her employer as soon as he entered. She was dreading telling him what had happened, but there was no way around it.

A moment later, the front door opened and she heard Charles's heavy boots on the hallway floor together with the light tap-tap-tap of his dog's feet.

She swallowed hard, giving him a few seconds to catch his breath and then she emerged from the living room to face him.

'Ah, Cate. How are you getting on?'

'I've cleaned the living room,' she told him with a weak attempt at a smile. 'It looks quite inviting now.'

He nodded and made to leave.

'Charles?'

'Yes?'

'I'm afraid I've had a little accident.'

'What sort of an accident?'

'With the vacuum. I seem to have... sucked something up.'

He frowned. He really was very scary when he frowned. 'Sucked up *what* exactly?'

'I'm not sure. It was one of those grey things you have all around the house.'

'A fossil?'

'Yes.'

'You sucked up a fossil?'

'It was an accident. It'll be in the cleaner, but I'm not exactly sure what I'm looking for or how to handle it. I thought I'd better leave it to you.'

Charles's face darkened. He didn't look pleased. 'Show me.'

Cate nodded and led the way into the living room. Rigs followed and jumped up onto the sofa. No wonder it had been so hairy, Cate couldn't help thinking.

She watched as Charles knelt down on the floor next to the vacuum cleaner.

'I'm so sorry,' Cate said.

'You really shouldn't be using this thing around the fossils.'

'Well, I know that now, don't I?'

'Is this how you do housework?'

'No,' she said, feeling annoyed by his condescending tone.

'Are you sure?'

'Of course I'm sure. It's just that this place is...'

'What?' He looked up from the vacuum.

'It's very dusty!'

Charles cleared his throat, suddenly looking embarrassed.

'A feather duster just won't cut it, I'm afraid,' Cate told him. 'You could probably use an archaeologist.'

'Well, I'm sorry I don't have time to keep my house clean. My work comes first.'

'I didn't mean to insinuate anything by that.'

'And yet you managed to do exactly that.'

Cate looked down at the floor, believing she was about to be fired even before she'd completed her first day. But, instead, he got on with the job in hand, wheeling the vacuum into the hallway and taking it apart. Cate winced as he plunged his hands into the interior. It was full of dust, dog hair and cobweb, but Charles didn't seem to mind. After a moment or two, he brought out the small grey ammonite.

'Oh, it's one of those!' Cate said. 'You wouldn't have missed it. You have so many around the place.'

His eyebrows rose a fraction.

'Sorry,' Cate said quickly, realising how rude she must have sounded.

'It's true enough, I suppose,' Charles told her. 'I do have plenty of ammonites, but this one's rather special.'

'Is it? Why?' Cate said, looking at the strange specimen he was holding with such care, but not being able to see why it might be more special than the hundreds of others he had.

'It was one of my first decent finds,' he told her. 'I remember the day I found it. I was about Eliza's age. I'd been on the beach for a good hour or so and finding only bits of broken belemnite. It was a rough day. The weather was pretty lousy and the light was fading and that's when I spotted this.'

Cate looked at it again, trying to imagine the young Charles on the beach all those years ago and his excitement at finding this ancient creature. He walked into the living room and carefully put it back on the newly-dusted shelf, and then he turned to face Cate.

'Listen,' he said, 'this house isn't an ordinary one. It'll take some getting used to, no doubt. But you need to move around it carefully.'

'Yes. I will,' she told him.

He gave her an incredulous look.

'Do you want me to promise?' she dared to tease him a little seeing as he hadn't fired her. 'I promise to move around Hollow House with more care in the future and not to suck up any more fossils.'

The tiniest of smiles tickled the corners of his mouth. 'I'm very glad to hear it.' He made to leave.

'Charles?'

'Yes?'

'When do I start on the admin work?'

He looked thoughtful for a moment. 'Once I can trust you with the vacuum cleaner.'

Cate moved around the house carefully after that, mindful of the precious things around her. They might have only looked like lumps of rock to her a few hours ago, but she had a new appreciation for them now and realised that they were important to Charles. Maybe they were even scientifically important too. Maybe they told us something about the history of the world. Anyway, she vowed not to suck any more of them up in the vacuum cleaner.

After checking in on Eliza and starting her off with her maths, Cate ventured into the dining room where she made a curious discovery that had nothing to do with fossils. She'd been gently dusting a rather fine piece of furniture that was only half-covered in fossils when she noticed one of the drawers had been left open a little. She tried to close it, but it wouldn't budge so she pulled it out and then tried to push it back in. That didn't work either, but she'd glimpsed something in the drawer and opened it again to take a look. It was a photo frame which had been placed face down. Cate knew that it wasn't her place to pry, but curiosity got the better of her and she lifted the frame out from the drawer, turning it over so that she could see the photo inside it. And what a beautiful photo it was too. There were three people in the picture and one of them was Charles. He was in the middle, his arms around the people either side of him. Cate looked in wonder at the woman to his left. She had long chestnut hair which was blowing in the breeze from the sea behind them and her smile was full. Charles was smiling too. But it wasn't the smiling faces that arrested Cate's attention, but the young boy to Charles's right. He looked to be a little younger than Eliza, Cate thought.

What was the photo doing lying in a dark drawer like that? Cate turned around as if Charles might be about to walk into the room to answer her question and, for a moment, she thought about putting it on a shelf somewhere. It was such a lovely, happy picture.

That's not your place, a little voice told her. Somebody – Charles most likely – had placed that photo in the drawer for a very good reason. Perhaps it held a painful memory.

Cate sighed and took one last look at the photo, her eyes focusing on the young boy. He had the same dark hair as Charles. The same eyes too. The resemblance was unmistakable, she thought, as she placed the photo back inside the dark drawer and closed it as best as she could.

Charles had a son.

CHAPTER SIX

Charles had been dreading the afternoon. He'd put things off as late as he could – going down to the beach in the morning for his usual perusal of the cliffs and the shore, taking care of some online orders back at home and, of course, sorting out the muddle that was Cate Rivers. He still couldn't believe that she'd managed to vacuum up one of his most beloved fossils. On her first morning. What other disasters lay in store for him, he wondered? He knew it had been a mistake letting her talk him into her and Eliza staying, but he'd made an agreement and would have to see the month out. Then he'd be free of her.

He sighed as he let Rigs out of the front door for a quick run before he left. He'd take the little dog with him if he could, but he wasn't allowed. Silly rule. Charles was quite sure he'd be most welcome and relieve some of the monotony of the day for the residents of the care home. He could leave Rigs in the car, but decided he'd be more comfortable at home. The old Land Rover was a cold place and Charles wasn't sure how long he'd be.

After giving Rigs a few more minutes of happy hunting in

the garden, Charles gave a whistle and brought the dog back inside. It was time to face up to his duty and the weekly visit.

After showering and changing his clothes, Charles grabbed a small bag from the kitchen and drove the short distance to Beeches. It was a modern building set in extensive grounds with a distant view over the Marshwood Vale towards Lyme Bay. It wasn't altogether unattractive as a building, Charles had to admit, but it lacked the personality of an older building. Still, it was clean and warm and the staff were kind and attentive. That was all he could ask for, he supposed.

He pulled up and parked in the visitor area and sat for a moment. Sometimes, he thought he should do that more often but, whenever he did, his mood became so dark as to scare him right out of thoughts and back into action again. That's why his job was so dear to him. It stopped him from brooding. But sometimes, like his weekly visits to Beeches, he couldn't stop the onslaught of the past.

First, three years ago, his father had died of a heart attack. It had been so sudden and unexpected that his mother had gone into shock. Charles had spent a lot of time visiting his old family home in Wiltshire, checking up on his mum and trying to make sure she was okay. But he'd begun to notice her lapses in memory. At first, he'd put it down to the stress of losing his father, but he'd soon suspected it was more than that and he'd taken her for tests. The news hadn't been good. She'd been diagnosed with dementia. Charles had realised then that his mother's health had been declining for a while, but he'd been so busy that he hadn't given it much thought. He remembered that even his father had joked about her appalling memory. They simply hadn't seen it for what it had been.

Things had been difficult after the diagnosis. Anna Thorner was a proud woman who didn't accept help easily and it had taken a while to persuade her to move into a care home in

Dorset where Charles could visit her more easily and she wouldn't have the worry of running the old family home anymore. Charles had organised for the house to be rented out and it went some way to covering the exorbitant fees of the care home.

He still couldn't believe how much had happened in the last few years. It was a wonder he was still sane. Father lost. Mother – well, she was lost too, wasn't she? There were occasional moments of lucidity, but not many. She wasn't his mother anymore, he knew that. But he had yet to make peace with it.

He shook himself out of his thoughts now, not wanting to think about the people he'd lost in the last few years. Grabbing the bag he'd brought with him, he made his way into the home.

There was a young woman on reception. She beamed him a smile and asked how he was. Charles gave a vague reply as he always did when signing in and then walked down the corridor of one of the wings that led off from the reception area. The carpet silenced his shoes and the smell of air freshener saturated the air. He hated that smell. Perhaps because it was associated with this place, but he believed he'd hate it anywhere – that unnatural sweetness. Charles virtually lived outdoors and nothing could compete with nature's blast of fresh sea air. He tried not to inhale too deeply and promised himself he'd drive home with his car windows wide open to decontaminate his lungs.

As he neared his mother's room, his footsteps slowed. He could see her door was slightly ajar and heard a voice coming from the room. Charles knocked and then entered.

'Hello,' he said to the young man inside who was fiddling with a tea trolley.

'Ah, Mr Thorner, isn't it?' the young man said. 'Can I get you a cup of tea?'

Charles had seen this man before, but couldn't remember his name and felt awful for having to peer at his name badge.

Alex.

'No, thank you, Alex.'

Alex nodded and left the room with the tea trolley, closing the door quietly behind him.

Charles turned his attention to his mother. She was sitting in a chair looking out of the window. He often wondered if she really saw what was out there or if her mind was elsewhere. It was impossible to know. It stung him to his very core whenever he saw her. At sixty-five, she was far too young to be lost to the world and he cursed the cruelty of the disease.

'Hello, Mum,' he said, bending to kiss her cheek.

She looked up at him, her eyes pale and misty with confusion.

'It's your son, Charles,' he said, hating that he had to introduce himself to his own mother. It was something he'd never get used to no matter how often he had to do it.

He pulled up the dressing table chair that was only ever used by him and sat opposite her.

'Are you not drinking your tea?' he asked, pointing to the cup Alex had left for her.

'Tea.' She repeated the word with no real understanding it seemed.

Charles waited a moment, seeing what she'd do – if she'd look at him or say anything. But she didn't. She stared resolutely out of the window.

'How are you feeling?' Charles tried, leaning forward and placing a hand on hers. She didn't respond to his touch at first, but then slowly turned her head and smiled.

Charles smiled back. 'Hello.'

'Hello, my dear. Have you been here long?'

'Just got here.'

She smiled again and it was such a lovely warm smile that Charles felt truly blessed. He didn't know how long this stage would last, for she could move from happiness and recognition to anger and confusion in a flash. But she was smiling now and Charles basked in the moment.

'You been out anywhere recently?' he asked, knowing that they sometimes had little trips from Beeches.

'I don't think so,' she said.

'I was at the beach this morning. Weather was atrocious,' Charles said.

'Beach? Why were you at the beach?'

Charles sighed. She'd gone again, hadn't she?

'For my work,' he told her, but he could tell she wasn't listening. Or not hearing, at least.

It was then she started looking around the room.

'Where's that nice boy?' she asked.

Charles braced himself, knowing what was coming.

'Where's Jamie?'

Out of all the things she'd forgotten, the fact that she still remembered this one name was a source of constant pain to Charles. She hadn't said his own name for several weeks now and yet she always seemed to remember Jamie.

Charles swallowed hard. 'He's not here, Mum.'

'Why doesn't Jamie come anymore? I want to see Jamie. I like Jamie, don't I?'

'Yes, Mum.'

'Where is he?'

Charles delved into the bag he'd brought with him. 'I brought you some cake. Look – it's your favourite fruit cake from the shop you like.'

'I don't want cake. I want to see Jamie,' she said, sounding like a truculent child.

'Well you can't see him!' Charles barked and then

immediately felt awful. It wasn't his mother's fault that she was like this. She wasn't trying to be difficult and she certainly wasn't trying to hurt him. The old Anna Thorner would have been absolutely mortified by this new version, he knew that.

Charles sighed and then his eyes caught sight of the CD player in the corner of the room. It had been a gift from his father to his mother and she loved it. Even when Charles had tried to persuade her to update her technology, she'd clung to the clunky machine for all she was worth. He got up and walked towards it now, smiling when he saw the disc of Strauss waltzes beside it. A favourite of his mother's. He put the disc in now and pressed play. Her response was almost instant and her face, which had been taut with anger a moment before, visibly relaxed now.

Charles returned to his chair and sat with her for a while, following her gaze out of the window. It was nice that she had this view of the garden, he thought. That had been important when he'd looked at homes. He'd wanted somewhere that was surrounded by greenery. Green was calming and she'd always loved her garden at home.

'Listen,' he said, 'I should go. You look tired.'

She gazed at him and then her eyes widened. 'Charles? Is that you?'

Charles's whole body went rigid. 'Yes, Mum,' he said, his eyes stinging with sudden tears. 'It's me.'

The first week at Hollow House was always going to be tricky, Cate reasoned. She and Eliza were getting used to a new home, a new job and a new routine. But, having been there several days now, Cate couldn't help thinking that the two of them had settled quickly into life in the old Victorian home, navigating their way around both it and its owner. Eliza was making good progress with her books and Cate hadn't sucked up any more fossils. Things, she thought, were going well.

Which was why she panicked one afternoon when Eliza wasn't anywhere to be seen. Cate had been washing the hallway floor and vacuuming the stairs and had been occasionally popping her head into the kitchen to check that Eliza was getting on all right. Only the last time, she hadn't been there. Cate stepped into the room. Eliza's history book lay open and Cate could see that she'd made a start with the questions in her exercise book, but where was she? She couldn't be upstairs because Cate had been vacuuming there and Eliza definitely hadn't passed her. Perhaps she was in the garden, Cate thought, making her way outside.

'Eliza?' she called. She didn't think it was likely that her daughter would have taken herself outside on such a day as this. Cate looked up into the battleship-grey sky. It was the kind of day where the sun refused to make an appearance and the whole of the county was cast into deep gloom. She went back inside, starting to worry now, the onset of paranoia nudging at her. No, she mustn't panic. Eliza must be somewhere in the house, she told herself. She just had to be methodical and search each room.

After leaving the care home, Charles headed home. He'd felt rain in the air and decided he had plenty to do in his workshop. He'd recently been commissioned to clean up a rather nice ammonite that a holidaymaker had found. The man had heard about Charles and had asked if he'd take the job on to surprise his wife on a special birthday at the end of the month. Charles had smiled inwardly, wondering if the wife in question would

want to be surprised with a fossil or if she had a piece of
jewellery in mind. In his experience, trying to pass a fossil off as
a gift to a woman didn't always go down well. Still, he was
making good progress with it so far and would have it ready in
time for the special day.

He'd just finished a particularly tricky bit with the air pen
when he'd looked up and seen Eliza standing in the doorway.
He didn't remember leaving the workshop door open and
wished he'd closed it now because he didn't like being disturbed
when he was working, but the young girl looked harmless
enough and he took pity on her standing there, her eyes wide as
she surveyed the room.

'Do you want to come in?' he asked her.

She looked surprised and a little scared by his invitation,
but the objects in the room obviously fascinated her and he
could see that she wanted to get closer to them, just as he would
if he were in her place.

'Come on – take a look if you want.'

Charles quickly looked around for possible child hazards
but, unless she picked up one of the larger fossils or geological
hammers and promptly dropped it on her feet, there wasn't
really much damage she could do.

Slowly, she entered and Charles turned his attention to his
work again to give her a bit of privacy, occasionally glancing up
to see where she was. He remembered the first time he'd gone
into a fossil hunter's workshop. He'd thought he'd entered
heaven. It was far better than any sweet shop or toy shop. And
that feeling had never left him. Every time he entered his own
workshop, or that of a colleague's, there was still that sense of
excitement.

He watched as she reached towards one of the fish fossils
he'd just started to work on, her fingers hesitant yet so
inquisitive.

'It's okay – it won't bite you!' he joked. 'You can touch it gently if you want to.'

He watched as she inched forward, her slender child's fingers reaching towards the object of fascination and touching it gently. And then she turned around, her eyes widening a fraction as if in question. Was she asking him something in that silent way of hers? She turned to the fossil again and then back to him, the same questioning look in her eyes.

'Oh!' he said, working it out at last. 'It's a dapedium. A fish from the Jurassic period. It was around at the same time as the dinosaurs.'

This seemed to satisfy Eliza and he continued with his work, letting her move around the room on her own. It was a couple of minutes later when he became aware that she was standing beside him, watching what he was doing. He found it a little unnerving, but her attentiveness touched him and he paused in his work.

'See this?'

She nodded.

'It was found on the beach near Lyme Regis after a big storm. The person who brought it in for me to clean was the first person to ever see it. And I'm the second and now you're the third. It's been hidden away in the rocks for about one hundred and eighty million years.'

He watched as Eliza's eyes rounded in wonder at this fact and then he saw her reach into her pocket and bring out a small notebook and pencil, watching as she wrote something down. A moment later, she showed him the paper.

Is it an amanight?

Charles smiled at her attempt to spell a word she'd probably never seen written down before.

'That's right. An ammonite,' he said. 'Let me write that for you.' He gestured to take her pencil and book. Eliza hesitated and he wondered if she was going to let him have them. He waited and she gingerly handed them to him and he wrote something down in the book.

'Ammonite – see?' He handed her things back to her and she looked down at the word he had written and nodded. 'The name comes from the Egyptian god, Amun, who had amazing horns like a ram, and people thought that these creatures looked like tightly curled horns.'

Eliza seemed to be taking this in.

'What do you think?' Charles asked and then realised that she wouldn't answer him. At least, not in words.

She nodded.

'You think ammonites look like curly horns too?'

She nodded and he smiled. 'Me too.'

She continued to stand over him and he got on with his work, conscious of her silent but very interested presence. He wasn't sure how long they continued like that, until Cate's voice interrupted them.

'Eliza! There you are,' she cried from the door. 'I'm so sorry, Charles. I hope she hasn't been disturbing you.'

'Not at all. She's just been finding her way around.'

'Well, she's meant to be finding her way around her history book!' Cate informed him.

'No greater history than in this room.'

Cate looked around it for the first time. She couldn't disagree with him. It was then that she saw her daughter writing something down, handing it to Charles. She watched as Charles read the message.

'No,' he said, his voice suddenly sharp.

'No, what?' Cate asked, stepping into the room and approaching the two of them.

'She can't come with me when I'm fossil hunting.'

'Oh, I see,' Cate said. 'Well, I'm sorry she asked.' She put a hand on Eliza's shoulder and guided her out of the room. 'We'll leave you to get on with your work.'

Charles watched as they left and immediately felt awful at having pushed the girl away, but what choice did he have? It was too dangerous and he didn't have time to keep an eye on a child. He was better off working on his own, especially after what had happened in the past.

Charles closed his eyes for a moment. Sometimes he hated the person he had become, but there was no other way to deal with things, he'd decided. He couldn't draw people to him. Not anymore. The damage he could do was untold. And yet there'd been that look in Eliza's young face that had spoken to him, reaching a part of him that he'd thought he'd safely locked away. He'd wanted to encourage her and to communicate his great passion for fossils.

But you can't, a little voice said.

He opened his eyes, picked up his air pen, and started his solitary work again.

CHAPTER SEVEN

Cate had thought she'd be too shy to invite herself round Allie's, but Allie had told her to call and Cate decided that she needed a friend. There was something she was still really mad about and felt she wouldn't be rid of until she talked it through with somebody. So, sitting in the living room of Hollow House on Saturday evening, she decided to text Allie.

Okay if I pop over?

Of course. Sunday morning good? I'll make a cake! Allie texted back almost immediately.

Allie's home was at the other end of Winscombe on the lane that led to the sea, and it was a pleasant walk from Hollow House on a fine autumn day when the beech trees were golden and the sun warmed all the bits of your skin that you were brave enough to bare. Cate and Eliza crossed the bridge and passed the church. They saw the little village shop and pub, and admired the many beautiful cottages that made up the village.

Allie's cottage was part of a terrace and was made from the deep iron-rich golden stone the area was famous for, with a chocolate-coloured thatched roof and porch. Cate saw joy dancing in Eliza's eyes when she caught sight of it.

'Isn't it pretty?' Cate said. It was certainly a less daunting place than Hollow House and Cate couldn't help envying her friend living in such a charming home. She suspected it would be a lot cosier in the coming winter months than Hollow House would be with its big draughty rooms.

Cate and Eliza entered the porch and knocked on the door. A moment later, Allie answered, a huge smile on her face, her hazel eyes warm and welcoming.

'Come in, come in!' She ushered them into a small hallway. 'Come through to the kitchen. There's cake waiting!'

Cate glanced around the house as they went. It was a sweet little home and the kitchen was warm and welcoming with a butler sink and multi-coloured tiles behind the cooker. A window overlooked a tiny back garden and was framed with red and white checked curtains, and there was a square pine table in the middle of the room on which sat a cake stand.

'Cherry and chocolate,' Allie announced. 'Two of my favourite things so I'm hoping for a taste explosion!' She giggled like a schoolgirl and Cate couldn't help but smile, remembering how much she'd missed her dear friend over the years and the pure joy that came from the warmth of her personality.

'Please – have a seat and I'll make us some tea.'

Cate and Eliza sat at the table and then Allie momentarily left the room.

'*Jack!*' Allie bellowed up the stairs. Cate jumped. She'd forgotten that, despite her small frame, Allie could yell when she needed to. 'Come and see who's here!' Allie came back into the kitchen. 'Sorry about that. He's probably plugged into something up there. You know what they're like.'

Eliza looked at Cate questioningly and Cate felt a little

guilty that her daughter had never been plugged into anything in her life.

Allie put the kettle on and, a moment later, loud footsteps were heard on the stairs and a tall, brown-haired boy stepped into the kitchen. He was wearing a striped jumper and jeans his feet were bare.

'Jack – this is my friend, Cate, who I was telling you about. We were at school together.'

'Hi Jack,' Cate said.

He nodded.

'And her daughter, Eliza,' Allie went on.

Jack and Eliza regarded one another for a silent moment and then Jack spoke.

'Can I get some cake now?'

Allie sighed. 'If you sit at the table like a civilised person.'

'I can't, Mum. I'm in the middle of something.' He pointed upstairs.

'You're not going to spend the whole day on that game, are you?'

'Dunno. Maybe.'

Allie sighed and brought a cake slice and a plate to the table, cutting a large chunk for her growing boy.

'Don't make crumbs!'

'Thanks, Mum!' He nodded to Cate and Eliza and left the room, his bare feet thumping up the stairs again.

'Obsessed!' Allie said. 'I have lost my son to a virtual world.'

Eliza reached out and touched Cate's arm, frowning at her.

'I'll explain it to you later,' Cate said, intending to do no such thing lest she lost her own daughter to it too.

'You said he's twelve?' Cate asked Allie.

'Yes.'

'He looks older.'

'Acts it too. It's terrifying!'

Allie got to work making a cup of tea for her and Cate and then poured a glass of orange squash for Eliza. She set the table with plates and forks and cut a good portion of cake for each of them.

'This is very kind,' Cate said. 'You shouldn't have gone to all this trouble.'

'I don't need an excuse to make a cake,' Allie said. 'Remember the one I made in Home Economics?'

'Didn't you double the ingredients or something?' Cate said, a vague recollection of a rather large cake nudging at her memory.

'We couldn't get it out of the oven! It had to be cut out! What a waste.' Allie shook her head, obviously still mourning for the lost cake.

'Well, this is delicious,' Cate said, taking another mouthful. 'Eliza?'

Eliza nodded her approval.

'Good!' Allie said. 'I'll put a gold star in the cook book so I know to make it again.'

'I meant to ask,' Cate began, 'how did you come to be in Dorset?'

Allie took a sip of her tea. 'Well, I was on a camping trip near Lulworth Cove shortly after sixth form and I really fell in love with the Dorset coast and started looking for work here. I took some pretty mundane jobs, just to get started, found somewhere to rent in Bridport. I then got myself a little car and started collecting sea glass on the beaches around here. I've always been obsessed with it and I'd fill my pockets, not really knowing what to do with it all until I saw some jewellery in one of the gift shops and decided that was it. So I booked myself on a course and started learning about jewellery making and, as soon as I could, opened my shop in Lyme.'

Cate smiled. 'I really admire you.'

Allie flapped a hand. 'Oh, there's nothing to admire. I simply did exactly what I wanted to. Don't we all?'

The question hung between them and Cate looked down at her plate.

'You've created a really beautiful life,' Cate said at last.

Allie reached her hand across the table and rested it on Cate's. 'Thank you!'

'I mean it. I'm a little bit in awe of you.'

'Oh, don't be silly! I'm only making a few necklaces and the shop is very small.'

'It's a *beautiful* shop and your things are gorgeous,' Cate said, her fingers flying to the amber necklace Allie had given her.

'Well, you're very kind.'

Cate smiled, hesitating with what she wanted to say next.

'What is it, Cate?' Allie prompted.

'I was just wondering – is Jack's dad on the scene?'

Allie glanced at Eliza and Cate read the message that the conversation was moving into grown-up territory.

'Eliza? Do you like rabbits?' Allie asked the girl.

Eliza nodded.

'Would you like to go in the garden and meet Carrot? She's in the hutch and you can lift her out and give her a fuss. She loves a cuddle. Take this too,' Allie said, going to the fridge and bringing out a crisp, juicy carrot. 'You'll be best friends forever if you give her this!'

Eliza quickly finished her cake and then took the carrot and went out of the back door into the enclosed garden beyond.

Cate smiled. 'She'll love that. You won't be able to get rid of her now.'

'So,' Allie said, 'you want to know about Craig?'

'Is that Jack's father?'

Allie nodded, a resigned look on her face. 'I'm not sure what to say about him except he comes and goes. But mostly he goes. He's a good guy, but he finds it difficult staying in one place long enough to make any kind of a life. I knew that when I met him and he was sure to tell me that when he found out I was pregnant with his son.' Allie shrugged. She seemed at ease with the situation. 'What can I say? I don't regret anything. I can't imagine my life without Jack and I don't feel I'm missing out on having Craig here full-time. This – what I have here – it suits me.'

Cate looked at her friend and she could totally understand why she was so content.

'Cate?'

'Yes?'

'How about you? I mean, Eliza's father?'

Cate should have known that the question was coming. After all, a fair conversation couldn't be one-sided.

'I've left him.'

'Yes, I can see that.'

'And I'm not going back.'

Allie nodded and pursed her lips tightly together. 'Did he – did he *hurt* you?'

Cate gazed down into her lap and nodded.

'And Eliza? Did he hurt her?'

'No, never,' Cate said. 'But he... he made threats.'

Allie swore under her breath. 'And is that why she doesn't speak?'

Cate nodded. 'Something happened.' Her voice was barely above a whisper now. 'Something happened and she just stopped talking.'

Allie sighed. 'Oh, Cate!'

'It's how she chose to cope with it, I guess.'

'How long hasn't she spoken for?'

'A few months.'

'And have you sought help?'

Cate nodded. 'The doctor I saw said that she'll speak when she's ready and not to put any pressure on her, but to give her all the time and space she needs.' It was Cate's turn to sigh. 'I've read a bit about it and everyone's experience is different, but I think – in her own way – this is Eliza trying to control things. She couldn't control what was happening around her, but this was something she could control.'

'But you'd think she'd start speaking again now, wouldn't you? I mean, now that you're away from... him. Now that you're safe here,' Allie said.

Cate shrugged. 'I hoped that might happen too, but she seems locked into this silence somehow. It's early days here, though, isn't it?'

Cate and Allie looked out of the kitchen window into the garden and saw Eliza with the enormous rabbit in her arms.

'I'm afraid Charles might have frightened her too,' Cate confessed. 'Eliza asked him if she could go fossil hunting with him.'

'She asked? I thought you said she wasn't speaking.'

'No – she writes things down sometimes, and it's wonderful that she felt confident enough to do that with someone who's virtually a stranger. It's a sign that she trusts him, I think. But he went and barked at her. I think it scared her a little.'

'Oh, no!'

Cate sighed. 'It wasn't really his fault, but it made me cross all the same. She shouldn't have disturbed him when he was working, I guess.'

'She was just being a normal child, showing an interest in things.'

'Yes, and it's a shame she got knocked back like that, but it must be odd for him having us in his house.'

'Not as odd as you'd imagine,' Allie said. 'You do know he was married, don't you?'

It was then that Cate remembered something else. 'I found a photo. In a drawer.'

'Of him and his wife?'

'Maybe,' Cate said. 'There was a young boy in it too. Looked like a mini Charles.'

A sadness suddenly filled Allie's eyes.

'He has a son?' Cate prompted.

Allie nodded. 'He had a wife and a son.'

Cate frowned, feeling anxious at the tone in Allie's voice and picking up on the word 'had' which she'd used. 'What happened?' she dared to ask.

'There was an accident,' Allie told her. 'At the local beach. It was one of those awful winter days. It'd been stormy – just the sort of weather fossil hunters like Charles love. He'd taken his son out with him. I don't know the details. But one of the cliffs just collapsed and the boy – Jamie – was killed.'

'Oh, God!'

'It was a horrible time. The whole village went into mourning and the church was packed for the funeral. I'll never forget it. The sound of crying in that cold, dark building. It was like a nightmare.'

'And how did Charles cope?'

'How do you think he coped? He'd lost his only child and, shortly after that, Sophie left him.'

'His wife?'

Allie nodded. 'Rumour had it that she blamed him for the accident.'

'Oh, my goodness. I had no idea.'

'Well, it's not exactly the thing you're likely to talk about to the hired help, is it?'

'I guess not.'

'No offence, Cate.'

'But to put that beautiful photo of his son in a drawer,' Cate said.

'Don't forget that his wife was in the photo too. I guess some memories are just too hard to be around.'

'Poor Charles. Did you know Sophie?'

'Not really,' Allie said. 'She bought some pieces of jewellery from me once and I delivered them to the house, but we weren't really friends. She was nice enough.'

'Where did she go?'

Allie shrugged. 'I'm not sure anyone knows.'

'She didn't have friends in the village who might know?'

'I heard that she left one night without telling anyone.'

Cate swallowed. She knew what that felt like.

As Cate and Eliza walked back through the village from Allie's cottage, Cate couldn't help thinking of what her friend had told her about Charles. She tried to imagine what that kind of loss did to a person. First his son and then his wife. How had he coped? *Was* he coping? Or was his perpetual gruffness tied in to what had happened in the past? Cate knew only too well that you should never judge anybody by appearance. You never knew the secret battles they were fighting or the things they'd endured.

Entering Hollow House, Cate couldn't help feeling the weight of sadness in the place. Had she felt it before? She'd only really been aware of the general mess and the fact that the house needed some attention, but now she could sense that there was something darker there. Perhaps it was just because Allie had told her, but Cate felt it was more than that. It came from Charles living on his own, surrounded by nothing but dead things that hadn't had a beating pulse for millions of years. It came from the fact that there were no photos, no little personal mementoes apart from the photo in the dining room drawer. Where were they all? What had he done with them? Few people could get through life without accumulating the sweet detritus like the paintings children did and the funny little things they made in clay or plasticine at school and then brought home for you to proudly display. Cate had had to leave all of Eliza's little school projects at their home when they'd fled, and she'd only managed to pack one photograph, but where were Charles's family things? Cate began to wonder if the locked room upstairs was something to do with the sad story from the past.

Was it Jamie's room?

The thought made her shiver. Charles hadn't said anything to her about the room. All she knew was that it was locked. She'd tried the door handle in an attempt to clean all the rooms upstairs and, when it hadn't opened, she'd just assumed it was a private space. Maybe some kind of office. Or just more fossils. But she was now convinced it had been his son's room.

Cate watched as Eliza ran up to their bedroom, blissfully unaware of the young boy who had once lived in the house. As it was Sunday, Eliza was allowed to do what she liked and that probably meant she'd choose drawing. Cate had a day off too, and she was wondering what to make them for lunch when Charles appeared in the hallway.

'Ah, Cate.'

'Hello, Charles,' she said, giving him a smile. He stared at her.

'Are you okay?'

'Yes, I'm fine.'

'You look – I don't know – different.'

'Do I?' She swallowed hard and tried to pull herself

together. 'Too much chocolate cake, perhaps. I've been to see a friend.'

'You have a friend here?'

'Yes, Allie. She lives in the village.'

'Allie?'

'Allie Kendall. She has a shop in Lyme. Gifts from the Sea?'

'Ah, right,' Charles said, seeming to know.

'It's Allie who told me about the job here.'

'I see.'

Cate saw a look pass over Charles's face. He suddenly seemed uncomfortable knowing that she had a connection to the village, and it was then that she guessed. He knew, didn't he? He knew that she knew. She'd been to visit a friend in the village – a friend who'd known about the job Charles had advertised. She was bound to know other things too – things she would naturally have told Cate. That's what Charles was thinking, wasn't it?

But neither of them said anything because it wasn't the kind of thing you just started talking about in the hallway on a Sunday.

Cate attempted to fill the awkward silence that had fallen between them.

'It's lovely out,' she said with a weak smile. 'The trees look so beautiful at this time of year, don't they?'

Charles didn't say anything. He seemed to be stuck – unable to move and unable to speak.

'We might take another walk later,' she said, knowing she was babbling now and saying nothing of any real interest. 'Maybe to the sea. Or down the lane before it gets too muddy. I read somewhere that it's a hollow lane – one of those ancient routes – is that right?'

Charles nodded.

'And that's how Hollow House got its name, right?' She

smiled hesitantly, but he didn't return her smile. Instead, he gave a nod and walked towards his workshop. A moment later, she heard the tap, tap, tap of his chisel and knew that, as ever, he had buried himself in his work.

Perhaps it wasn't a good idea to work with a chisel when one's hands were shaking, Charles thought. But he didn't know what else to do with himself. When he was stressed, he worked. When he was happy, he worked. Work was the way he made sense of the world. Work was the thing he lost himself in. Only it didn't seem to be helping this morning. He laid his chisel down.

She knew, didn't she? Cate knew what had happened. Whoever this Allie Kendall was, and he was only vaguely aware of her, she'd gone and told Cate all about his past, hadn't she? You couldn't live in Winscombe and not be aware of what had happened. In a small village like this, it was impossible to keep things private especially when they were of such magnitude as losing a son and then your wife walking out on you.

But they didn't know everything, did they? Because it had only been Charles on the beach that day. Nobody except Charles knew everything.

And nobody ever would if he had his way.

CHAPTER EIGHT

After settling Eliza at the kitchen table with a heap of books on Monday morning, Cate found herself in Charles's workshop. She guessed she'd passed the vacuum cleaner test and that he now felt he could trust her with the administration work.

'It's pretty simple really,' he told her. 'I have a small office here,' he said, leading her through to a room off his workshop.

Cate tried not to gasp at the mess. There was a table on which sat a computer and there was some sort of in tray. At least that's what she guessed it to be – it was hard to tell under all the papers and envelopes that were stacked upon it. The table was weighed down with a heap of papers too, as well as fossils. Were they being used as paperweights or was he meant to be doing something else with them?

He cleared his throat. 'It might need tidying up in here.' He looked vaguely around the room.

'You might be right,' Cate told him.

'Well, take a look at the system I've got going. There's a filing cabinet, but I haven't used it recently. Perhaps you could put it to good use?'

Cate nodded and watched as he pulled the office chair out for her to sit on, moving a stack of padded envelopes first. He then showed her his online shop which he ran via his website and which he advertised via a Facebook group.

'You haven't posted here for a while,' she told him, looking at the date of the last photo he'd put up on Facebook.

'Maybe that's something you could take over. Do you like photography?'

'I can take a picture,' Cate told him.

'Well, that's something I'm happy for you to do although you'd better check with me for the names of things before you post. Some of the people on the group know their stuff and won't take kindly to any vague descriptions.'

'Understood.'

He then showed her how the orders came in and how all his specimens were labelled. Some of the packing material was kept in a cupboard behind the desk and there was a massive roll of bubble wrap too.

'I'll take charge of the larger pieces. The ones that need to be crated.'

'You have them that big?' Cate asked.

'I get a few pieces from trade shows and sell them on. They can be very large. So don't worry – I'll do the dinosaur heads myself.'

Cate frowned. She couldn't tell if he was joking or not. He didn't seem to be the joking kind.

'I try and do one or two post outs each week, but I'm afraid that hasn't happened recently,' he went on. 'But that's usually enough to keep on top of things and the customers seem happy with that.'

'And you use the post office in the village?'

'Yes. Closed on Wednesday afternoons. They're used to me and all my odd-shaped packages.'

'Good to know.'

'So, if you have any questions, just ask, but I think there's plenty for you to be getting on with.'

'Yes, thank you,' Cate said, hoping she'd understood everything.

'I'll leave you to it, then. I hope you don't mind a bit of noise. I'll be working in there,' he said, motioning to the workshop. 'You can shut the door. Oh, and you can plug that heater in here. I don't like it too hot around the fossils, but we can't have you freezing, can we?'

She watched as he walked through to his workshop and she turned around to face her own work. Where to start? Well, she'd have to clear a space for herself to work in first which would mean sorting out all the heaps of papers. She got to work. Invoices, receipts, household bills – they were thrown together and it took some time to sort through them all, filing them away neatly in the cabinet so that Charles would be able to find them at a moment's notice. How had he been coping, she wondered? It was a miracle he was able to run any sort of a business. Still, if he had managed, he wouldn't have needed her so she guessed she should be grateful that he was so disorganised.

Once the papers had been tidied away, Cate checked on Eliza who was happily working in the kitchen. She then returned to the office and familiarised herself with the computer and the online shop orders. Charles had put all of the smaller specimens out on a table at the end of the room. They were clearly marked up and it was Cate's job to print out the envelope labels and receipts, and to carefully wrap each fossil. She soon discovered that the fossil sales were the fun bit of her job. There were some really pretty things and each had its own label telling of its provenance. Some had been found locally by Charles. Others, like the quirky trilobites that looked like massive black woodlice trying to crawl out of the rocks they were in, and the golden-brown shell-like nautilus had been sourced from abroad.

Cate marvelled at the variety of things Charles sold, wondering how she could have lived on the planet so long and not been aware of all of these fascinating creatures. She decided, then and there, to school herself. Not only was she genuinely interested, but she knew she could make herself more useful to Charles if she was knowledgeable. And he'd be less likely to let her go at the end of the month. She'd seen plenty of books about fossils around the house and was determined to learn what she could.

As she carefully wrapped each piece that was to be posted, popping in one of Charles's business cards, she couldn't help remembering the time in her previous life when she'd tried to take an evening class. It hadn't been anything particularly academic that would involve tons of books and endless essay writing, but her husband had shaken his head.

'What do you want to do a silly class for?' he'd said. 'You don't need to go back to school and sit in a stuffy classroom in the evenings, do you?'

Well Cate had wanted to, but she'd learned not to push things when he objected to them, especially in that belittling way he had – making her feel stupid for even bringing the subject up.

But he wasn't around now, was he? And, if Charles didn't mind, she could read all the books she wanted. It might even help Eliza with her schoolwork. They could learn together. Suddenly, Cate felt excited, which was a feeling she hadn't had in a very long time. Excited and hopeful, she thought, believing that the future might not be so scary a place as she'd imagined it to be.

After she'd packaged everything up, she tapped lightly on

the door between the office and the workshop and Charles looked up from the bench he was hunched over.

'What time does the post go here?' Cate asked.

'Four o'clock.'

'I'll take this batch down now, shall I?' she said, motioning to the packages she'd prepared. He got up and took a look at her work.

'Very impressive.'

'Just doing my job,' she said with a smile.

'I should have hired you months ago.'

'I wish you had,' Cate said without thinking. She could feel herself blushing. 'I'll get going then.'

Charles nodded. 'Here – take this cash. It should cover that little lot. There are a couple of big bags under the desk. Good and sturdy to get the fossils out to the car.'

'Car? I was going to walk.'

'Oh?' Charles seemed surprised.

'I'm enjoying walking. I didn't used to do it much at... before I came here.'

'It's a bit of a hike with heavy fossils,' he warned her.

'It'll do me good,' she insisted. 'Besides, I haven't got any dinosaur heads. Not today at least.' She gave a little smile and he nodded.

She retreated back into the office and, finding the two bags under the desk, she carefully placed the packages inside them while silently cursing herself. Why on earth had she said that about him hiring her months ago? She'd had no intention of highlighting her desperate need of this job and yet that's exactly what she'd done. But maybe it was a light-hearted enough comment and he either hadn't noticed it or had forgotten it already.

Smiling briefly as she walked through his workshop, she popped by the kitchen on the way out.

'Fancy a walk to the post office?' she asked Eliza, thinking she might welcome an escape from her school books. But her daughter shook her head and pointed to Rigs who was snoring in his basket. Cate nodded in understanding. She could never compete with a dog, could she?

It was a cool autumn day, much crisper than Sunday had been, and Cate felt it nip lightly at her fingers and nose. She'd have to think about getting some new gloves at some point. A new winter coat too. Hers was woefully thin and the lining was horribly torn. She tried to remember how old it was. She'd had it when she'd been pregnant with Eliza so that made it at least nine years old. She'd once dared to mention its decrepit state and had got a slap across the face. Her husband hadn't liked to spend money and, as Cate hadn't been allowed to earn any of her own, she'd had to make the winter coat last from year to year. Perhaps she'd be able to save up for a new one now. In the January sales.

The post office was at the back of the small village shop which sold absolutely everything you could imagine from daily newspapers and magazines to fresh baguettes and boiled sweets. There was a little queue for the post office counter and Cate waited her turn, looking around at the goods on offer and the people ahead of her in the queue.

'Why do children always move to Australia?' the woman being served was asking.

'Or Hong Kong?' the postmistress answered.

'Ah, yes. How's Molly?'

'I wish I knew! Haven't heard from her in at least a week.'

The woman tutted in sympathy as she handed over her money and then turned to leave the shop.

Cate was up next.

'Hello,' Cate began as she approached the counter with her bags. 'I've got a few packages for you. From Charles Thorner.'

'So you'll be posting the fossils from now on, will you?' the woman said. 'He told me to expect you.'

'He did?'

'Oh, yes. One of our best customers is Mr Thorner. I reckon this place may well have shut down years ago if it hadn't been for that website of his.'

'Really?' Cate was amazed to hear that. All the more reason for her to work hard for him and to help him make a success of his business, she thought as she handed the packages over and watched as each was weighed and processed. When it was all done, Cate paid with the cash Charles had given her. It was an eye-watering amount but then there had been a lot of packages and each, she hoped, was making Charles a good profit.

'Thank you,' she said when it was all done and the post mistress smiled at her.

'I'm Dora,' she said.

'Cate.'

Dora nodded. 'It's nice to see a new face in the village. I hope you'll be happy here.'

'I think I will be, yes.'

And that was it. Cate's first trip to the post office. It felt like a little milestone and she felt light and free as she walked back to Hollow House and not just because she was no longer carrying the heavy packages. This was to be the pattern of her new life, she thought. She'd got the hang of the housework, she was learning how to run Charles's office, Eliza was working well and gaining confidence every day and Cate was becoming very fond of the village she was living in.

It was even colder now and Cate reached up to adjust her scarf, wincing at the tender spot at the back of her neck where the bruises were. They were perhaps some of the worst. And the last, she told herself. Not quite the last because he'd grabbed her left wrist after that, hadn't he? She pulled her sleeve back to look at the angry blue and purple marks on her pale skin. She could almost feel his fingers again now, but he wasn't there. She was safe.

She did her best to try not to think about him, but his dark shadow would often creep up on her, forcing the breath out of her lungs as she remembered the fear that would course through her body when he simply walked into the room. It hadn't always been that way, but the early days of their relationship, when he'd been sweet and attentive, were buried under so many years of abuse that they might as well have never happened. Indeed, Cate believed that they'd never been real at all and that sweet side of him she'd seen for all too brief a time had been nothing but a façade: something he'd put in place for a purpose. And it had worked. He'd reeled her in so very easily.

Cate took a deep breath, focusing her gaze on the present moment instead of conjuring up the past. The last thing she wanted was for him to pollute the new space she had found for herself. She looked at the golden beech trees that lined the lane, the deep green fields that undulated gently, and the dark ribbon of road, slick with the rain that had fallen earlier that day. She might not be able to change the past, but she could do her very best to bury it.

When Cate got back to Hollow House, Charles wasn't in his workshop. She was walking through it on her way to the office, but stopped when she noticed what looked like an enormous pile of rubble under the table in the centre of the room. Bending down, she took a closer look at the grey rocks that she hadn't noticed before.

'Unfinished projects,' Charles said as he entered the room behind her, a mug of tea in his hand.

Cate gasped and stood back up. 'But you've got enough here for a lifetime.'

'One or two lifetimes, I should think,' he admitted.

'So why do you still go out when you've got all this here?'

He took a sip of his tea. 'Because I know what these are, but you never know what's still out there.'

'Ah, I see. The shine's worn off these pieces, then?'

'Not exactly. But they're safe.'

'Rainy day fossils?'

'Something like that although I've never minded the rain.'

She smiled. 'Charles?'

'Yes.'

'I've noticed all the books around the house. Would it be all right if I read some of them?'

'The fossil ones?'

'Yes.'

'You're interested in learning about them?'

'I really am.'

He took a moment to consider this. 'Okay. Just – erm – be careful with the older books. They're... delicate.'

Cate nodded. 'I won't go near them with the vacuum cleaner.' She saw Charles blanch at the mere mention. 'I'm joking!'

His eyes widened. He really wasn't used to humour, was he? Mind you, Cate wasn't used to teasing anyone and was surprised that she enjoyed it so much.

She looked around the room again, expecting to see the terrier with his master.

'Where's Rigs?' she asked.

'In the kitchen. It's warmer in there,' Charles said, 'and I think Eliza gives him more attention than I do.'

Cate smiled. 'You might have lost your dog there.'

'I think you're right.'

Cate frowned. 'Rigs. That's an unusual name, isn't it?' She saw a dark look cross Charles's face and realised she probably shouldn't have pried. 'It's none of my business,' she quickly added.

He shook his head. 'It's from the opera *Rigoletto*. He's called Rigs for short.'

'Oh, I see.'

She saw Charles swallow. 'It was my wife's favourite opera.'

'Oh,' Cate said. It was the first time he'd ever mentioned her.

'She liked Verdi,' Charles added, looking decidedly awkward.

'I'm afraid I don't know much about opera.'

'You're not the only one,' he said with an attempt at a smile.

They stood awkwardly for a moment, half-glances passing between them.

'I'd better check on Eliza,' Cate said at last.

She left the workshop and made her way through the house towards the kitchen, planning to tell Eliza about the books they could enjoy reading together. But she was stopped from entering the kitchen by an unfamiliar noise coming from the room. Cate froze in the doorway, not daring to go in for a moment. The noise continued. Was it really Eliza? Well, it couldn't be anyone else, could it? And it certainly wasn't Rigs.

Cate peered into the room, not wanting to disturb her daughter, and saw that she was crouching over Rigs's basket. The little dog was on his back, presenting his furry belly to his new friend, and Eliza was beaming down at him. But she was doing more than smiling.

She was laughing.

CHAPTER NINE

Cate stood staring at Eliza, not quite knowing how to respond. What she'd read about her daughter's condition suggested that you shouldn't make a big deal out of this sort of thing. It could have the effect of making the person feel self-conscious, causing them to retreat back into silence once again. So Cate watched Eliza quietly and, as soon as Eliza got up, Cate left, not wanting her daughter to know she'd been seen.

But she couldn't settle after that. She just had to tell somebody so she returned to the workshop and knocked gently on the door, then louder as she heard the sound of chisel on rock.

'Charles?'

'Cate?'

She stepped into the room. 'I didn't want to disturb you, but I just heard Eliza laugh.'

Charles looked up from the fossil he was working on, obviously confused by this declaration. 'And that's unusual?'

'*Yes!* She hasn't made a noise – not a single noise – for months. *Nothing.* Not a pip!'

'And she just laughed?'

'Yes!' Cate was aware that her hands were clasped to her face like a bad actress in a melodrama and she could feel tears in her eyes.

'Was it a little laugh or a big belly chuckle?'

Cate thought. 'It was light and high and sweet. Not long. But such a happy sound.' The tears were falling now – unchecked and unrepentant. She just couldn't help it.

'And she was doing her school work when this happened?' Charles asked with a frown.

'Heavens, no! She was tickling Rigs.'

'Animal therapy?' Charles said. 'So Rigs is acting as some kind of therapist?'

'I guess he is,' Cate said. 'I just can't believe it! We've only been here such a short time and yet–'

'Maybe you should have bought her a dog some time ago,' Charles suggested.

Cate shook her head, trying not to think about the time that she'd tried to persuade her husband to get Eliza a guinea pig. The black eye she'd been given in response had made sure she'd never asked again.

'So, you think she'll be talking soon?' Charles asked.

Cate felt her throat constrict with emotion. 'I don't know!'

'Perhaps it's a bit early to expect that.'

Cate nodded.

'Cate – are you all right?'

She nodded again, but she could feel more tears threatening to spill. 'My girl!' was all she could say. 'Sorry!' She noticed Charles was looking a little lost.

'It's okay,' he said, but he was definitely looking awkward.

'I'll just finish tidying up,' Cate said, leaving the poor man alone and making her way to the office where she closed the door so she could trumpet her emotional nose without disturbing him too much. She did her best to concentrate on her job, but it was hard when she'd witnessed such an incredible breakthrough with Eliza. Did little Rigs know how grateful Cate was to him? Perhaps she could buy him some special dog treats. Maybe she could give them to Eliza to give to Rigs. That could further cement the special relationship that was obviously developing.

Cate was filled with so much excitement and hoped that this was the beginning of Eliza's healing process.

But the joy wasn't to last. That night, after Cate had read a few pages about some of the early scientific discoveries along the Jurassic Coast and promptly fallen into a wonderfully deep slumber, she was woken by the sound of a long, shrill scream.

'Sweetie!' Cate cried. She turned her bedside lamp on and, feeling disorientated for a moment, saw the terrified face of her daughter staring up at her from the bed. Eliza was hugging her ragdoll Jemima closely to her and her cheeks were streaked with tears.

'It was just a dream, darling! It's over now,' Cate promised her. 'You're here with me. *Safe* with me.' She wrapped Eliza up in a big tight hug, feeling her tiny frame shaking against her own. 'It's all right. Nothing can harm you here. We're both safe.'

It was then she heard a door open and guessed that they'd woken Charles. A light tapping on their bedroom door confirmed her suspicion a moment later.

'Come in.'

Charles's dark hair was tousled and his expression was anxious. 'What's happening?' he asked, pulling a jumper over his T-shirt and pyjama bottoms.

'Eliza had a nightmare – that's all,' Cate said, doing her best to play it down. 'I'll take her downstairs for a warm drink if that's okay?'

Charles nodded. 'Anything I can do?'

'I don't think so,' Cate said.

'Are you sure?' He glanced at Eliza, seemingly moved by the child's distress.

'That's kind of you, but I think we can manage. Go back to bed. We didn't mean to disturb you.'

He nodded and she watched as he left the room, probably wondering, yet again, why he'd agreed to have these people living in his house.

'Come on, sweetie – shall I make you a cocoa?'

Eliza nodded and the two of them wrapped up warm and headed downstairs.

Rigs, who was in his basket by the Aga, was happy to see them, giving his stubby tail a thump and Eliza knelt down beside him as Cate heated up some almond milk for cocoa.

The scream might have been the second noise Eliza had made that day, but it wasn't one to be encouraged, Cate thought, hating that her little girl had been so scared. And what a horribly different noise from the happy laughter Cate had heard earlier that day. Had her nightmare reversed the glorious effect of the laughter? Could Rigs be relied upon to help his new best friend find her way back to happiness? He seemed to be doing his best with his belly presented to Eliza in joyful surrender.

Milk warmed, Cate got out two cups and the tin of cocoa together with some sugar. She wasn't going to worry about sugar spikes in the middle of the night right now. Comfort and sweetness were what they both needed.

'Here we are,' she said a moment later and they sat together at the table, Eliza keeping a watch over Rigs as he closed his eyes once more. 'Test it a little first. It'll still be hot. But you can warm your hands on the cup,' Cate told her, realising how very cold it was to be up in the middle of the night at Hollow House. Even the Aga couldn't keep the chill at bay. Or maybe it was just the cold grip of fear that Cate was feeling. Eliza didn't seem cold, she thought.

Once again, Cate found herself wanting to apologise to Eliza for the terrible father she'd had. It was one thing for Cate's husband to have ruined *her* life, but it was too painful to see how he'd impacted Eliza's life too. No youngster should be having nightmares like that. Nightmares induced by a parent.

How many times had Cate wished she'd never met him? And yet, she wouldn't have Eliza if she hadn't and she couldn't regret that, could she? She looked at her daughter, so pale and fragile in her dressing gown, and wished with all her heart that she'd been able to create such a being on her own. But at least she had the consolation that her daughter didn't have an ounce of her father in her.

As they sipped their cocoa in the quietness of the night, Cate thought back to how she'd met Eliza's father. It had been through a mutual friend, Amanda. She'd been hosting a party at her parents' home when they'd been away. It wasn't one of those wild parties where the neighbours are forced to call the police, but there had been loud music which had made Cate want to escape. She'd never liked anything too loud and she'd been secretly curious about the garden that sloped down towards the river. And that's where she'd met him. She'd been watching the clouds darken from peach to orange when she'd become aware that somebody was behind her. Even on that first meeting – even before she'd seen him – he'd managed to scare her.

She'd leapt, physically leapt, wine glass in hand.

He'd laughed, looking handsome in a crisp navy shirt, but he hadn't apologised for scaring her had he?

They'd introduced themselves and watched the sun setting together. It had been one of those significant life moments when two people shared something that felt so much bigger than themselves. And how he'd charmed her. He had been so easy to be around and he'd made her laugh. So much. Where had that man gone? Had he even been real? Those were questions that Cate had asked herself oh so many times in the years that followed. Maybe it had been an act. Maybe he'd known that women were attracted to men who made them laugh.

The other question was why had she stayed with him so long? That was a hard one to answer. At first, she'd overlooked the jibes and the barbed comments. He worked hard, she told herself. He was tired. And she shouldn't have left that mess in the kitchen, should she? She should have ironed that shirt better. She blamed herself for all the little faults he pointed out in her. She hadn't been good enough and she'd done her best to live up to his expectations of her. But then he'd started to punish her. At first, it was a slap. She'd been stunned, staring at her red cheek in horror in the bathroom mirror. He'd cried after that. He'd physically broken down, crumpling in a heap on the bedroom floor, his arms wrapped around his head as he'd wept.

'You made me do it! Why did you make me do it?'

Cate had been confused and frightened and she'd found herself comforting him because she didn't know what else to do. He'd hit her and she'd been the one to comfort him. What a fool she'd been! Instead of packing and leaving that very moment, she'd been trying to understand him and to mould herself into what he wanted. She'd later found out that many victims of abuse did that. Her online research into it taught her that it was a normal survival technique.

Then there was the fear. The fear of not being able to make it on her own. He'd always gleefully told her that she wouldn't be able to survive without him and, for a long time, she'd believed him. There'd been the fear of being caught leaving too and the ramifications of it. If he'd ever found out what she was planning, he would punish her or – worse – punish her by keeping their daughter. She hadn't been able to bear the thought of that. But the fear of him hurting Eliza one day had been the catalyst to get her out of there. And that's why they were here now.

Cate and Eliza finished their cocoa and Cate washed the cups and put them on the draining board.

'Time to go back to bed,' she told Eliza, watching as she said goodnight to Rigs in her gentle, silent way and the two of them went back upstairs, snuggling close under the duvet.

Cate listened to the soft breathing of her daughter for a while, making sure that she had fallen into a safe and carefree sleep before allowing herself to close her eyes.

When Charles had allowed Cate and her daughter to stay at Hollow House for a trial month, he'd expected his days to be interrupted, but he hadn't expected his nights to be disturbed. He'd slept pretty badly after being woken by Eliza's cries. Indeed, he could still hear them echoing around his head as he left the house early the next morning. Poor child, he thought. He'd never forget the ghost-like face of the girl, sunken deep into her pillow, clinging on to her mother as if she were a life raft in a storm-tossed sea. It pained him to see a child in distress and he'd feared it would set his own nightmares off if he'd closed his eyes again. So he'd slept fitfully and shallowly and felt pretty ghastly as he drove down to Charmouth with Rigs by his side.

'Did you look after her, Rigs?' Charles asked the little dog, hoping that Eliza's journey to the kitchen in the night for a warm drink and a bit of Rigs therapy had given her the peace that she'd looked so desperately in need of.

He spent a couple of cold hours scouring the cliffs and

stopped to chat to a fellow fossil hunter who had just discovered two vertebrae in a loose slab of rock. They weren't in very good condition, but there was always the promise of the rest of the body just waiting to be uncovered.

Charles was glad to get back in his car and head home. He was cold and tired and his heart wasn't really into the hunt that day. He'd be better off holing up in his workshop with a hot cup of tea beside him.

So that's where he found himself half an hour later, bending over a workbench, examining the fore paddle of a plesiosaur which he was in the process of cleaning. It was a beautiful specimen. It was just a shame that it was the only bit of the creature he'd managed to find so far. But that was the nature of the game. Sometimes the creatures you unearthed would have been destroyed millions of years ago and you were lucky to discover the pieces that remained, and Charles felt lucky to have this one precious section.

He was just about to start work on it when he became aware that there was somebody behind him. Turning, he saw Eliza was standing on the threshold of the workshop. He must remember to shut his door, he thought to himself, and then felt mean at having such a thought.

Charles noticed that she had more colour in her face this morning and was relieved to see it. He only hoped that whatever horror had woken her in the night had left her now.

'You okay?' he asked her. She nodded. 'Want to see this?' She nodded again and he beckoned her inside. She stood a little distance away from him. 'Come closer and you'll see it properly.' She looked anxious, but moved forward. 'Do you know what it is?' She shook her head. 'It's called a paddle which is like a flipper you'd see on a turtle or a dolphin today,' Charles went on, 'and it belonged to a large sea creature called a plesiosaur that used to live off the coast here about two hundred million years ago.'

Charles found a scrap of paper and pulled a pen from his jacket pocket, quickly sketching an image of the creature for Eliza.

'It was funny looking with a long thin neck a bit like a giraffe.' He saw the beginnings of a smile tickling Eliza's mouth. 'Can you imagine seeing this creature for the first time? You know it was first discovered by a woman?'

Eliza shook her head.

'Mary Anning, who lived in Lyme Regis, discovered some bones in 1823. Nobody knew what to make of them. Was it a kind of fish? Did it still exist in the depths of the deepest oceans?' He paused, watching as Eliza's fingers reached out to touch the bubble-like texture of the paddle. 'They're very rare creatures,' he told her. 'You're a hundred times more likely to find an ichthyosaur than you are a plesiosaur.'

He walked to the other side of the workshop and reached for a cardboard folder from a shelf above one of his benches. He brought it over to Eliza and pulled out a photograph.

'This is an ichthyosaur. Notice how the ichthyosaur paddles are totally different in shape from the plesiosaur. The plesiosaur's are much longer and you can easily see the five long fingers. Almost like a human hand, aren't they?' Charles said, outlining the fossil on his bench. He then pointed to the ichthyosaur paddles in the photo. 'Much more rounded, aren't they?'

Eliza nodded.

'Now, somewhere in here is my plesiosaur,' Charles said, hunting through the paper clippings and photos he'd stashed away in the folder. 'Here we are,' he said a minute later. 'It wasn't complete, but it's my best find to date.'

Eliza looked up at Charles and then back down at the photo he showed her.

'Like it?' he asked and she nodded and then looked around the room and back at Charles. 'I had to sell it,' he said, guessing she was wondering where it was. 'It's hard to let my finds go sometimes but, if I didn't sell a few, I wouldn't be able to go on looking for more. Anyway, there's always the future, isn't there? And the promise of something bigger and better, which is why this paddle over here is so exciting.' He guided her across to another bench where yet another paddle sat. 'See how big this one is? And the paddles on the one in the photo here are a lot smaller. It's an ichthyosaur's. So what that's telling me is that somewhere, if we're very lucky, the rest of this creature is just waiting to be discovered. And it'll be a monster. I call it The Big One! It'll be one lucky fossil hunter who finds it.'

Eliza seemed to be examining him for a moment and then she took out a pencil from her skirt pocket and wrote something down underneath the drawing of the plesiosaur Charles had given her. He inched forward to read it when she'd finished.

You will find it.

He laughed. 'You think so?'

She nodded.

'Maybe,' he said. 'Or maybe you will. Perhaps you'll be the next Mary Anning.'

Eliza bent to write something else on the paper. Charles read it.

Okay.

Charles smiled. 'Well, promise me you'll let me see it if you do.'

He watched as she carefully wrote the words, *I promise.*

It was later that day when Cate popped her head round the kitchen door to check on Eliza. Cate had been working upstairs, changing all the bedding and doing her best to keep the cobwebs at bay which was no easy task in the old house with its tall ceilings. Still, it was a good workout, she told herself.

When Cate saw her daughter concentrating very hard on a drawing at the kitchen table, she decided not to disturb her. She wasn't one to spy on Eliza, but she stood watching her for a moment, fascinated by the look of concentration on her daughter's face, her eyes fixed to the paper and her fingers grasping the felt tip pen. She loved her pens. Cate would have to buy her new ones because she got through them so quickly. She was always drawing and Cate encouraged it. It was good that Eliza had this outlet, she thought – that she could express herself in this way. She might not talk, but she could put all her thoughts and feelings into her art.

As Cate continued to watch, she became aware that Eliza was only using one pen for her picture and it was moving fast over the paper as if she was colouring the whole thing in. Cate became curious as to what her daughter was doing and took a step closer. It was then that she saw the pen Eliza was using. It was the black one and it was moving across the page in unrelenting swiftness. Cate stifled a gasp. It was all black. There was nothing else. Just black.

Cate closed her eyes, fearing the worst. What exactly was happening in that young girl's head? Cate might have physically removed her from the source of danger, but the poor child was still processing it all, wasn't she? And then there'd been the nightmare just last night.

Slowly, Cate walked closer still.

'Eliza, love! What are you doing?' she asked gently, seeing that her daughter had drawn a tiny figure in the bottom right hand corner of the paper that was clearly meant to be her. Cate grimaced. It was, perhaps, even worse seeing that image there than if it had been a totally black drawing. It seemed as if Eliza had painted herself with the black weight of the world on her young shoulders. And she wasn't done yet. Cate watched as Eliza's pen continued, not stopping until the last piece of white paper was swallowed up. She then turned it over and Cate feared the worse – that she was going to do the same to that side. But she didn't. Instead, she put the black pen down, picked up the red one and wrote two words very carefully in her best handwriting.

Cate read them.

Deep Time.

Eliza looked up and smiled and then handed the piece of paper to her mother.

'Thank you,' Cate said, not quite sure what to say or what to make of it.

Eliza picked up her notebook and wrote something down which she handed to her mother a moment later.

'Charles told me,' Cate read. 'He told you what? Something about Deep Time?'

Eliza nodded, looking terribly pleased with herself.

'Well, I'll ask him to tell me sometime,' Cate said.

It was later that evening when Cate met Charles in the kitchen. Eliza's books had been tidied away to a corner of the dresser and Cate now walked over to it and pulled out the drawing Eliza had done.

'I hear you've been teaching Eliza a thing or two.'

Charles turned around from the kettle and frowned. 'I have?'

'Yes.' She handed him the piece of paper which he took and

examined, a puzzled look on his face as he stared at the unrelenting black image. 'Turn it over,' she added.

He did and it was obvious that he was struggling to hold back a smile.

'I thought she was having a dark episode when I saw her colouring a page black. I'm hoping you can shed some light on it. So to speak.'

'About Deep Time?'

'Yes.'

'Well, it's a term used to describe geological time, first coined by a man called James Hutton in the eighteenth century. I was telling Eliza that the Earth is approximately 4.5 billion years' old and Deep Time makes up most of the Earth's history and that, by comparison as humans, our lives – which may reach one hundred years if we're very lucky, are but a fraction of a second when measured against the history of the Earth.'

Cate chewed her lower lip. 'And that didn't worry her?'

'Why should it?'

'Because it makes our lifespan seem so insignificant.'

'Yes, it does. But I usually find that children can cope with that concept better than most adults. If anything, I'd say she was interested to know more.'

'Really?'

'I think so. She looked interested.'

'And that's why she drew herself as so small in the bottom right of the picture? To represent the shortness of a human's life in comparison to the age of the Earth?'

'I guess so.'

Cate thought about this for a moment. This was a very unexpected development, she couldn't help thinking, and perhaps it was one she could use to her advantage.

'Charles?' she asked, a little hesitantly.

'Yes?'

'How would you like to...' she paused, wondering if she had the nerve to ask after all.

'What?'

'Teach Eliza?'

'What do you mean?'

'Teach her some science, some geology, some fossil stuff. She's obviously interested.'

'Oh, no!' he said, shaking his head emphatically. 'I'm not a teacher.'

'But it sounds like you are to me.'

'No, no. I was just talking to her.'

'But that's all teaching is really. Talking with enthusiasm.'

He shook his head. 'It's not for me.'

'Why not?' she asked gently.

'Why not? Look, I don't want to sound rude, but I don't think I have to give a reason for not doing a job I don't want.'

She suddenly felt bad. She shouldn't have pushed him like that. It wasn't fair of her.

'I'm sorry,' she told him. 'I shouldn't have asked. It's just that – well – I've not seen Eliza so fired up about anything for a long while. It's like she's coming alive again. It's so wonderful to see. And I just thought you might want to pass on the knowledge you have.' She bit her lip again, knowing she was still being pushy, but not able to help it when it came to her daughter. Eliza was her whole life.

Charles looked confused by what she'd said. 'But I do share it,' he insisted. 'I share it with collectors who buy my pieces. The knowledge I have all feeds into what I do in the field.'

'Yes, but think how exciting it could be to enlighten a young mind like Eliza's. She's like a little sponge and it's obvious that she's made a connection to you.'

Charles stared down at the picture Eliza had drawn and

Cate watched, wishing she could tell what he was thinking in those few silent moments.

'I could pay you something. You could deduct it from my salary if that's easiest.'

He shook his head. 'It's not that,' he said, finally glancing up. 'Look, I'm not going to promise anything, okay? She's welcome to join me in the workshop and I'm happy to show her what I'm working on. But it'll be more of a natural conversation than anything approaching a lesson.'

'I understand,' Cate told him.

'I won't be sitting down with text books or giving her homework or anything like that.'

'I wouldn't expect that of you. Anyway, home tutoring is *much* more informal than that.'

'I won't suddenly find a school inspector knocking on the door?'

'Goodness, no!'

Charles ran a hand through his hair. 'You know, this isn't what I expected when I advertised for a housekeeper,' he confessed.

Cate could feel her cheeks flaming and worried that she might just have jeopardised her position at Hollow House and that Charles might very well be planning on kicking her and Eliza out once the month was up.

'I think you'll enjoy it,' she said, managing to sound far more confident than she was feeling.

'You think?' There was a slight edge of humour in his voice, wasn't there? She wasn't sure, but she'd tell herself that there was.

'Definitely!' she told him. 'You're going to be a great teacher.'

CHAPTER TEN

Charles wasn't sure how to start with Eliza. He felt awkward and uncomfortable now that he'd been given a proper role and, no matter how many times he told himself that this was all just informal, he felt a responsibility towards the child. A responsibility he hadn't asked for.

He looked at her standing there beside his work bench. She looked as awkward as he felt. It wasn't her fault, but he couldn't really blame Cate for asking, could he? She was just looking out for her daughter.

'So, where shall we start?' he asked, looking at the young girl as if she might have an idea of how this all worked.

She gave a little shrug.

'I've not done this sort of thing before,' he confessed, and then wondered if he should have said that. Surely it was part of his role as a responsible adult to put the child at ease.

'How about we look at some of the jobs I'm working on? I can tell you a bit about what I'm doing and you can ask me any questions you have? Would that work?'

Eliza nodded and relief flooded through him. Good. They were on their way.

Cate had hung around the hallway outside Charles's workshop for a little while under the pretence of sweeping the floorboards. But, really, she was listening to Charles, feeling his discomfort and keeping her fingers crossed that this idea of hers wasn't going to turn out to be a disaster. Finally, after a bit of faffing about, Charles and Eliza seemed to be settling down to something and she heard his anxious tone change into a patient one. It would do Eliza good to have someone teaching her who wasn't her own mother, and an even more wonderful idea for that person to be a man. Heaven only knew that good male role models were lacking in the young girl's life.

Cate left them to it, smiling as she walked up the stairs, her duster in her hand. It was dark in this part of the house. A great slope of hill cast a shadow on the rooms and the late autumn day was a gloomy one so Cate switched on the lights, noticing the pictures on the walls properly for the first time. They were sweet botanical prints, simple but beautiful and very feminine. She doubted very much that Charles had chosen them and wondered if they'd been left by his wife.

For a moment, Cate thought about all the things she'd left behind in her old home: the little bits and bobs she'd collected over the years like china cups and saucers, pretty lampshades and cushions. She hadn't been able to take them with her on her quick escape, and the truth was that she hadn't really wanted to either. For her, they represented her old life – the one she'd needed to get away from and, however pretty those things had been, they hadn't been things she associated with happiness.

Looking at the framed prints of flowers hanging on the wall

of the landing, she wondered if, in their own small way, Charles's wife felt the same way about these. Had she left Hollow House with only the bare essentials? Had everything else been too painful to take with her?

Cate glanced at the room at the end of the landing. It had to be Jamie's bedroom. It was the only room in the house she hadn't been into. Charles hadn't said not to go inside, but the fact that the door was locked was a clear indication that it wasn't meant to be disturbed.

Cate stared at it. Was there anything more seductive than a locked door?

She continued to dust around the landing. There was a small table under the landing window on which sat a large ceramic bowl covered in swirling fish. She gently sent the duster around it and that's when she noticed there was a key inside. She lifted it out and gave it a dust, feeling its weight in her hands and wondering – just wondering – if this was the key to the locked room.

She looked around as if Charles might pop up at any moment, but of course he didn't. He was downstairs with Eliza. So she stood there for a few moments, holding the key in her hand and knowing exactly what she was going to do, but a little afraid to actually do it.

Taking a deep breath, she walked along the landing.

What was it that drew her to the room? Was it simply the fact that it was locked and her nosiness was getting the better of her? Was it a mother's curiosity? She knew it wasn't anything to do with her role of housekeeper, although instinct told her that rooms should be aired and taken care of, and there was a part of her that believed she should run a vacuum through it and give it the once-over with a duster. But it was more than that, wasn't it? This room represented a great sadness that permeated throughout the whole house and something drew her towards it.

Perhaps it was the sadness that she was carrying inside her that was connecting herself to this room. Whatever it was, she knew she had to look. If the key fitted.

It did.

Cate turned it slowly and opened the door. A wall of coldness hit her. Hollow House was a big, cold house, even when the central heating was on full, but it was obvious to her that this room hadn't been heated in a long time.

Cate had already guessed whose room this had been and there was no mistaking it now that she was inside. From the pale blue walls and carpet to the football posters on the walls and the bucket of Lego in the corner, this was a young boy's room. There was a black and white football on the floor by the bed and, on the bedside table, there were several silver trophies for sporting achievements.

She entered slowly, noting that the bedding looked fresh on the neatly-made bed. The curtains were open and the view out across the garden was a particularly pretty one, taking in the slice of sea that was visible in the distance.

She could feel tears stinging her eyes as she looked, once again, at the little bed. The bed no longer being slept in. What was it like to lose a child, she wondered? Unimaginable. It was every parents' nightmare, wasn't it? It was a pain you carried with you always no matter how many years had passed, and this loss was a recent one.

She moved towards a little table at the far side of the room. It looked to be set up as a desk and she saw an exercise book lying there. A homework diary, perhaps. She peered closer, reading the name neatly printed in blue ink on the front. Jamie Thorner.

A hard lump formed in her throat as her fingers gently touched the book. Did Charles ever come in here and do the same thing? Could he still feel his young son's presence? Cate could feel it and she couldn't help wondering if that was a curse or a comfort to Charles.

It was then that she caught sight of a small shelf filled with books and felt herself naturally drawn towards them, tilting her head to read the titles. There were a few novels, she noticed: adventure titles and fantasies, but the collection seemed to be mostly non-fiction and – unsurprisingly – there were a number of books about fossils and geology. Cate's hands reached towards those books, pulling them out one by one. Eliza would love these, she thought. Her interest in Charles's ancient world had opened a new door for her and Cate believed these books would enhance Eliza's learning. Excitement filled her as she chose some of them, making a neat pile on the bedside table.

She collected six books to begin with. That would be enough and she thought it was probably best to make sure Charles didn't mind before she took any more. Gathering them up in her arms, she took one last look around the room before leaving and locking the door behind her. She then returned the key to the bowl by the landing window and made her way downstairs.

As she approached Charles's workshop, she could hear him telling Eliza something about coastal erosion and could tell that he was pausing to allow Eliza time to write any questions she had for him. She didn't want to disturb them so she took the books to the kitchen instead, placing them on the table for Eliza to look at later.

It was just after eleven when she heard Eliza and Charles coming out of the workshop. Cate had been sorting through a pile of papers in the dining room which really should have been in Charles's office and not scattered over several dining room chairs. She put them down when she heard Charles's voice and joined him and her daughter in the hallway.

'I thought it was time for a break,' Charles announced as he saw her.

'Getting on all right?'

'Yes, I think so.'

'Not asking too many questions, is she?' Cate asked, winking at her daughter.

'Enough.'

Cate smiled. Her daughter might not talk, but that didn't mean she wasn't an active participant in lessons.

'She loves learning,' Cate told Charles. 'Loves books too.' She bit her lip, knowing that she'd have to reveal to Charles what she'd done sooner or later, and that it would probably be sooner as they were almost at the kitchen now.

'What is it?' he asked, obviously sensing her unease.

'Nothing,' she lied. 'Shall I put the kettle on?'

They walked through to the kitchen together, Eliza skipping ahead to greet Rigs. As Cate passed the kitchen table, she glanced at the books. Charles hadn't seen them yet, but he would in a minute.

'Biscuit?' she said, opening a cupboard and bringing out a packet of shortbread.

'Thanks.'

Eliza nodded.

Cate got a plate and laid out a few fingers of shortbread and then she filled and switched the kettle on. Tea and biscuits first. Confession later.

'So, what have you both been doing this morning?'

'We were learning about...' Charles stopped and Cate knew why. He must be looking at the table.

'What were you learning about?' Cate prompted.

But Charles wasn't to be dissuaded. 'What are these doing here?'

Cate didn't turn around immediately. Instead, she pulled out a teaspoon from the drawer and grabbed a couple of teabags.

'Cate?' Charles said.

'What is it?' she asked feigning innocence.

The kettle was boiling now and Cate could see that Charles was fast approaching boiling point too.

'Where did you get these books?'

He clearly knew where the books were from, but she couldn't blame him for asking and he could probably see the guilt etched across her face.

'From the bedroom at the end of the landing.'

'And who said you could go in there?'

'I found the key and thought the room might need a clean.'

'That room is kept locked for a reason,' he said.

'I know. I just thought I should–'

'You're not paid to think. You're paid to *do*.'

Cate blanched at his tone. 'I'm sorry, Charles. I didn't mean any harm. I saw the books and–'

'Put them back!'

'But they were just sitting there and Eliza would love to use them.'

'Put. Them. Back.' His tone was cold and stern now, making Cate put down the mug she had just picked up, and Eliza stand up from where she'd been kneeling beside Rigs.

'Charles – I didn't mean any disrespect.'

'You shouldn't have gone in there.'

'I know. But I thought it might be a good idea to see if the room needed airing.'

'It needs nothing. It needs to be left alone.' He was leaning forward now, his hands resting on the table as if he was slowly sinking into himself.

Cate felt dreadful and rather frightened. She knew she'd taken a risk going into the room and taking the books, but she'd sincerely hoped that Charles might be pleased that they were being used and it would form a connection between his son and her daughter, especially now that he was teaching her. But she could clearly see that she'd misjudged the situation horribly.

Without saying another word, she moved to the table and scooped the books up in her arms.

'Eliza – come upstairs with me.'

The two of them left the kitchen, Cate looking back to see the ashen face of Charles as he stared resolutely into nothing.

Cate's whole body felt heavy with sadness as she traipsed up the stairs with the books, Eliza behind her.

'Go and sit in our room,' she told her daughter when they reached the landing. Eliza looked at her questioningly. 'I'll be with you in a moment.' She watched as Eliza made her way into their bedroom and then Cate went to get the key from the bowl, letting herself back into the ice-cold room. She felt a weight of sadness putting the books back and guilt at having made Charles so mad. How naive she'd been. How would she have felt if the situation had been reversed? She couldn't begin to imagine.

When she returned to join Eliza in their bedroom, her daughter had written something in her notebook and thrust it under Cate's nose as soon as she was in the room.

Why is Charles so cross with you?

'I did something I shouldn't have done,' Cate told her.

Eliza scribbled furiously.

What did you do?

Cate sighed, not quite knowing how to answer. Honestly, she told herself. 'I went into a room I shouldn't have gone in.'

Eliza frowned.

'You know the room at the end of the landing?'

Eliza nodded.

'It's locked, but I found the key and went inside. That's

where I found some books and I thought Charles would let you use them. They're children's books, you see.'

Eliza grabbed her pad again.

Who do the books belong to?

'They belonged to Charles's son,' she paused. 'But he died.'

Eliza seemed to take this on board.

'I shouldn't have taken them,' Cate said, 'and he's right to be annoyed with me.'

Eliza was writing again.

Will he stop teaching me now?

'Oh, sweetie! I hope not!' Cate gave her a hug and silently cursed herself, hoping that she hadn't spoiled things for Eliza.

It was then that her fingers instinctively clasped the pendant she was wearing. Hadn't Allie told her that amber was meant to protect the wearer? Cate sighed. Well, one thing was for sure – it hadn't protected her from her own stupidity.

Living so close to the coast could be both a blessing and a curse. In autumn when the sea raged and the wind pummelled the little villages that lay huddled inland, it was a punishing environment. On days like that, Allie would wonder what she was doing there and contemplate the logistics of moving to the Mediterranean or somewhere where you didn't get beaten up by the weather on a regular basis.

But could she ever really leave Dorset? She remembered when she'd met Craig Alexander on Charmouth beach. He'd been out surfing and had looked mighty fine in his wetsuit. There'd been five minutes of flirtation on the windy beach that afternoon and a promise to meet each other in a local pub that evening. She'd drunk too much white wine and the rest was history. She'd found herself pregnant five weeks later.

'Wow!' was what Craig had said. 'That's – like – *fast!*'

Allie had seen the glazed look of fear in his eyes and had known she would be on her own if she decided to keep and raise their child. And of course she was going to keep it. She might not have planned to have a baby quite so early in a relationship, but she saw the child as a gift and she was going to make the very best of it.

Craig had upped and left shortly after the birth. He'd stayed around just long enough to see Allie settled. His parents had been thrilled at having their first grandchild and had made sure Allie had all that she needed. She still remembered the day Craig had left. He'd picked his son up, said, 'He's a cute little fellow, isn't he?' He'd kissed Allie quickly on the cheek and had got on his motorbike and disappeared. He was one of life's drifters. There'd been no malice in the way he'd left, Allie had seen that and, although it was hard for her to accept that the father of her son didn't want to be around, she'd realised that she'd never be able to change Craig and that it would be foolish to even try.

Some of her friends had been outraged at Craig's behaviour and couldn't believe how calm Allie was in her response to his infrequent visits. But what else could she do? You couldn't put shackles on somebody or make them stay by forcing them to feel guilty. That wasn't any kind of life, was it?

Anyway, the truth was, Allie liked being a single parent. Her decisions were never challenged – well, other than by her son Jack himself. She could raise him exactly the way she wanted to. Her parents and Craig's visited occasionally, but they weren't the sort to interfere. Allie couldn't help thinking that Craig's parents were a little embarrassed by their son's behaviour and that kept them away. Perhaps his mother thought Allie would always be asking them where Craig was. Well, Mrs Alexander needn't have feared on that score.

It was funny when she thought about it. Craig had left his native Dorset, but Allie the interloper had stayed. Today, as she left her cottage for the daily walk down to the beach, she thanked Mother Nature for the mild autumn day she'd blessed Lyme Bay with. It was days like this that kept Allie going through the long, cold months of winter, and when she might arrive a little late at her shop in Lyme Regis because the loveliness of the day had made her walk on the beach all the more difficult to end. Besides, these were often the best days for finds because she relaxed into her walks more, allowing her pace to slow and her eyes to focus on the treasures under her feet.

Was there anything more alluring than that glint of wet sea glass in the sand? Whether it was the opaque milky-white pieces or the bright emerald-green, Allie found it impossible to ignore and would fill her pockets with the little jewels even though she knew she had enough for several lifetimes. Still, they always came in handy when she ran the occasional class in her shop. She never tired of her students' joy when she got out the glass containers she kept her beach treasures in. Gasps of wonder would greet her and she would feel that bubble of joy rising in herself as if for the first time, knowing exactly how her students were feeling.

Spotting a piece of green glass, Allie stooped to pick it up. It was large and had that salty roughness about it that made it so wonderful to touch. She held it for a moment, the pad of her thumb rubbing over it in delicious appreciation. It would make a lovely focus for a piece of jewellery, she thought, holding it up to the light to admire its full potential. She then dropped it into her pocket where it clinked against the other treasures she had stored there.

She continued along the beach, finding more green and white glass and a few small pieces of the elusive blue which sparkled like sapphires in the sand. But it wasn't just glass she was after. Allie loved to spot anything that was pretty and she soon had a fine collection of little shells.

Checking the time, she gasped as she realised she had been on the beach for over an hour and hurried back to the cottage to collect her car. How quickly the time passed when there were only the waves for company. She'd seen barely anybody that morning, but she had recognised a fossil hunter. She'd been lost in her own little world – just as Allie had been. It was funny the way the beach united people in that unique way. You could spend hours of your life just a few feet away from somebody and yet not really know them at all. Allie supposed that it was kind of like an open plan office where you could be working alongside your colleagues without really communicating with them. Only this open plan office was the most beautiful in the world, she thought. Not for her the confines of a building – some airless room filled with computers and phones and stress. Oh, no. Allie counted herself very lucky to be running her own shop and working with beautiful, inspiring things that made her happy.

Driving the short distance to Lyme Regis, Allie parked and walked to her shop, turning the sign round to 'open' at long last. She switched the alarm off, turned the lights on and took off her glass-laden coat.

Then the day's work began. Starting with unpacking a recent acquisition. She'd placed an order for several pendants from a local jewellery maker and she brought them out of their box now. They were large blue stones set in silver and they were lovely. Some were made of blue lace agate and, with its lilac-blue and cream stripes, it reminded Allie of the tide coming in. The others were a stone called larimar which was the most celestial of blues and looked just like the Caribbean Ocean from where the stone came. Allie was hoping these would prove popular with her customers in the run-up to Christmas and was tempted to buy a couple for herself. That was the problem when you worked in a place surrounded by such beautiful things: it was easy to spend all your profits before you even got a chance to pay the household bills.

As she dusted a shop shelf, she became aware of somebody looking in one of the windows. She was used to that, of course, but this person had been standing there for some time now and Allie glanced up to see what had caught their eye.

She hadn't expected what greeted her. It was a man. A tall, handsome man with bright eyes and a smile that never failed to charm her.

It was Craig Alexander.

CHAPTER ELEVEN

Allie could feel her heart doing a tango in her chest as her shop door opened and Craig walked in.

'Hello Allie,' he said, as if he visited her shop every day and not once in a blue moon.

Allie tried to speak, but her voice died somewhere in her throat before the words could come out.

Craig was coming closer and, before she knew what was happening, he'd taken her in his arms and kissed her fully on the mouth.

'Don't do that!' she told him, finding her voice at last and pushing him away.

'Why not?' he asked, taking a step back from her. 'Are you seeing somebody?'

Allie glared at him. 'That is *none* of your business.'

The left corner of his mouth tilted upwards in that cocky way of his that she used to find so attractive, but was now just winding her up.

'That means you're not,' he said.

'That means you're overstepping the mark.'

He seemed to consider this for a moment. 'Aren't you pleased to see me?' he asked.

'I'm puzzled rather than pleased.'

'Ah!' He grinned. 'Well, I was going to call, but I thought I'd surprise you instead. You used to like surprises, didn't you?'

She couldn't help thinking that he was asking the question as if to jog his own memory. He couldn't really remember if she liked surprises or not, could he? It just went to prove that they knew so little about each other which was only to be expected when they'd hardly spent any time together.

But then she thought of Jack, her son. *Their* son. This man – her one-time partner and the man she'd loved so dearly if briefly – had given her the greatest of gifts. She must never forget that. For all his faults, she would always be eternally grateful to him. And perhaps he was here to see Jack. She couldn't stop him if that's what he wanted and there was a part of her that desperately wanted to encourage that. But there was another part of her that was, perhaps, even stronger – the part that wanted to stop Craig from going anywhere near Jack because she knew that Craig wouldn't be staying for long. He'd just be passing through. And that had the potential to do more damage to Jack than if he never saw his father at all.

A customer came in and Craig moved across to the other side of the shop. Allie nodded to the woman who smiled and proceeded to look at the collection of sea glass jewellery on display. Allie opened her sketchbook up. She'd been working on some new designs for bracelets, but it was hard to concentrate with Craig in the shop and she kept glancing up from her sketches to look at him. Damn it, but he was still so handsome with that shock of rock star hair – a little too long and a little too wild. He was wearing a scruffy biker's jacket and his jeans were ripped and faded. In short, he was a bit of a mess as far as Allie was concerned, but what a handsome mess he was.

She watched as he shuffled around the shop awkwardly in his biker boots, picking up a seashell photo frame and almost dropping it and then clumsily bumping into a low table on which perched some of her favourite pieces of pottery in swirling blue and green glazes. She could hardly bear to watch him. But then he moved towards the dresser, picked up one of the felt octopuses and, grinning, made it do a little dance on the dresser top. Allie did her best not to laugh, but a part of her wanted to reprimand him, and she probably would have if there hadn't been a customer in the shop.

She returned her attention to her sketchbook, wondering if there was a market for hat pins these days and quickly deciding that there probably wasn't. A shame really. Hat pins, cravat pins and cufflinks could be a beautiful addition to her sea glass repertoire. For a moment, she mourned for the lost world of fashion accoutrements. How wonderful if they were to have a resurgence, she thought.

She was just idly sketching a perfectly redundant hat pin when the customer approached the till.

'So lovely!' she said, holding one of Allie's sea glass pendants out towards her.

'Thank you.'

'Do you make them?'

'I do.'

'Well, they're gorgeous. It was hard to choose just one.'

Allie smiled. It was always heartening to hear that her pieces resonated with others. Carefully, she wrapped the necklace in tissue paper and popped it into a paper bag. The customer paid and left the shop.

'Thought she was never going,' Craig said, walking over to the table the customer had spent so much time poring over. 'So, you still making these funny sea glass things?'

Allie did her best not to flinch. Craig had never understood her need to create and used to make fun of her endless trips to the beach.

'Isn't it obvious?'

He gave a little laugh. 'And it's paying?'

'We do all right,' she said, feeling quite defensive now and then she noticed that Craig was still holding the felt octopus.

'Could you put that down, please?'

He looked at his hand, seemingly surprised by the fact that he was still holding something.

'Oh, right. Actually, I was thinking of getting it for Jack. What do you think?'

Allie frowned. 'Are you being serious?'

''Course I am.'

'He's twelve, Craig. He isn't going to want a soft toy.'

'Oh.' Craig looked down at the creature. 'Sorry, mate. You're not wanted.' He then replaced the octopus in the open dresser drawer, facing the wrong way so that Allie had to straighten it.

'What's he into then – Jack?' Craig asked.

'Music. Games. Books. He likes to read.'

'Does he?' Craig sounded surprised.

'Fantasy mostly. And science fiction.'

'Blimey.'

Allie tried not to sigh audibly at the lack of knowledge about his own son. After all, she'd known this about Craig all along and she should be grateful that he was showing an interest now.

'I thought I could pick him up from school and then walk back home with him,' Craig went on.

'Walk back from Lyme?' Allie said in surprise.

Craig frowned. 'No – the village school.'

'Craig – Jack's at secondary school here in Lyme Regis.'

'Is he?'

'Yes!' she cried, her frustration bubbling up inside her.

'Wow! That happened – like – fast! How long have I been away?'

'Well, if you don't know–'

'Hey! I've been busy. It isn't easy finding work on the road these days especially not in some of the places I've been.'

Allie really wasn't interested and started fiddling with some of the shells she'd pulled out of her coat pocket in an attempt to calm herself down – only it wasn't working like it usually did.

'What do you want, Craig?' she asked him, sounding more blunt than she'd intended, but she needed to know.

Craig came closer, placing his hands on the table she was working at and leaning forwards slightly.

'I want to spend some time with him, Allie. I know I haven't been the best father in the world, but I'd like to put that right.'

They stared at each other for a couple of moments and Allie could see the expression of earnestness in his eyes.

'Please – help me do this right,' he whispered. She looked down at the table top because his gaze was too intense.

'He doesn't know you,' she said at last. 'You've been away so long.'

'I know.'

'He was a small boy when you last visited.'

'I know that too.'

'And I'm scared that you're going to let him get close to you and then go again. Like you always do.'

He shook his head. 'Not this time.'

She looked up at him. 'How can I be sure?'

He blinked. 'What do you want from me? A contract signed in blood?'

'That would be a good start.'

He laughed, but then his expression became serious. 'Look, I know I've no right to do this to you both.'

'No – you do have a right,' Allie interrupted him and she was rewarded with a little smile from him.

'Thank you.'

'Just – just don't mess him about. Don't make promises you can't keep.'

He nodded and Allie sighed. This was the very last thing she'd expected to happen when she'd come into the shop this morning.

'Where are you staying?' she asked him casually, expecting he'd be at his parents' place in Dorchester.

'Actually, I was hoping I could crash at yours.'

Allie couldn't believe what she was hearing.

'Craig – you can't just turn up like this out of the blue and expect me to make up the spare room for you. Anyway, there isn't a spare room.'

'I can kip on the sofa.'

'No you can't.'

He frowned. 'Why not?'

'Because it's our home and – forgive me for putting it so bluntly – you're a stranger.'

He shuffled his boots from side to side.

'Can't you stay with your parents?' she asked.

'They've got friends over from Canada.'

'Oh. Well, can't you pitch a tent up somewhere?'

He glared at her as if she was mad. 'In this weather?'

'What? It's been lovely!'

'Look,' he said, 'give me one night to get myself sorted. I won't make a nuisance of myself. I'll even cook you both dinner. How's that?'

Allie remained unconvinced.

'I'll take Jack to school in the morning.'

'On your bike?' she asked in horror.

'I've got a spare helmet.'

'You're kidding, right? Anyway, he gets the bus.'

'Okay. I'll walk him to the bus stop.'

'You really don't need to.'

'I'll pack his lunch box.'

'Craig!'

'Please, Allie – just one night!'

If she gave in to him now that one night could so easily turn into two and then three and then...

'*One* night, okay?' she said at last, holding up a solitary index finger as if to make herself absolutely clear.

Craig grinned. 'Okay,' he said.

Allie sighed. She knew she was letting herself in for a world of trouble.

Cate was still feeling emotionally bruised after Charles had shouted at her for taking Jamie's books and was anxious that he might ask her and Eliza to leave at the end of the month. She'd been steadfastly avoiding him, but that could only last so long when they were living and working together under the same roof.

Later that morning, Cate was working in his office, processing some of the orders from his website, when she heard Rigs barking and guessed that Charles was back. He'd been down on the beach for hours and she couldn't help wondering if part of the reason he'd been there so long was to avoid her.

She waited a moment, listening as he came into his workshop, and then she took two deep breaths for courage before going to face him.

'Charles?' she said, her voice small and reed-like.

He looked up from the central table where he'd just placed

a boulder-like stone. His hair looked damp from a recent downpour and his face was pinched with the cold.

'Yes?'

'I want to apologise for the other day.'

She saw him swallow.

'I shouldn't have gone into Jamie's room. And I shouldn't have taken those books – not without asking anyway.'

'No, you shouldn't have.'

'I'm sorry.' She looked down at the dusty floorboards of his workshop and made a mental note to tackle them later. She waited for him to accept her apology, but he didn't. Perhaps he wasn't going to accept it. Perhaps they weren't going to be able to move on from this.

'Well, I just wanted to say I was sorry. That's all,' she repeated and then withdrew to the office. She turned her attention to the computer and continued with her work.

'Cate?'

Charles was standing in the doorway.

'Yes?' She couldn't help feeling nervous and half expected that he was about to give her her notice. Maybe he'd let her see out the promised month, but that would be an end of things. She and Eliza would have to go.

'I wanted to apologise too.'

She frowned. '*You* apologise?'

'I shouldn't have shouted like that. The last thing I want to do is scare Eliza.'

There was a pause while they both stared at each other, not quite knowing what to do next.

'Then we're both sorry and we both accept each other's apologies?' she asked, thinking it was best if they were absolutely clear about this.

He nodded and Cate felt relief surging through her.

'And will you go on teaching Eliza?'

'Of course.'

Cate smiled, unable to hide her joy. 'Thank you!'

'Perhaps...' he paused.

'What?'

'Perhaps I could choose some books for her. From Jamie's room.'

Cate's mouth dropped open. 'Really?'

'Just a few. To begin with.' He gazed down at the floor for a moment and Cate stared at him, wondering what was going through his mind, and a part of her wanted to cross the space between them and take his hand in hers to give him some comfort because she could see how difficult this was for him.

'She'd *love* that,' Cate told him, bringing him back into the moment.

Charles looked up again. 'Because they're just sitting there, aren't they?'

Cate nodded and then gave him a tender smile. 'I think that... well, that books should be read. It shows that you love them.'

Charles glanced down at the floor again. 'Yes.'

'That's what I think anyway.'

He nodded and then sighed. 'Listen – I have to go out for a bit.' His hand came up and clutched at the door, his fingers drumming on it.

'Back to the beach?' Cate asked.

'No.' The drumming continued. 'No,' he said again.

'I'll see you later, then.'

He seemed to hesitate before leaving as if he wanted to say something else. But he thought better of it and simply nodded and left.

🐚 🐚 🐚 🐚 🐚

Charles went upstairs and changed quickly out of his tatty old fossil hunting clothes and put on some tatty but clean clothes. He really should invest in a new wardrobe, he thought, but it seemed such an extravagance as, besides the beach and the care home, he never really went anywhere and who was there to see him? Other than Cate and Eliza, that was? No, his old clothes would have to do. He didn't have money to splash out on new things.

Leaving the house a moment later, he couldn't help feeling relieved that the awkwardness between him and Cate had lifted. As angry as he'd been at her for entering Jamie's room, he couldn't help admitting that she might have helped in some small way. Perhaps it was time to stop treating that room like some kind of museum to Jamie. He wouldn't have wanted that, would he? Jamie – like himself – had always been a practical boy and he would most likely have detested his beloved books being left on a shelf when somebody could have been enjoying them just as much as he had.

Jamie.

A hard lump of sorrow formed in Charles's throat and he did his best to swallow it down which wasn't easy. Some days were worse than others and today felt like a bad one. Talking with Cate had forced him to remember things he'd thought he'd locked safely away. But nothing was truly locked away, was it? Anything could bubble up to the surface at a moment's notice. That was the terror of grief. You were never in control of it no matter how hard you tried to convince yourself that you were.

But Charles couldn't give in to grief today. He had things to do. And so he got in his car and drove.

How quickly each week went by, Charles thought, as he made his way to the care home to see his mother. The truth was, he was glad to get out of Hollow House even if it was just for a couple of hours. He might well have smoothed things over with

Cate, but the house still felt heavy with their altercation as well as the sadness Cate had forced to the fore of Charles's mind.

He followed the coast road and then turned down the lane that led to the care home, parking a moment later on the gravel driveway alongside the other visitors' cars.

He hesitated before he went inside, preparing himself mentally for how he might find his mother. Would it be a good day or a bad day or even an indifferent day? Those were, perhaps, the worst – when she'd just sit there saying nothing and doing nothing. Charles found those particularly gruelling.

He took a deep breath, grabbed the box he'd left on the passenger seat, and went inside.

The receptionist nodded and smiled at him as he entered and signed in. Then he followed the long, carpet-silent corridor towards his mother's door. It was ajar. Perhaps somebody was keeping an eye on her. He looked around, but nobody seemed to be about so he knocked gently before going inside.

His mother turned around and smiled at him as he walked into the room, which was encouraging.

'Hi Mum!' he said, bending to kiss her. 'You smell good.'

'Perfume,' she said.

'Perfume?'

'One of the girl's gave me a squirt.' His mother chuckled and Charles smiled. He couldn't remember the last time he'd seen her so happy. She seemed almost normal again – as if she'd slipped back into her old self – and it was such a wonderful moment that Charles realised how very stressed he'd been coming to see her today and that he really shouldn't be. He shouldn't expect his visits to be doom-filled because he didn't know how this disease would affect her from moment to moment, and it wasn't fair to expect her to always be difficult or uncommunicative.

'Mum,' he said, 'I've brought you your favourite chocolates.'

She wowed him with a smile. 'Oh, thank you!'

'Would you like one now? I've taken the cellophane off.'

She looked at the box, her eyes alight. 'No. Best not. After tea perhaps.'

Charles nodded and placed the mint chocolates on her bedside table.

As he sat down in the chair opposite her, he noticed her glance out of the window and he swallowed hard. There was something about looking out of the window that seemed to carry her away to another plane and he prepared himself to lose her again. Well, it had been nice while it lasted.

'Mum?' he said softly, hoping against hope that he might call her back into the present moment, but her gaze was fixed on the middle distance. 'Mum?'

He was surprised when she finally spoke.

'I saw your father today.'

Charles blinked, wondering if he'd heard her right.

She motioned outside with her left hand, her wedding ring, which she never took off, flashing. 'He was over there by the tree. Waving at me.'

Charles couldn't help looking out of the window. There was nobody there, of course, and probably never had been.

'Mum?' he began, but he was too late.

She suddenly turned and stared at him.

'Where's Jamie?' she demanded, her calm expression replaced by one of perplexity.

Oh, God, Charles thought, closing his eyes in despair. Not again. Not today.

He took a deep breath in an attempt to remain calm. 'He's not here, Mum.'

'Why doesn't he visit me anymore?'

'You know why.'

'I don't know why.' Her perplexity was fast turning into

rage. 'Tell me why! *Why* doesn't my Jamie come and see me anymore? Are you keeping him from me?'

Charles could see the colour rising in his mother's face as she worked herself up into one of her frenzies.

'No, of course I'm not keeping him from you.'

'Then why isn't he here? Why doesn't he come?'

Charles was aware of a facial tick pulling at the skin by his mouth. He was feeling jittery and anxious. His palms were hot and his back felt clammy.

'Mum – please don't keep asking me that.'

'I want to know where Jamie is!' She was stamping her feet now like a child throwing a tantrum.

'Please–'

'Tell me where he is!' Her feet were thumping on the floor, the shockwaves making Charles feel as if he was about to have a heart attack.

'He's DEAD, Mum! He's dead and you'll never see him again, okay?'

Charles was on his feet now and hadn't realised he'd been shouting until one of the carers came into the room.

'Mrs Thorner – are you all right?' she asked.

His mother was rocking in her chair now, her hands twisting around themselves.

'Yes, she's all right!' Charles snapped and then felt bad at the sight of his mother so frail and vulnerable.

'Mr Thorner!' the woman said, turning to face him. 'Would you like to come with me?

He ran a hand through his hair, suddenly feeling anxious. Where was she taking him? Maybe he was going to be banned from the home. He couldn't say he'd blame them.

'Mum?' he called softly. 'Mum? I'm sorry.'

The carer took his arm and guided him from the room.

He was led into a small office which overlooked the

courtyard where some of the residents were walking around in the autumn sunshine. As he watched them, he heard hushed voices in the corridor outside and could only imagine the conversation that was taking place about him. He dropped his head to his chest and sighed. Some days, he felt like he was unravelling and this just happened to be one of those days.

When he heard the door close behind him, he turned around to see Philip Orton, the manager of the care home. He was a pretty decent sort of chap. Late forties, hair receding, a slight paunch, but always a kind face.

'Please, take a seat,' he told Charles as he came into the room and his kind tone made Charles immediately feel guilty at what he'd done.

'Before you say anything, I'm sorry. I didn't mean to shout at her. It won't happen again.'

Philip shook his head and, instead of going to sit behind his desk, he sat on the chair next to Charles.

'It's okay,' he told Charles.

'No – no, it's not. I shouldn't have lost my temper like that.'

'Don't blame yourself. We can't always be in control of our emotions and your mother's condition is a pretty emotive one.'

Charles took a deep breath and let it out slowly, deflating his anxiety just a little. 'I had to tell her – she kept asking me. It's nearly every visit now.'

'About your son?'

Charles nodded. 'I don't know – I just couldn't cope today. She kept asking and asking why I don't bring Jamie to see her anymore. It was driving me crazy! Why can't she remember?'

Charles was aware that his voice had risen again and Philip leaned forward in his chair and gently patted Charles's hand. It was so unexpected and tender a gesture that Charles almost felt like crying.

'I'm afraid patients with dementia can be unpredictable.

They seem to retain the strangest information while the big important things in life like who their own family members are can be totally forgotten. And all that changes from moment to moment. I'm sure you've seen that.'

'Oh, yes,' Charles agreed. He'd seen it all too often.

'And I'm afraid that's unlikely to change,' Philip went on. 'The only thing we can change is our response to it.'

Charles swallowed hard. What Philip was telling him in that compassionate way of his was that Charles's outburst had achieved nothing.

'I'm sorry,' Charles said. It seemed to be a day filled with apologising for his bad behaviour.

'It's okay,' Philip assured him. 'This is a stressful condition for relatives to cope with and please don't think we're judging you for your behaviour. That's the last thing we'd do. I simply wanted to make sure that you're okay.' Philip paused and Charles wondered if he was expected to say something although he could think of nothing other than to apologise again.

'Is there any way we could support you better in this?' Philip asked. 'Perhaps it would be easier to see your mother when she's in the communal area? Or maybe you'd like to join us on one of the trips we take residents on?'

Charles flinched inwardly. That was the very last thing he wanted.

'Don't feel you have to commit to anything today. Just give it some thought.'

Charles nodded, feeling relieved.

'Well, I'm afraid I have a rather dull meeting to attend,' Philip said, standing up and Charles took that as his welcome cue to leave.

'Thank you,' he said as Philip reached a hand out to shake his. 'You've been very understanding about all this.'

'Not at all.'

Charles was glad to leave the care home. He drove directly to the coast, parking his car and sitting for a moment with his window open, listening to the calming crash of the waves. It was high tide and not the time for fossil hunting, but he decided to go for a walk on the little strip of beach that the sea had left, hoping that the roar of the waves would silence the roar in his head.

It had been a wet autumn and you had to be careful not to walk too close to the cliffs for fear of rock falls. It was an autumn that reminded him so horribly of the events just two years ago when the accident had happened.

Charles stopped walking and stared out into the grey waves as he remembered the first time he'd taken Jamie fossil hunting. He'd been four years' old. Sophie had protested, but Charles had insisted that the young boy was ready to see what his father got up to. Indeed, Jamie had been asking for months if he could go with his daddy.

Gazing out to sea, Charles could remember it as if it were yesterday, and he could almost feel that small hand tightly encased in his own right now. So much so that he looked down as if he might discover his son beside him.

He closed his eyes and smiled sadly as he thought of how Jamie's little arms had been stiff with the many layers Sophie had wrapped him in that the poor boy had hardly been able to move. Charles had unzipped his coat a little and had decided that the scarf that obscured half his face wasn't absolutely necessary.

It had been a bracing walk that day. Charles had shown Jamie some of his favourite places along the cliffs and they'd picked up endless belemnites and ammonites together. And Charles had told Jamie about The Big One – the fossilised remains of a beast of such proportions as had never been seen before.

'It's waiting for us, Jamie. I just know it is.'

'Where is it, Daddy?'

'It's sleeping in the cliffs along this coast. Waiting for its time to reveal itself to the world.'

'And you're going to find it?'

Charles had smiled down at his son.

'*We're* going to find it,' he'd told him.

Only Jamie had never lived to see it.

Charles turned away from the sea and glanced up at the cliffs, wondering if The Big One was any closer to being discovered. Then, head down against the icy wind, he walked towards his car.

When he got back to Hollow House, he could hear Cate talking to Eliza in the kitchen. Rigs, who usually welcomed his master if he'd been out without him, didn't make an appearance. Traitor, Charles thought, but he would make use of the opportunity of not being accosted by anyone. The truth was, he wasn't ready for company just yet, even that of his little dog.

Charles headed upstairs, knowing exactly where he was going. Perhaps that was why he was feeling so odd all of a sudden. But it was the right thing to do. He felt that now.

Reaching the top of the stairs, he made his way to the bowl on the landing and plucked out the key. He then walked towards the door, placing the key in the lock and his fingers around the door handle. Slowly, he opened it and went inside. He'd been into the room many times since that dreadful day, but it never seemed to get any easier.

Time. Everybody had told him it took time. But how much time? He sometimes thought if he lived to be as old as the fossils he found, it still wouldn't be long enough to get over the death of his son. And were you meant to get over such a thing? It seemed barbaric to him that he should even think of a life after

Jamie. What right did he have to be happy again when his son lay in his grave? What right did he have to begin again?

Charles walked over to the little shelf and stared at the volumes there, remembering what a great bookworm his son had been. He took a book down and he could feel tears forming as he flipped through the pages and saw a little doodle Jamie had made in the margin. It was of a dinosaur and Charles could remember reprimanding Jamie for having misused his book in such a way. But – oh – how glad he was to see that little doodle now, his fingers touching it lightly.

He chose a few more titles and then sat on the edge of the bed, feeling the full weight of his sorrow. It had been a long, hard day. They came from time to time and he had to live with that.

He could only hope that tomorrow would be easier.

CHAPTER TWELVE

Allie had asked Craig if he'd give her a few minutes with Jack before he called round. Craig hadn't been keen to oblige, but had reluctantly agreed. He'd still wanted to pick his son up from school and bring him home on the back of his motorbike, but Allie wasn't having any nonsense like that.

She was restless and anxious when Jack arrived home, doing her best to busy herself in the kitchen.

'Hey Jack!' she called when she heard the front door opening.

'Hi Mum.'

'Want something to eat?'

'No thanks.'

She heard his footfall on the stairs and came out into the hallway to see his shoes and bag by the door. She'd been hoping she could have a little chat with him over a cup of tea and some biscuits, but he was too eager to get up to his room and his computer.

'Jack?' she called as she went upstairs, tapping on his door a moment later.

'What?'

Allie entered the room. 'Jack! Don't say *what*. Say *pardon*.'

Jack nodded without looking away from his bright screen. Allie sometimes wished they had more power cuts in their village. She'd love to know what life would be like without the influence of that dreadful box.

'Jack? Look at me, darling.'

Jack sighed and turned away from his computer.

'There's someone who wants to see you.'

'Who?'

Allie could feel her throat tighten and wondered if she'd be able to get the words out.

'Your dad.'

Jack frowned. 'My dad's here?'

'Yes. He's outside.'

'You mean the guy hanging around with the bike? That's my dad?'

'Yes. Do you want to see him?'

Suddenly, Jack looked like a vulnerable little boy rather than the slightly sulky lad he was rapidly turning into as he neared his teens.

There was a pause before he answered. 'Yes.'

Allie nodded. 'Do you want to come downstairs?'

Jack got up from his chair, looking as if he'd been summoned by the headmaster, and Allie wanted to give him a hug but didn't think he'd appreciate that.

'He's very keen to see you.'

'Is he?' Jack said. 'Why?' His voice was laced with suspicion. 'I mean... why now?'

Allie sighed, truly not knowing what to say. 'I'm not sure. Maybe he's just ready now.'

'Where's he been?'

'I'm not sure.'

'You don't know much about him, do you?' Jack said, not in an accusatory tone at all. He was genuinely perplexed.

'Your dad is what we call a free spirit. He comes and goes. He does what suits him when he wants.'

Jack muttered something under his breath.

'And that doesn't make him a bad man, darling – it just makes him... different. But he's here now and he wants to see you. But only if you want to see him, that is.'

Allie smiled encouragingly although she still had grave misgivings about the whole thing.

Once downstairs, Allie went to the front door and opened it. Craig was standing on the opposite side of the road with his head down against the wind, his hands deep in his pockets. Allie beckoned him over.

'It's freezing out here!' he said, his accusatory tone suggesting that he should have been allowed in before now.

'He's ready to see you,' Allie said, 'but, if you mess this up in any way, you'll have to leave – understood?'

'I'm not going to mess it up.'

Allie gave him a look which she hoped would help him to understand exactly how she felt about this situation.

'Take your boots off,' she said as he stepped into the hallway behind her.

He tutted, but did as he was told.

'You know, I'm actually quite nervous,' he whispered and Allie blinked, almost feeling sympathy for him. Almost, but not quite.

'Come on through. He's waiting for you,' Allie told him, leading the way into the kitchen. 'Jack?' Her son was standing by the sink, his lanky body all awkward angles.

'Hey!' Craig said, moving forward as if to hug Jack, but stopping as he read Jack's body language. Allie flinched inwardly as her son inched backwards a little, a frown etched on his face. 'How are you?'

Jack didn't answer.

'How's school?' Craig tried again with that old chestnut of a question adults ask when they don't have a clue how to talk to a child.

''S'okay,' Jack said.

For a moment, Allie thought it was all over and that Craig was going to give up at the first hurdle and leave. But he didn't.

'I got you something,' Craig began again, reaching inside his jacket pocket. Allie was dreading what he was going to produce after the soft toy octopus incident. Luckily, it was something more suitable: a huge bar of nougat. 'You like it?' He handed it to Jack.

'Sure,' Jack said with a grin, and Allie couldn't help being a little disappointed that her son had been bought as easily as Edmund was by Turkish Delight in *The Lion, the Witch and the Wardrobe.*

'Thought you might,' Craig said, sounding more confident now that he'd made an inroad with candy. 'I used to live on it. My mum – your grandma – used to tell me all my teeth would drop out before I was twenty.'

'And did they?'

Craig opened his mouth in an exaggerated smile and Jack smiled right back at him.

'Don't eat it all in one go,' Allie told him, kind of wishing Craig had bought him the octopus after all.

'Well, shall we sit down?' Craig suggested.

'I'll make some tea, okay?' Allie said.

'Milk, two sugars – remember?' Craig said.

'I remember.'

Allie got three mugs out of the cupboard and filled the kettle, fiddling with tea bags, milk and sugar as Craig shifted in his chair and cleared his throat, working up to ask another unsuitable question, no doubt, Allie thought uncharitably.

'So, what's your favourite subject at school?'

And there it was. Allie almost laughed.

'I don't know,' Jack said.

'You must like one more than the others,' Craig persisted.

Allie saw Jack shrug. 'Science, I guess.'

'Oh, we have a budding scientist, do we?'

'Jack wants to work with computers,' Allie told Craig.

'Is that right?'

'I guess.'

'But there's plenty of time to make such important decisions,' Allie said, serving the tea and giving her son's shoulder a gentle squeeze.

'The last time I saw you, you were still riding a bike with stabilisers on.'

Jack grimaced at being reminded of being a kid.

'Do you have a bike?' Craig asked.

Jack shook his head.

'They're expensive, Craig,' Allie told him.

'I don't need one anyway.'

Craig looked upset by this admission. 'But a bike means freedom.'

'It means danger on the roads around here,' Allie cut in before Craig got himself any ideas about buying Jack a bike.

'It's not dangerous if you take care. Listen – I'll take you out on the motorbike, okay? Give you a taste of what it's like.'

Allie felt her blood run cold. 'You will not!'

'He'll love it, Allie!'

'I will, Mum!'

'Not happening,' Allie said emphatically.

Craig ran a hand through his hair. 'We'll have to think of something else to do, Jack.'

'Yeah, I guess so.'

'What did we do together the last time I saw you?'

'He was probably too young to remember,' Allie said, a twist of cruelty in her voice that she couldn't quite help.

'I'm sure it was something fun, wasn't it?' Craig asked.

Jack shrugged. 'I don't really remember.'

Craig sighed.

'Oh, wait,' Jack suddenly said, 'was it you who took me swimming that summer when I found that jellyfish on the beach and–'

'No, darling,' Allie interrupted, 'that was Ben, a friend of mine.'

'Oh.'

Craig looked put out by this. 'I can't believe you don't remember me. I have visited, you know.'

'Craig!' Allie used her warning voice. 'It's not his fault.'

'No. It's all *mine*, I suppose.' Craig snapped, getting up and leaving the room. They heard the front door open and slam shut, the sound of his motorbike starting up a moment later.

Allie looked at Jack who seemed angry and lost.

'Great idea, Mum!' he said and fled upstairs and, a moment later, Allie heard the sound of his bedroom door slamming.

'I can't believe I let him into our home so readily,' Allie told Cate as they walked along the beach, their hands in their pockets and the wind in their faces, Eliza skipping ahead of them. It was Friday morning and Allie had called a crisis meeting and, luckily, Cate had been able to respond, leaving a note for Charles in case he missed them. He'd told her that she was free to make her own timetable, as long as each day's work got done, and Cate valued the freedom of being able to come and go as she pleased.

'I had my reservations, of course, and I knew it wasn't going to be easy,' Allie went on, 'but I didn't think it would be quite as bad as it was. But at least he didn't stay the night like he'd threatened to.'

'And he just stormed out?'

'Yep! Like a stroppy teenager. In fact, out of Craig and Jack, I'd say that Jack handled the whole thing with far more maturity than his father.

'Oh, Allie – I'm so sorry.'

'It's my fault.'

'No it's not!'

'It is! I shouldn't even have let him into my shop when I saw him outside it. I should've locked the door on him and pulled the blinds down,' she paused. 'Even though I don't have blinds.'

Cate couldn't help smiling.

'Honestly, Cate, he brings nothing but trouble with him.' She groaned. 'Why oh *why* did I let him near Jack?'

Cate glanced at Allie as they walked and put a gloved hand on her friend's shoulder.

'You were trying to do your best for everyone. That can sometimes be impossible.'

'You're telling me!'

They continued to walk, Eliza ahead of them, bending at intervals to examine the stones and sea glass beneath her feet.

'How did we get so unlucky with the fathers of our children?' Allie cried into the wind.

Cate swallowed hard.

'I mean, what did our children do to deserve that fate?'

'Nothing!' Cate told her, 'but we're doing okay on our own, aren't we?'

'That's my one solace in this,' Allie said. 'I look at Jack

sometimes and can't believe the last twelve years have happened. I remember how terrified I was when I found out I was pregnant. That was scary enough, but it was even scarier when I realised I was going to have to raise him on my own.'

'But you're doing an amazing job.'

Allie smiled, looking genuinely surprised by this praise. 'Really? I'm not sure some of the time. Perhaps that's why I let Craig back in. I worry that Jack's missing out not having his father in his life.'

'But he has everything he needs,' Cate told her friend. 'A loving mother, a wonderful home, food in his belly and even a rabbit to cuddle.'

Allie laughed, but her smile soon faded. 'But is it the same? Does a child not need a father too?'

'Not like the one Eliza has.'

They stopped walking and Allie turned to face Cate. 'God, I'm sorry! Here I am moaning on about my little problem when you're the one who really knows what trouble is.'

'It's okay,' Cate assured her. 'But something I've learned is that it's far, far worse to be in a destructive relationship than none at all. I feared leaving for so long. I wasn't sure I could cope on my own and, well, let's just say that he didn't exactly help to build me up over the years. In fact, I think he wore me down quite a bit.' Cate paused, staring down at the pebbles and the sand.

'I noticed that when you came into the shop,' Allie said gently.

'You did?' Cate looked up.

'You seemed – I don't know – more fragile. And you were never fragile before. You were always so strong and happy and vibrant.'

Cate felt like she was on the edge of tears as she listened to

Allie. It had been one thing to acknowledge the change, but quite another to hear about it from somebody else.

'I don't know what happened,' Cate said hopelessly. 'No, that's a lie. I do know. He wore me away little by little. Like the sea on the cliffs. With each tide, he'd expose more of my insecurities. He'd tell me things about myself that weren't true and I believed him because he told me over and over again. I started to believe his lies that I wasn't a good person, that I didn't deserve to have friends and that I shouldn't be out in company at all.'

'God, Cate! How did you put up with that for so long?'

Cate shrugged. 'I thought I loved him.' She gave a hollow laugh. 'I thought that was love. All those things he said to me and did to me – I thought that was his way of guiding me. I really managed to convince myself of that.'

'Oh, Cate!' Allie reached out a hand.

'It's okay. I know how stupid I was now.'

'Not stupid – *never* stupid.'

'Then why did I stay all those years?'

'Because you'd built a life together and because you had Eliza.'

Cate sighed. It was true. She'd made a home and had to admit that a part of her had been terrified of walking away from that and going where exactly?

'But you're still strong, Cate,' Allie went on. 'You escaped, didn't you? You're here. And you and Eliza are safe and happy.'

Cate blinked her tears away and looked to where Eliza was bent double, her eyes fixed on the beach, a look of intense concentration on her young face.

'I wish I could be sure,' Cate said, voicing the fear she harboured deep within her – the one that kept her awake late into the dark, Dorset nights. Even though they had managed to leave Cambridgeshire and she had done everything in her power not to be traced, she couldn't help worrying. Were they truly safe here? Would he somehow manage to track them down and come after them? And, if he did, what would he do? Cate was terrified when her thoughts strayed into that territory because she knew his retribution could well be the end of her. She did her best to hide her fear from Eliza, of course, but she sometimes wondered if her daughter knew exactly what she was thinking for she would often come up to her and simply hug her, as if instinctively knowing that was exactly what she needed at that moment.

'Cate?' Allie called softly, her hand reaching out to touch her shoulder.

'Sorry!'

'You left me there for a minute. You okay?'

Cate nodded and then she thought of Charles. 'You know, all this talk of rotten fathers and we're forgetting Charles. I'm sure he was a good father. You can tell by the guarded way he acts around everything to do with Jamie.'

Allie nodded. 'You're right. He doted on that boy. I'd often see him on the beach with him.' Allie gave a smile. 'I remember this one time – Jamie got his wellies stuck in some of that awful mud at the base of the cliffs. Charles was struggling to get him out and another fossil hunter came along to help. It was quite a scene!'

'But he was okay? I mean, he was okay then?'

'Oh, yes. Charles popped him up onto his shoulders after that, muddy wellies and all.'

'But should he have been so close to the cliffs if there was a danger of getting stuck?'

'Probably not,' Allie said. 'But he was his father's son and those cliffs are the family business.'

Cate glanced up at the dark cliffs that stretched along the beach.

'Eliza!' she called. 'Come and hold my hand.' Her daughter was nowhere near the cliffs, but Cate suddenly needed to have her close.

'You know what?' Allie said. 'I could really use a cup of tea before I go into work. Shall we get off this beach?'

Cate smiled. 'That sounds like a very good idea indeed.'

Later that day, after Cate and Eliza had returned from the beach and Charles was back from making a delivery, he called Eliza through to his workshop.

'I've got something for you,' he said, placing the books in front of her as she sat down at the corner of one of his workbenches which he'd cleared for her as a place to work. 'These belonged to my son, Jamie.' He paused, very aware of Eliza's large blue eyes watching him intently. 'He would have... he would have wanted you to use them.'

Eliza looked at the books and then back up at Charles, and then she picked up her pencil and wrote something in her notebook, handing it to Charles a moment later.

I will look after them.

Charles smiled. 'I know you will.' He picked up one of the books. 'I thought you might like to start with this one. It's got a very good chapter about Mary Anning. Remember we talked about her? She was the nineteenth-century fossil hunter who made some really important early discoveries.' Charles opened the book and presented the chapter to Eliza. 'Have a read of that and then I'll show you something, okay?'

Eliza nodded and Charles moved across to the other side of the room and began his work, glancing round every so often to make sure Eliza was getting on all right.

It was about twenty minutes later when he heard her chair scrape back and he turned to see her standing up.

'Finished the chapter?'

She nodded.

'Okay, good.' He motioned to her to join him at his bench. 'I want to show you something rather special. It's something I've been working on for a while now.'

Eliza joined him and peered closely at the pile of bones in front of her.

'This is an ichthyosaur. You know what they look like now, don't you?'

Eliza nodded.

'Well, it's *part* of an ichthyosaur. It's missing some of its tailbone, I'm afraid.'

Eliza scribbled a note.

Where is it?

Charles smiled. 'Well, it might have been washed out to sea recently or even millions of years ago if it was broken. Or maybe it was eaten by a predator so that, when the bones settled on the seabed, it had already lost its tail. I guess we'll never know.'

Eliza scribbled again.

This is what Mary Anning found.

'That's right,' Charles said. 'She and her brother Joseph found some of the first ichthyosaurs. Just think – this one here might have been friends with the one the Annings found.'

Eliza gave a tiny smile as did Charles because he wondered how on earth that thought had popped into his head.

'You see how it's in very soft shale and its bones are all over the place? The bones from its paddle have come away and are scattered amongst the ribs here, see? It's waiting patiently to be put in the right order and it takes a while to get it right particularly if some of the pieces are missing. That's what you don't really know until you start working.'

Eliza passed him her notebook again.

How long will it take you?

'Well, that's the big question,' Charles said, scratching the back of his neck. 'I'm a bit of a flitter. I tend to work on several pieces at once, but I should get this done in the next couple of months, all being well.'

He watched as Eliza gazed down into the pile of rubble-like bones.

'Would you like to have a go?' he asked her.

Her eyes widened with surprise.

'You've done a jigsaw puzzle before, haven't you?'

She nodded.

'Well, it's just like that really only – well – bonier.'

For one wonderful moment, Charles could have sworn Eliza was on the verge of laughing, but she didn't and Charles couldn't help feeling a stab of disappointment. He wasn't quite as clever as Rigs was, obviously.

He stood back, giving Eliza some space to work.

'Don't be afraid. You have nice small fingers which are made for this sort of work. Not like my fat clumsy ones.'

A sound.

Charles did a double take. There'd been a definite little pip of sound from Eliza then. Not quite a laugh, but certainly something that might precede a laugh. He grinned. He must tell Cate.

'Eliza – I'm just going to make a cup of tea for your mum, okay?'

She nodded, but didn't turn around as she was too absorbed in her work. Charles was delighted that he'd introduced her to this special creature. But then she stopped what she was doing and, picking up a pencil, wrote something down quickly in her notebook.

Can we look for one together on the beach one day?

Charles read the question, his heart slowly sinking inside of him as he passed the notebook back to her.

'Let me think about it,' he told her and he left the workshop, heading to the kitchen to make some tea.

But he didn't make the tea for a few minutes. Instead, he thought about Eliza's note. It wasn't just the note – it was the way she'd looked at him with those intense blue eyes of hers. She had a way of expressing so much even without the use of words and he found that rather unnerving, he didn't mind admitting.

But he couldn't. He just couldn't.

After that dreadful December day on the beach, he'd vowed he'd never trust himself to take a child fossil hunting again. It was too dangerous to risk. And – yes – his scientific mind told him it had just been appalling bad luck and the odds of anything like that happening again were unlikely, but the parent in him was still terrified to the core.

Parent. Father. Was he those things now? Could you still be called those names when your child had died? There wasn't a name for that, was there? When you lost a wife, you became a widower; when a child lost their parents, the child became an orphan, but what did a parent become when they lost a child? Other than completely helpless and hopeless?

Charles took a deep breath. It was all too easy to fall into desperate thoughts and he didn't want to go there. So he returned his thoughts to Eliza, trying his best to be rational. After all, Eliza wasn't Jamie, was she? For a start, she was two years older than Jamie had been and, if they did go to the beach, Cate would be there with them because Charles wouldn't dream of taking Eliza by himself.

So, was he going to suggest it?

He put the kettle on and then went to the foot of the stairs. He could hear a vacuum cleaner above and so waited for a few moments. Finally, it was switched off and he called up.

'Cate?'

She appeared at the top of the stairs. 'Am I making too much noise?'

'No. I was just making a cup of tea. Want one?'

'Please. I'll be done in a mo.'

Charles returned to the kitchen and it suddenly occurred to him that this was the first cup of tea he'd offered to make for Cate. In fact, he probably hadn't made anybody besides himself a cup of tea for about two years now.

He pulled two mugs from the cupboard. He'd have to ask how she liked it. He was just taking the milk out of the fridge when Cate came into the room.

'Thank you, Charles,' she said. 'Milk, one sugar.'

He nodded, doing his best to lock that little piece of information away as he put tea bags in the mugs and added hot water.

'Eliza okay?' she asked.

'Fine. I've left her with a practical task.'

'Oh?'

'She's piecing together the bones of an ichthyosaur.'

Cate laughed. 'You're kidding me!'

'I assure you, I'm not.'

'And she's okay with that?'

'She seems like a natural. She even made a little noise.'

'She did?' Cate beamed him a smile. 'What sort of noise?'

'It was tiny. Just a pip of excitement really.'

Cate seemed to ponder this for a moment. 'Maybe we have a young palaeontologist on our hands. Maybe this new interest of hers will encourage her to talk.'

'Maybe.' Charles handed her a mug and then took a sip

from his own. 'She asked if she could go fossil hunting with me again.'

Cate frowned. 'Oh, Charles – I'm so sorry. I'll have a quiet word with her. She knows she's not meant to pester you.'

Cate turned to leave the room right there and then when he stopped her.

'No, wait a minute.'

She looked back at him.

'Maybe – I mean – perhaps we could all go together.'

He watched as her face slowly broke into a smile. 'To the beach? Fossil hunting?

'Yes.'

'Really?'

'Well, we won't be hacking out pieces of the cliff or anything like that. I think that's what Eliza might actually have in mind after seeing this ichthyosaur. But I thought we could look for some easier pieces to find.'

'Like ammonites?'

'Yes.'

'Charles – she'd *love* that! I'd love it too.'

'Don't get her too excited. We won't be making any scientific breakthroughs.'

'Well, you never know.'

'True, but I don't want Eliza getting her hopes up. I've been filling her head with Mary Anning and I don't want her to be disappointed if she only finds a broken belemnite.'

'She won't be disappointed, I promise.'

CHAPTER THIRTEEN

It had been a long time since Charles had had anyone in his Land Rover other than his dog, Rigs, and it felt strange having Cate sitting next to him with Eliza in the back. Rigs, who was sitting next to Eliza, seemed totally unfazed by this new development – less fazed than Charles at least.

'This is a bit like a school field trip,' Cate announced as they set off. 'Only better.'

'Is it?' he asked.

'Of course. There are no teachers on this one.'

'But I thought we were teachers now?'

'Yes, but not boring old teachers with rule books and worksheets.'

'Ah, I see.'

'Although I have been doing my research, you know?' Cate announced.

'You have?'

'Eliza isn't the only one who's been reading about Mary Anning. I've been finding out a bit about her from one of your books.'

'Really?'

'And she sounds like a pretty fascinating woman.'

'Oh, she was.'

'To have made all those discoveries and stood her ground in a world dominated by men. And then,' Cate said, her voice raising a little, 'to have one of her finds ridiculed by that dreadful Frenchman!'

'Georges Cuvier.'

'What a prat! Just because he'd never seen anything like her discovery before didn't mean that it wasn't real.'

Charles nodded. 'It was a pretty remarkable find, though. It had around forty vertebrae in its neck. Just imagine what that looked like to the scientists at the time. They'd never seen anything so strange.'

'But to have her work questioned like that. What kind of dinosaur was it again?'

'A plesiosaur,' Charles said. 'Not technically a dinosaur. It was a marine reptile. Dinosaurs lived on the land.'

'Well, anyway – to be accused of cobbling together bones from other beasts and passing them off fraudulently – it might have ruined her,' Cate said.

'Indeed.'

'It's so wrong. Why should she have been discredited like that?'

Charles shrugged. 'Things were tough if you were a woman back then. And even tougher if you were a working-class woman.'

'It's not right,' Cate said.

'I agree,' Charles told her. 'You know there's a statue of her in Lyme Regis now.'

'Well, I should think so!' Cate said.

Charles smiled. 'I like that you feel so strongly about our local heroine.'

'I do.'

'Just...' Charles stopped.

'What?'

'Don't get your hopes up. It's very unlikely that we'll find anything like that today.'

'But there's always a chance, isn't there?' Cate said.

Charles didn't answer.

'Charles? Isn't there? That's why you go out so often, isn't it? Because you never know what's waiting for you each day.'

He sighed. 'Yes. You never know.'

Cate nodded. 'So, today might be our lucky day. Mightn't it?'

'Anything is possible, I guess.'

It didn't take long to reach Charmouth. It was, perhaps, the most famous destination for fossil hunters – both professional and amateur – along the whole of the Jurassic Coast but, on an overcast day towards the beginning of winter, there were only a few cars in the car park: brave dog walkers, braver surfers and foolhardy fossil hunters such as themselves.

'Wrap up warm now,' Charles said, opening the car door to a blast of icy air. 'It's a long walk and we'll be down on the beach for an hour at least.'

Cate got out of the car and helped Eliza on with her hat and scarf. Eliza did her best to push her away and Cate smiled, realising her daughter was too old to be babied anymore.

'You need to keep snug, sweetie,' she told her, wrapping her own scarf tightly around her neck.

They crossed a wooden bridge over a wide river and made their way down to the beach. Rigs ran ahead of them and was the first to arrive, promptly chasing after a couple of gulls who had dared to land on the shore.

'We want to go as far as possible while the tide is going out and then make our way back as it's coming in,' Charles told them. 'Always remember that. *Don't* get cut off. The most important thing is to be aware of the sea and what it's doing. We've timed it well today. It's low tide and we'll be safe for the time we're here.'

'That's good to know,' Cate said.

'The other thing – don't go too close to the base of the cliffs. It's been wet recently and they'll be eroding which is good for fossil hunting, but bad for personal safety.'

'Okay,' Cate said.

They walked on together, the roar of the wind in their ears.

'Is this your favourite place to fossil hunt?' Cate asked, raising her voice to be heard.

Charles shook his head. 'Too many people usually. But it's good enough for beginners and it's not so crowded today.'

Cate tried not to take offence at being thought of as a beginner because she realised that that was exactly what she was.

'Where do you like to go?' she asked Charles.

'Where people aren't,' he replied.

He wasn't going to tell her, was he? Perhaps it was like those people who hunted for truffles and would guard their spots with their lives. This was his livelihood after all, she reminded herself. Not that she had any real ambition to take up fossil hunting on a level beyond that of a beginner. Still, the thought of uncovering something spectacular was very appealing.

They continued to walk with Rigs leading the way. They passed a few people who were obviously out to do the same thing as them. It made Cate wonder how there was anything left to discover on the beach if people were constantly plundering it throughout the seasons, but then again, the constant coastal erosion meant that new finds were being thrown up on the beach after each storm and, if it wasn't for the fossil hunters, much of it would be lost to the sea.

'Okay,' Charles said at last. 'I think this will do us.'

Cate looked back along the stretch they'd walked. The car park was far in the distance now, and she could just make out the town of Lyme Regis along the coast. The tide was safely out, but she was very aware of it now that Charles had pointed out the dangers of being cut off.

'The trick is patience,' Charles told them, pushing his hat away from his face. 'There's no point just charging up and down the beach hoping that something will leap out at you. You'll be very lucky if it does. You've got to slow down – your body and your mind. Look at the ground until your eyes start to familiarise all the shapes there are to be found. It might take a while, but they'll start to emerge – the long thin shapes of belemnites and the glorious round ammonites. They'll seem distinct once you've got your eye in. Just pick a patch of ground and give it your total attention. And aim for the areas of black sand – that's where the pyritised ammonites are found.'

Cate smiled. She liked listening to Charles. He was so earnest and she could hear the passion behind his words. She glanced at Eliza who seemed to be rapt too and then she noticed that Charles had walked off and was already scouring a patch of beach.

'Come on, Eliza – let's get to work.' She didn't want to be left behind and she was quite determined to come up with some good finds. Okay, so they might not unearth an ichthyosaur or plesiosaur today, but she was hopeful that they would at least find an ammonite.

It was a strange experience spending so long on a beach without having the intention of either walking along it or sitting down upon it. Instead, she and Eliza adopted an odd kind of posture with their heads bent down, their shoulders hunched against the wind and their eyes focused on the ground. Eliza, Cate thought, had a distinct advantage: being young, her eyes were sharper, but she was also much closer to the ground and it wasn't long before she'd found a few thin pieces that looked promising.

'Charles!' Cate called above the wind.

He looked around from where he'd been searching and walked over to them.

'Show him what you've found, Eliza.'

She opened her clenched hand and Charles nodded.

'Belemnites – broken, but nice pieces for an amateur.'

Eliza looked confused and looked up at Cate.

'He says, well done, sweetie!' she told her. She looked back at Charles. 'Have you found anything?'

Charles delved into his pocket and he brought out a little bag in which were three beautiful pyritised ammonites.

Cate gasped. 'You found those just now?'

'Yes.'

'Where?'

'Over there.'

Cate grasped Eliza's hand and strode further down the beach to where Charles had just been, beginning their search again. If anyone knew what a good spot looked like, it would be Charles.

The sea was still a long way out, but the gentle roar of it in the background was a mesmerising soundtrack and lulled her into a trance. Being out on the beach, eyes fixed to the ground, the sound of the waves filling her mind, was a feeling like no other Cate had ever experienced. She could see how addictive this could be – how one could easily spend half of one's existence on this lonely stretch of beach.

Glancing up, she saw the other people who were shuffling along the beach in the same hunched pose. Fossil hunters' stoop, she'd call it. Nobody had come here for the views out to sea or the one back to Lyme Regis – they were here to find treasure.

For the next half an hour, Cate's world focused on a few square inches of beach. It was a very good way to switch off. The outside world with all its stresses and strains simply disappeared as her vision, her attention was almost completely absorbed in the task of finding fossils.

Cate completely lost track of time as she scoured the beach. She was half aware of Eliza who was a little way ahead of her on the beach, and of Charles who was some distance apart from them now with Rigs at his heels. They'd stayed away from the base of the cliffs which looked dark and dangerous, running with water and looming broodily over the shingle below. It was a landscape Cate had never seen before and it reminded her, once again, of how little she had seen of the world. How very isolated she'd become since getting married. She'd allowed herself to be hidden away like that from all the beauty and adventure of life.

For a moment, she forgot about fossil hunting and stared out towards the grey sea. She was being too hard on herself. She hadn't allowed herself to be hidden away – she'd had no choice in the matter. She had been made a prisoner in her own home. Both her and Eliza. Well, no more, she thought. They'd escaped.

Cate felt a tugging on her arm and looked down to see Eliza staring up at her with wild excitement in her eyes.

'What is it?'

Eliza opened her hand to reveal the most perfect ammonite, glinting gold. Cate gasped.

'You've found one! Eliza! I've only been finding bits of them – look!' Cate delved into the pocket of her jacket and brought out the little curved sections of broken ammonite she'd found.

'See – all broken. But yours is wonderful, sweetie. Where did you find it?'

Eliza pointed and Cate took her hand. 'Shall we show Charles?'

Her daughter smiled and nodded and they walked towards him.

'Charles?' Cate called as they approached. He had his head bent against the wind, eyes to the ground and Cate realised that her voice had been carried far out to sea on the wind and hadn't gone anywhere near him. 'CHARLES!' she tried again. This time, his head came up. 'Come and see what Eliza's found!'

Charles approached them and Eliza opened her clenched hand for his inspection.

He nodded. 'Very nice.'

'It's complete, isn't it?' Cate asked.

'It certainly is.'

'How old is it?'

'About a hundred and ninety-five million years.'

Eliza's mouth dropped open in a silent gasp.

'And to think that it was waiting for all those years for you to come and find it,' Cate told her daughter.

'Nothing ever beats that first fossil,' he told them. 'Take good care of it and keep it somewhere safe. You don't want to drop it.'

Eliza shook her head. There was no way she was going to lose this precious find.

'When we get home, soak it in water for a few days – that will get rid of the salt and stop it from disintegrating,' Charles went on. 'So, are you ready to leave now you've found one?'

'Are you kidding?' Cate cried. 'We've only just got going!'

Charles gave a little smile as if recognising that sentiment. 'You've got the bug, that's for sure. Want another half hour?'

'At least!' Cate said. 'As long as that's okay with you, boss?'

He smiled and nodded. 'It's okay with me.'

They continued searching. They didn't find anything much after Eliza's wonderful ammonite, but the fun they'd had searching more than made up for that. And there was always next time, wasn't there? That was the thing about fossil hunting. Nobody knew when that next find would be waiting for them. Each new day, each new tide and storm could promise the most wonderful gifts.

Returning to the car, frozen but happy, the three of them drank tea from the two flasks Charles had made up for them. It had been a good idea of his to have this waiting for them. Cate's fingers had never felt so cold, but the warmth from the tea as she held the little cup made them tingle with life again.

She glanced at Charles as he drove back through the wet country lanes. She had a new respect for what he did now. It took real dedication to go out there in all weathers with absolutely no guarantee that there'd be anything to find. She admired that and she'd had just a little taster of what that life must be like. Eliza too. She seemed to be hooked, judging by the frown on her face when she'd been told it was time to leave the beach. Cate had promised her that this was just the first of many trips.

The sky had darkened dramatically by the time they made it back to Hollow House and the first raindrops were beginning to fall. The three of them trooped in through the front door, followed by Rigs, who immediately ran to the kitchen, had his tea and then took refuge in his basket. It felt good to be home, Cate thought, acknowledging the fact that Hollow House really was beginning to feel like home.

In the kitchen, Eliza found a little bowl which she filled with cold water and gently placed her fossil in it. Cate watched, her daughter's face etched with concentration.

'That's a wonderful find,' Cate told her. 'Perhaps you can do a painting of it.'

Eliza beamed at the idea and went in search of her paintbox.

'Charles?' Cate said as he walked into the kitchen. 'Thank you for today. Eliza loved it.'

He nodded.

'I loved it too,' she added. 'Despite being cold and wet and not finding anything much. I had a really great time.'

As a self-employed single mother, Allie was always doing her best to economise and that usually meant making her own packed lunch for work. But, sometimes, a home-made egg mayonnaise sandwich on day-old bread just wasn't enough to get you through a cold November day. So Allie closed the shop for five minutes and nipped along to the high street where she treated herself to a large cheese straw and a millionaire's square from her favourite bakery. She'd walk them off on the beach the next morning, she told herself.

She was just licking the last of the delicious caramel-coated crumbs off her fingers when she saw a figure crossing the street towards her shop. She sighed. It was Craig.

She really hadn't thought she'd see him again, believing that he wouldn't have the nerve to show up after storming out on her and Jack the way he had. Well, she'd been wrong. He had more nerve than she'd given him credit for.

For a moment, she thought about flying towards the door to lock it, but it was too late because he'd seen her and had picked up his pace. She dusted herself down of crumbs and waited, wondering what the next few minutes would bring and hoping that she'd manage to control her temper.

Opening the door, Craig stepped inside. He gave a weak sort of smile.

'Hi.'

Allie didn't say anything, but sighed inwardly when he produced a bunch of flowers.

'I wanted to say sorry,' he said, taking a step closer to her. 'For the other day.'

Still, Allie didn't speak.

'I shouldn't have walked out on Jack like that.'

'No, you shouldn't have,' Allie said at last, her anger slowly bubbling up inside at the mention of her son.

'I just got upset that he didn't remember me.'

'Well, that's not exactly his fault, is it?' Allie told him.

Craig hung his head and sighed. 'Of course not.'

Allie waited for him to speak again or at least offer her the flowers he'd brought with him.

'I was hoping to try again,' he said. 'With Jack.'

Allie shook her head, not trusting herself to say anything that wouldn't be extremely hurtful and harmful to both of them.

'Here,' Craig said at last, shoving the flowers towards her.

But she just couldn't hold back. 'If you think a lame bunch of flowers is going to persuade me to let you see Jack again, you've got another thing coming.'

'*Lame?*' He glanced down at the bouquet, turning the flowers this way and that. 'They cost me nearly a tenner!'

'Give them to your mum, Craig, because I don't want them.' Allie turned her back on him and began to tidy things on her table that really didn't need tidying.

'I want to see him, Allie,' Craig said behind her. 'I want to see him and you can't stop me.'

Her hands froze and she closed her eyes briefly.

'Why did you come back?' she asked, turning to face him again.

'What do you mean? You know why. To see you and Jack.'

'But what do you hope to gain?'

He frowned. 'I don't need to answer these silly sorts of questions.'

'You'd be asked more probing ones in a job interview. I think I've a right to know what your intentions are before I risk you upsetting my son again.'

'Our son, Allie. He's *our* son.'

'Well, he doesn't want to see you,' she told him.

'He said that?'

Allie bit her lip. 'He didn't need to. You should have seen him after you left. He was furious. I don't ever want to see him go through that again. You crashed back into his life for all of ten minutes and left a trail of chaos behind you.'

'I've said I'm sorry.'

'Not to Jack you haven't.'

'Then give me that chance. Let me see him. Perhaps he'd like these flowers,' Craig said with a weak smile at his attempt at humour. 'Please, Allie. Let me try again. I won't mess up, I promise.'

'How do I know you won't? How do *you* know?'

'Because there's too much at stake here. I want my son in my life, and I'm not talking about co-parenting or visiting every single weekend. You know what I'm like. But I want it to be more than it has been. I want him to grow up knowing I'm there for him.'

'Even when you're a thousand miles away?'

'Yeah. Especially then. I've missed him.' He paused. 'I've missed you.'

'Don't!'

He held her gaze for a moment, a softness in his eyes that she still found disturbingly attractive.

'One more chance, Craig – that's all you're getting!' Allie said at last.

He nodded. 'Okay.'

'If you mess it up again...'

'I won't mess it up.'

She gave him her best glare – her mother lion glare. 'You'd better not,' she told him.'

Allie wasn't quite sure how she was going to tell Jack that his father was coming round again and so she spent the rest of the week dithering, leaving it until Friday night when she casually mentioned it after giving him a second slice of Bakewell tart.

'He what?' Jack said in disbelief.

'He said he wanted to see you again. Maybe go out somewhere with you.'

'Why?'

'Why? Because he's your father.'

Jack made a funny sort of snorting noise and Allie couldn't help agreeing with him. Still, she supposed that it was her role as mother to encourage him to give this his best shot.

'If you're unhappy about anything – at any time – you give me a call, okay?'

'I don't understand why he's come back after all these years,' Jack said and his previously pained expression had turned into one of mistrust and fear. It made her remember just how young and vulnerable he was even though he put on a tough exterior most of the time.

'It's as baffling to me as it is to you,' Allie told him, 'but I think we should give him a chance, shouldn't we? He might not deserve it after ignoring us for so many years, but he isn't a bad man, I promise you that. He's just... different.'

Jack seemed to be taking this in. 'Our form tutor told us it's good to be different and that you shouldn't try to squeeze yourself into a box you don't fit in just to please those around you.'

Allie smiled. 'Well, your form tutor sounds like a very wise person. Just think of your father like that then – he doesn't fit in anybody's box but his own.'

Jack ate the last of his Bakewell tart. 'I suppose I could see him. Give him a chance.'

Allie reached her hand across the table and squeezed his. 'Has anyone told you you're completely fabulous?'

Jack grinned and it was a grin so like his father's that it almost took Allie's breath away. 'Yeah, they have,' he said, 'but this is the first time today.'

CHAPTER FOURTEEN

Weekends still felt odd for Cate at Hollow House. She wasn't used to having so much time and space to call her own. Charles was usually out or in his workshop, and Cate and Eliza had the old Victorian house and grounds to themselves. At first, they'd mostly stayed indoors, reading books or watching television together or baking in the kitchen which was so much bigger than that of their previous home. There was room to spread out and Cate took great delight in watching Eliza rolling out pastry on the long work surfaces or getting to work with a sieve and mixing bowl. There was room to breathe here, Cate thought, in every way possible.

When they'd lived in Cambridgeshire, he'd be home at the weekends and Cate would be forced to spend time with him. They never went out together and the claustrophobia of being made to share a small space with somebody you feared was a constant strain on her. She could never be who she truly was for she was always moulding herself to be what he wanted – repressing her identity so as not to get hurt. What kind of a life was that? It made Cate shudder when she thought about how many years she'd endured it.

And then there'd been the added pressure of Eliza being there with them both at the weekends. When he was out of the house during the week, Cate and Eliza would have a few precious hours together and Cate had been able to see the difference in her daughter during those times.

And she could see it now too. She was a different child at Hollow House. Although painfully shy and still not speaking, Cate could see that she was slowly opening herself up. She seemed to move with a certain ease now – running down the stairs which was something she never would have dreamed of back in their old house. She'd done it once and had been shouted at by her father as if she'd committed some appalling crime. The tears had spilled down her rosy face and she'd crept down the stairs on silent feet after that. But not anymore. Now, she could be a normal child. Not that she ran screaming into rooms or tearing around the house. She'd never be that kind of child, but you could see the freedom in her body language now and it was a joy for Cate to witness.

Slowly, as the weeks passed, they'd become bolder and decided not only to explore the beaches but the myriad footpaths surrounding their village. Cate had bought them some wellington boots and they found that they enjoyed tramping around the fields no matter what the weather was like. In fact, mud became their new friend and would make them smile and laugh together, for Eliza was learning to laugh even more now.

But there was one place Cate had been meaning to explore ever since she'd got her car stuck there on the day of their arrival. The place held a fascination for her and she'd wanted to return, but hadn't yet mustered the courage for its name was just a little foreboding. The hollow lane – the lane after which the house had been named. Cate had been reading about it online. Hollow lanes, she'd learned, were ancient tracks naturally formed in soft ground after centuries of use by people and animals and vehicles. They were often called "holloways" – the word coming from an Old English word, hola weg, meaning sunken road. They could be hundreds or even thousands of years old.

When Cate had told Eliza this, she'd seen her daughter's eyes light up with excitement and knew that the one at the end of their village had to be explored. And so they set out one Saturday morning, coats, hats and wellies on for their adventure.

The entrance by the farm, where Cate had dared to drive her car, was as muddy as she remembered it – if not worse after all the recent rain. She looked around the farmyard, half dreading seeing the old farmer and feeling her face flame in embarrassment, but there was nobody around.

The track led on, passing in between two steep fields until the trees took over. Cate gasped when she got her first real glimpse of it. She could clearly see where the track had sunk deep down into the valley over the years, causing the banks on either side to look so tall, held together by the roots of the trees which towered above her and Eliza.

It was a strange place with an eerie kind of beauty to it. It wasn't welcoming exactly, but there was a sheltering feel about it – a sense that you were cut off from the rest of the world. Of course, being almost winter, the trees were mostly bare, but she could imagine how beautiful it would be in the height of summer when the leaves were in their full green glory, making a cathedral roof over the lane.

Cate glanced down at Eliza to see what she made of the place. Her face was pale as she took it all in.

'What do you think?'

Eliza stared at her mother and shook her head.

'You don't like it?'

She shook her head again.

'It is a bit spooky, isn't it?'

They walked on, marvelling at the twisting tree roots and the sandy-coloured earth that surrounded them and Cate couldn't help trying to imagine all the people who had walked here before them – the farmers, the drovers, the cattle and the carts going to market. And now her and Eliza. She smiled at the thought of the two of them there – in a place that felt it belonged to another age and which had very little to do with the fast-paced technology-filled world that existed now. But how important it was that these places still existed, she thought – that you could find them and almost reach out and touch the past. To follow in footsteps that had long vanished, to see the same sights and hear the same sounds.

It was then that Cate remembered something.

'I read that there's a little footpath that goes from here to the sea,' she told Eliza. 'Shall we try and find it?'

Eliza nodded.

Rather than glancing at her phone for the time, Cate looked up at the sky when they reached a gate that led into a field. She was getting pretty good at working out how much daylight was left by the position of the sun and judged that there was time to make their way to the beach and back again. After all, it couldn't be far.

'It must be this way,' Cate said, noticing a stile opposite the gate that led downhill.

The stile was slippery with moss, but they made their way safely over it and walked across the field before finding a little track.

'I think this must be it,' Cate said confidently.

It was something of a relief to leave the shady, shadowy holloway behind them and to have the open sky high overhead and Cate breathed in the clear air that smelled so different from the leaf-laden lane. She could already taste the salt-tang of the sea and, a few minutes later, the track opened out and they found themselves on a little beach. The tide was in so there wasn't much room for walking, but it was a beautiful place. However, as Cate turned and saw the great cliffs looming further down the beach, she remembered that Allie had told her that it had been this beach where Charles had lost his son. By those very cliffs.

She gazed up at them now, noticing how wet and dangerous they looked after the recent bad weather, and she grabbed Eliza's hand.

'Let's go, shall we?'

Eliza nodded. She looked tired after their walk.

Luckily, there was another way back home from the beach which meant they didn't have to retrace their route through the hollow lane. With the sun fast slipping from the sky, it might have tested their nerves just a little more than they wanted.

Charles's Land Rover was there when they got back and he greeted them at the door.

'Been out walking?' he said.

'How can you tell?' Cate laughed, gesturing to her muddy boots before taking them off in the porch. 'We wanted to give our boots a proper workout.'

'Where did you go?'

'Along the hollow lane.'

'That's brave of you.'

'Actually, it wasn't too bad considering all the rain we've had,' Cate said, as she took her and Eliza's coats and hats and hung them up in the hallway. They were greeted by Rigs who scampered towards them to sniff where they'd been without him, looking suitably put out when he obviously realised it had been a great, muddy adventure down squirrelly lanes and across rabbity fields.

'You been out too?'

'Just along Monmouth Beach.'

'Good hunting?'

'Not today.'

He looked a little subdued and Cate thought it wise not to mention the fact that they'd been to their local beach.

It was as she was making them all a hot drink that something occurred to her – surely her probationary month was over by now? For the first couple of weeks, Cate had been all too aware of the passage of time and had been mentally ticking the days off until that awful deadline Charles had set. But, slowly, she'd relaxed more and the days had passed by gently and easily. They were, she believed, happy to live and work together and, although she must never forget that he was her boss and could ask her to leave at any time, she couldn't help thinking that they were slowly becoming friends too.

'Charles?' she said, passing him his mug of tea as they all sat down at the table together.

'Yes?'

'Do you realise what day it is?'

'Erm... Saturday?' he said, obviously wondering if this was a trick question.

'No, I didn't mean that.'

'What did you mean?'

'I mean, it's a month since I started working here. It's over a month actually. I'd kind of lost track of the time.'

'Right,' Charles said, still seemingly not following her train of thought.

'Well, you said a month, didn't you?'

'Did I? In what context?'

'In the context that you'd see how we both got on with this

new role and whether or not you wanted me – *us* to stay.' She glanced at Eliza who was sipping her hot chocolate, hoping that having her big blue eyes watching Charles might work in their favour.

He took a moment to take this in. 'Oh, I see! A month. Right.'

'That's right,' Cate said, and then she suddenly felt nervous. Maybe she shouldn't have brought it up seeing as he'd clearly forgotten about it all. Now, however, she'd given him the perfect opportunity to decide that her time was up. Maybe he'd ask her to leave once she'd washed their mugs up.

'Well,' he said, 'I think – erm – we've been getting along all right, haven't we?'

Cate nodded, aware that her palms were sticky.

'All of us, I mean,' he said, glancing at Eliza who nodded too.

'Yes,' Cate said, anxious to get this over and done with.

'So,' Charles said, having the audacity to sip his tea before finishing his sentence, 'would you like to stay?'

Cate gasped in relief. 'Really?'

'Yes, really.'

'You're making this a permanent post?'

'Well, as permanent as anything can be in life,' Charles said and Cate nodded.

'Thank you, Charles. We've been very happy here, haven't we, Eliza?'

Eliza nodded and Charles smiled.

'You've done some good work, Cate. The house is so clean and organised, and my office – well – it's a weight off my mind knowing that's taken care of.'

'And a weight off mine knowing we can stay.'

Charles frowned. 'There's just one thing.'

'Oh?' Cate felt her heart lurch in anxiety.

'If you're both to stay here permanently, shouldn't we think about Eliza having a room of her own?'

'Well, I hadn't really thought about that. I mean, we're cosy enough as we are, aren't we?' Cate looked at Eliza.

'I think she'd like somewhere to call her own, wouldn't you?' Charles asked and Cate couldn't quite believe it when Eliza nodded.

'But there isn't anywhere,' Cate pointed out, mentally counting the rooms she'd seen in the house. Surely he wasn't going to offer Eliza Jamie's room.

'Ah, that's where you're wrong. Come with me.' He stood up and they followed him out of the kitchen. Rigs followed too, sensing something fun was about to happen.

Charles led the way upstairs and Cate began to wonder if she'd somehow managed to miss a room in the house, but couldn't think how. It was when they reached the landing that Charles stopped and looked at a bookcase at the far end.

Cate frowned. 'I don't understand.'

'Watch this,' Charles said, motioning to the bookcase. A moment later, he was standing in front of the shelves and reached out to remove a handful of books. Cate and Eliza watched as she saw a door handle appear in the gap he'd made.

'Is there a room behind here?'

'The loft.'

'Why did you put a bookcase here?'

'Just lazy, I guess. I wasn't using the space and it seemed better to have the books here than in my room, but I can easily move them in there.'

Cate helped him to move the books, putting them into neat piles on the landing floor. They then moved the bookcase carefully to one side and Charles opened the door to reveal a short flight of stairs up into the loft. He switched a light on and led the way up. Cate, Eliza and Rigs followed closely behind, emerging into a long room with a low, sloping ceiling punctuated with two skylights.

Cate, who'd been looking to the right, now glanced left and gasped.

'Oh, my god! 'Is that – *real*?' she asked, noticing that Eliza's mouth was agape.

Charles laughed. 'No! It's papier-mâché. But I'm very pleased you thought it might be real. His name's Dennis. Dennis the dinosaur and me and Jamie made him. We were hoping to make a complete dinosaur only, well...'

Cate glanced at him, feeling his sadness at time running out.

'He's wonderful,' Cate told him, moving closer to the enormous dinosaur head.

'Yes, but perhaps Eliza doesn't want to share a room with him.'

Cate glanced at her daughter whose face was full of joy. 'No, I think she does. Do you, Eliza? Do you want Dennis up here with you?'

She nodded vigorously.

'What is it, exactly?

'Well, it started off as one thing and ended up becoming something else. I think I'd made one suggestion and then Jamie had his own ideas.'

'It's a Dennis,' Cate said.

'Exactly. It's its own thing, isn't it?'

Cate took a step closer and reached out to touch it. 'I'll give it a dust,' she said.

'And maybe we can move it into the corner to give Eliza more space. And get a bed up here.'

'Oh, yes, a bed would be a good idea,' Cate agreed.

'We've probably got bits of furniture around the house that can come up too. If I move a few fossils.'

Cate smiled, amazed that he was willing to disrupt his fossil displays in order to make a cosy room for her daughter.

'And we can get that radiator over there going. It's quite warm up here when it's on, and the light's good too with the skylights and I've got a spare lamp Eliza can have. Anyway, I'm sure she'll make it her own.'

Cate looked around, still a little unsure about this new set-up. She was used to having Eliza close to her. But she had to let her daughter make the decision for herself.

'You won't be too lonely up here on your own, sweetie?'

Eliza shook her head.

'Okay,' Cate said and then she looked at Charles. 'She'll take it!'

Saturday might have been going very well for Cate but, as far as Allie was concerned, it was a nightmare.

First, Craig had turned up late for his day with Jack, and Jack had been convinced his father had forgotten him. Allie had texted Craig at least half a dozen times, only for him to turn up half an hour late, his phone switched off, and totally unaware that he wasn't on time.

Allie was relieved to see that Craig had, at least, borrowed his father's car and she made him swear that he wouldn't take Jack anywhere near a motorbike. She'd spent five whole minutes making Jack promise to text her at regular intervals to let her know he was okay. She'd then stood on her doorstep to wave them off with the distinct feeling that she'd made the worst mistake of her life.

She couldn't concentrate on anything much once they'd left. There were the household chores to do, of course, but she did them half-heartedly, her mind spiralling out of control as she thought of all the awful things that could be happening with her son. As the day wore on, she checked in with Evie who was running the shop for her. Allie should have been able to relax a little more, but she couldn't. She'd sincerely believed that Craig might have given up after just an hour or two and brought Jack home, so she told herself it was a good sign that he hadn't.

It *was* a good sign, wasn't it?

As the hours ticked by, another fear crept up on her as she calculated just how far away the two of them could be by now. Craig might actually have abducted Jack. Oh, god! She'd never forgive herself if that had happened.

It was an hour after sunset when she heard a car pulling up outside the house and she ran to the front door.

'Oh, thank goodness you're all right!' she cried as Jack got out of the passenger door.

'Why wouldn't he be all right?' Craig asked.

'You didn't text me!'

'Aw, Mum! We were busy.'

'Too busy to let your mum know you're okay?'

'He was fine. We were just having a good time, weren't we, Jack?' Craig explained.

'Yeah. Pretty good.'

Craig grinned and then he shuffled his boots, looking expectant. Allie read the signal. He wanted to stay. He wanted her to invite him in for tea. He wanted to get his feet under her table. Then tea would turn into spending the evening, and the evening would end in a nightcap... and then he'd never leave.

'No,' she said bluntly.

'Pardon?' Craig said, looking surprised.

'You can't stay for tea.'

'But I didn't ask,' Craig said with a nervous kind of laugh.

'Say goodbye to your father, Jack.'

'Bye, Dad.'

'Bye, Jack.'

Allie was all too aware that she was acting like an angry teacher marching a kid out of a classroom, but she couldn't help herself. She had to remain in control.

'Allie!' Craig hissed, once they'd reached the door. 'What's going on?'

She took a deep breath, trying to calm herself. 'It's just time to leave, okay?'

'Hey!' Craig said, reaching out and placing a hand on her arm in a gentle gesture. 'What's the matter?'

She'd been avoiding eye contact with him but, now, she looked at him. 'Nothing.'

'Allie, come on. You're acting all weird. I'm not going to steal Jack away from you!'

'Don't even joke about it.'

'We just had a nice day out together and now he's safely home, isn't he?'

Allie supposed she couldn't argue with that and yet she still had misgivings about this whole situation.

'And what next?'

'What do you mean?'

'Are you leaving?'

'Well, it looks like I'm leaving here, doesn't it?' he said with a shrug.

'I mean, are you leaving on your travels again?'

'I've just got back. Don't pack me off before I'm ready. I want to spend some time here.'

Allie folded her arms across her chest, knowing full well what message she was giving out by doing so.

'Allie – you've got to trust me. I can't make any promises to be around forever, but I'm here now and we had a great time today. He's a good kid and you're doing a brilliant job with him. But I'm still his father and I need to do this. Please, help me do this.'

Allie took a moment to digest his words. 'Okay, but you've got to let us know your plans. In advance! Don't just run off in the middle of the night and then send a postcard in six months.'

'I won't.'

'You've made a commitment by coming back.'

'I know I have.'

They stood in silence for a moment and then Craig leaned forward and kissed her cheek. 'I won't let you down,' he whispered and she watched as he left, feeling only a little less uneasy about things.

She walked through to the kitchen where Jack was buttering himself some toast.

'So, did you have a good time with your dad?' she asked him.

Jack wiped his mouth with the back of his hand. 'Yeah. It was all right.'

Allie sighed. Sometimes, it was so hard getting information out of her son. She would often remember how easy it had seemed when he'd been a young boy. He'd tell her everything and be so excited when he came out of school, reciting his whole day and telling her all about his friends' antics. Not anymore, though. She was lucky to get a "yeah" these days. Still, that was all part of growing up, wasn't it?

'So – what did you do?' she pushed, determined to find out something more.

'We went to see Grandma and Grandpa for a bit and then went into Dorchester for a pizza.'

'Are your grandparents okay?' Allie asked, aware she hadn't seen them for a while.

'They're good. Grandpa fell asleep in his chair and snored like a lion and Grandma gave me some chocolate.'

'And what did you do after lunch?'

'Just walked around for a bit. Went to some shops. I showed Dad some of the new computer games I like.'

'Did he get you one?'

'Nah. He said he didn't have any money.'

Well, that sounded about right, Allie thought, and then felt bad for being so mean. After all, time was far more precious than money and Craig had made a real effort today.

'Mum?'

'Yes?'

'He's all right, you know,' Jack said with a smile and, taking one more bite from his toast, he left the room, his feet thudding up the stairs and his bedroom door closing a moment later.

CHAPTER FIFTEEN

It didn't take long to get the loft ready for Eliza. Charles bought a single bed which was delivered the next day and Cate got to work cleaning the space, opening the skylights to let some fresh air in, and Eliza helped Charles to paint the walls with a dusky pink paint he'd found under the stairs, a big smile on her face as she worked beside him. Cate had to pinch herself as she watched the progress they were making. It really felt as if they were becoming a little unit of sorts. A group of lost souls who'd been brought together after a life of loss and pain.

Finally, the loft was ready and the three of them stood back to admire their work, taking in the newly painted walls, the lovely old ceramic lamp Charles had assured Cate he never used, and the sweet little bed with brand new linen and a big fluffy pink cushion studded with sequins which Cate had treated her daughter to. Jemima the ragdoll, who was sat up against it, looked most appreciative. And, of course, there was Dennis the dinosaur to keep Eliza company. It really was a beautiful room – pretty yet quirky which, Cate thought, was the perfect fit for her daughter.

But how strange it was to spend that first night in the double bed without Eliza. Cate tossed and turned and tutted until she was quite worn out, but still sleep wouldn't come. She turned the lamp on and stared up at the ceiling, wondering how Eliza was getting on up there on her own. She hoped Dennis the dinosaur was taking good care of her.

At around quarter to three, Cate had been able to bear it no longer and had got out of bed, popped a jumper on over her nightie and walked out onto the landing, hovering by the door to the loft which had been left ajar. Cate waited a moment, listening for sounds that her daughter might be awake, pacing up and down in fear or crying in her sleep. But all was quiet and Cate went back to her own room and crawled into bed, staring at the ceiling for a while longer before falling into a fitful sleep.

The next morning, Cate went upstairs bright and early.

'Eliza?' she called as she entered the loft. 'Did you sleep okay, sweetie?'

Eliza yawned as she got out of bed and nodded, her blonde hair falling around her face. Cate smiled. She looked like a messy cherub.

'I missed you last night! Did you miss me?'

Eliza shook her head, making Cate laugh.

'Charming! Well, I'm glad you slept well.'

They got washed and dressed and had breakfast. As usual, Charles was out and Rigs was with him, but he arrived back just as Cate was setting up Eliza with her morning's study, which was good timing as she'd got a text from Allie asking if they could meet to talk.

'Would it be all right if I popped out for a bit?' Cate asked.

'I can pick up some shopping . We could use some new dusters for a start.'

'Worn holes in mine already?' Charles teased.

'They are mostly holes now, yes!'

'Okay. Eliza can work with me if you like.'

Eliza nodded. She did like.

'Thanks, Charles. I won't be too long.'

Cate drove into Lyme Regis and met Allie at Gifts from the Sea.

'Let's get some air,' she said, closing up her shop. 'I'm in need of ozone.'

It was a bright sunny morning and they walked along Marine Parade towards the great grey arm of the Cobb – the harbour wall which stretched out to sea.

'Guess what? Craig took Jack out for the day,' Allie said.

'Did he?' Cate said.

'He did,' Allie said. 'And he's been round for tea too.'

'Really? And how did that go?'

Allie sighed. 'It was okay.'

'Just okay?'

'Good. Actually. He didn't mess up and he and Jack seemed really at ease together. You wouldn't think Craig had been away for so long. It all seemed...' she paused, 'really natural.'

Cate thought for a moment. 'Forgive me for saying, but you don't sound happy about all this,' she told Allie, watching the emotions flitting across her friend's face.

'I know!' Allie cried.

'But it's going well. Isn't that what you wanted? For them to build a good relationship together and for Jack to have his father in his life?'

'I thought I did,' Allie said.

They'd reached the Cobb now and climbed the steps up to the top, marvelling at the view along Monmouth Beach to their right and the sweep of the harbour to their left. The wind picked up as they walked and Cate watched Allie carefully as she seemed to be struggling with something. Was it the wind in her face that was making her eyes water or was she crying?

'Allie?' Cate prompted. 'What is it? What's the matter?'

They stopped walking and Allie turned to face her, her hair blowing around her face.

'I'm afraid,' she said in a voice that was almost whipped away by the wind before Cate heard her and so she stepped closer.

'Afraid? Of what?'

Allie shook her head and shrugged at the same time. '*Everything!*'

Cate frowned, anxious for her friend. 'Oh, Allie!'

'I've been alone for so long, bringing up Jack *just* the way I want,' Allie explained. 'Nobody's ever interfered with that. It's been me and my boy, and we're a good team, you know?'

'I do know!'

'And now Craig's on the scene and he's getting really comfy around the place. I guess I'm just not used to it. It feels like a kind of invasion.'

'And how does Jack feel about it? Is he happy?'

'Yes! That's the thing that's bugging me the most. Jack's *perfectly* happy that his father – who did a runner when he was a baby and has barely been around since – has turned up now to stake his claim.'

'Are you worried that he's going to run off again?' Cate asked.

'Yes, of course I'm bloody worried!'

Cate grimaced. 'Forgive me, but I think you might be overreacting slightly.'

Allie frowned at her. 'Oh, you do, do you?'

There was a sharpness in her voice which Cate didn't recognise.

'Allie – listen–'

'How would you feel, Cate? How would *you* feel if your husband turned up to see Eliza? Wouldn't you *overreact* slightly? Wouldn't that be slightly awkward?'

Cate dropped her gaze to the ground. She wasn't quite sure what she'd done to deserve that, but she suddenly didn't want to be anywhere near Allie and started to walk away from her.

'Oh, God – Cate – what am I saying?' Allie called after her. 'I didn't mean that for real. I was trying to make you see my point of view.'

Cate couldn't respond. She could feel that she was shaking now and knew she had to get home. Right now. To Eliza.

'Cate! Please!'

Allie's voice faded behind her as Cate's pace quickened and no apology could reach her. The damage was done – the seed was planted in Cate's mind. Of course, she'd thought of it a hundred times already, but she was finally beginning to feel safe in her little corner of Dorset. Why should he find her? It had been over a month since they'd left Cambridgeshire and she'd been telling herself that he didn't care and that he had no interest in finding them. That's what had been keeping her going – constantly telling herself that she was safe, even in the middle of the night when she would wake up after a dark dream and lie there shaking under the bedclothes.

Cate couldn't remember anything about the drive back to Hollow House from Lyme Regis, but it wasn't until she was back that she realised she'd forgotten to go shopping. She didn't feel much like it now. She just needed to get inside.

Locking her car, she crossed the driveway and let herself in kicking her boots off, but keeping her coat on because she felt so cold. She'd felt cold since leaving the Cobb in Lyme Regis and now she couldn't remember very much about what had happened. Had she left Allie standing there on the Cobb? All she'd known was that she had to get back to Hollow House and Eliza.

'Eliza?' she called now, running through to the kitchen. But her daughter wasn't there. 'Eliza?' Her voice was more panicky as she headed to check another room.

'Cate?' Charles appeared in the hallway just as she was leaving the kitchen. 'You're back. Come and see what Eliza's drawn,' he said.

'Is she okay?'

'Yes. Of course she is.'

Cate pushed past him and went into his workshop. 'Darling!' she cried, crouching down beside her daughter and hugging her close.

'Cate?' Charles was beside her. 'Are you all right?'

Cate was still holding Eliza, her hair hanging over her daughter's face. Eliza made to push her away.

'Cate? What is it?' Charles asked, reaching out to touch her arm.

Cate gasped, pulling away as if she'd received an electric shock.

'My God, you're shaking!' Charles said. 'Come with me. Eliza – are you all right to stay here?'

Eliza nodded.

Cate felt Charles's hand on the small of her back, guiding her into the kitchen and towards a chair at the table. 'Sit there,' he said softly. 'I'll make you a hot drink, okay?'

Cate could hear his kind words, but she couldn't yet respond to them. It seemed as if she'd lost the power of speech.

She felt horribly swimmy, as if she might pass out at any moment. She heard the kettle boiling and the sound of a spoon in a mug. She could smell tea and, a moment later, she wrapped her hands around the warm mug Charles handed her and then he sat down opposite, giving her a few moments before he spoke.

'Did something happen?' he asked gently.

She shook her head. 'It was...' she stopped. 'Nothing. I'm being silly.'

'I don't believe that for a moment,' he told her. 'Tell me, Cate. What's going on?'

She took a sip of her tea. Her fingers were still trembling which was ridiculous. She was back now. Safe. Wasn't she?

'I went to see Allie.'

'Your friend from the village?'

'Yes. We met in Lyme. She's got a shop there and we went for a walk along the Cobb.' Cate could feel herself becoming more anxious as she remembered what had happened. 'We were just talking, Charles. You don't need to know anymore.'

'I might not need to, but I'd like to.'

Cate looked across the table at him, noting the concern etched across his face.

'Did you have a fight?'

Cate sighed. 'Yes.'

'Did you push her off the Cobb?' Charles' mouth twitched into a tiny smile and Cate couldn't help but respond.

'No! I didn't push her off the Cobb.'

'Well, that's something. I was getting worried for a moment that I was harbouring a fugitive.'

Cate sipped her tea. It was sweet and hot – just what she needed, and Charles's weak attempt at humour had helped her to relax a little.

'Cate? Something's upset you. What is it?'

She hesitated, knowing that – if she told him – there would be no going back. She might well have been viewing him more as a friend than a boss recently, but telling him about her past was moving into new territory.

She took a deep breath. It was time she told him the whole truth.

'I'm scared, Charles,' she began. 'I'm scared of him. What if he comes for her?'

'Who?'

'What if he wants Eliza?'

'You mean her father?'

'He might find us.' She could feel herself shaking again at the mere thought of him.

'You ran away from him, didn't you?' Charles asked.

Cate nodded. 'He wasn't a good man.' Again, she hesitated, a part of her wanting to hide the truth forever instead of releasing it. But what would be the point of that?

'He... he hurt me,' she said in a voice barely above a whisper.

'I thought he might have,' Charles told her, surprising her.

'Why did you think that?' Cate asked. As far as she was concerned, she'd given no hint to him that she'd been a victim in her previous life. She'd made no reference to running away or having to start afresh.

'I saw the bruises,' he said, his eyes flashing briefly to her wrist.

Cate's hand instinctively flew to the sleeve on the wrist which had been so horribly tainted by her husband's brutality.

'Did he ever hurt Eliza?'

'No,' Cate said. 'But the fear was always there. I couldn't risk it any longer. He was getting worse, you see.' She shook her head. 'I shouldn't have left it as long as I did. I should have got away sooner.'

'Well, you're here now,' Charles said.

'And there's nothing to link me to this place, is there? I was very careful. He didn't know I had a phone and I didn't leave a paper trail. I even changed our names.'

'Then you're safe.'

'Am I?' Cate could feel the panic rising again.

'How else could he find you? Are you even sure that he *wants* to?' Charles asked.

These were the questions that tormented Cate over and over again.

'He didn't love us,' Cate said. 'Not in any sort of normal way. But he was so possessive. He might try and find us just because he sees us as belonging to him.'

'Then you should tell the police.'

Cate shook her head. 'I don't want to let anyone know I'm here. He... he has a way of finding things out.'

She took another sip of her tea.

'Cate? Do you mind me asking how it all started? Was he always violent, I mean?'

Cate shook her head. 'Not at first although he always seemed to have a violent mind if that makes sense.' She sighed as she thought back. 'It started off small with insults. He'd call me clumsy or say I wasn't good at something. Like when I once attempted to help him with his accounts. "You're not a natural with figures, are you?" And he'd say it with this horrible sneer and it was unmistakably an insult. But then he'd seem to check himself and give a nervous laugh and ruffle my hair in apology, and I'd think I'd imagined it. At least, that's what I told myself.' She paused, taking a deep breath.

'It wasn't long before it became physical,' she went on. 'I'll never forget the shock of that first slap. The sting, the redness – both of those were bad enough. But it was knowing that he had that thing inside him – that rage – and that he could direct it at me. That was the scary thing. And I let it go on for years. The slaps, the punches. He broke one of my front teeth once.'

'Were the police never involved?'

'No. I couldn't. I feared what he'd do to me if I spoke to anyone and so I kept quiet. I hid my bruises and never said a word.'

'But Eliza? How did she respond to all this?'

'How do you think? She did her best to hide away from it all in her room, but she must have heard things. I'd tell her to keep away from her father when he was in one of his moods. I'd say he was tired and that she shouldn't bother him and she seemed to accept that, but I often wondered how much she knew.'

She paused again to sip her tea. 'I guess we were always going to be heading in the wrong direction. I kind of knew that. It was never going to end. He wasn't suddenly going to get better, was he? You don't become cured of a personality trait like that. And, even if you can be, you have to want to be and I don't think he'd ever want to change. I did suggest it once. I suggested that we go and see a counsellor together.'

'And did you?'

'No. Of course not. And I never even dared to mention it again after he took my suggestion out on my left shoulder.'

She heard Charles swear under his breath.

'Then, one night, he came in late from work,' Cate went on. 'I could tell he'd been drinking but, when I confronted him, he denied it. He was a very bad liar.' She gave a wry smile. 'He went through to the kitchen and I followed him. Stupid, stupid!' She cursed herself. 'I should have left him alone, but I was upset. I was standing up to him because he'd made a promise to our daughter and he'd broken it. She'd been in a school play that evening. Even before all this, she was a shy little thing, so it was a big deal for her to have a speaking role and I'd promised that we'd both be there. But, of course, he didn't show up. So I told him how disappointed Eliza was – how he'd let her down.' She stopped, looking down into her lap. 'He never liked being challenged like that. You were never meant to tell him if you thought he was wrong about anything. Anyway, I did that night. I think I'd been hoarding a whole host of things for years and I let it all gush out. Why did I do that? I should have known better. I really should!'

Cate took another deep breath. She felt drained remembering it all, but there was no going back now – not when she was so close to finishing her story and bringing it up to the present day with her sitting in a warm kitchen opposite Charles.

'In a normal household, you should be able to leave a bread knife out without fearing what it might be used for,' she said. 'But ours wasn't a normal household. And it was stupid of me to have left it out. I didn't normally for fear of accidents with Eliza and also because I always used to fear the worst would happen one day.'

Cate closed her eyes, fearing recalling that dreadful scene in the kitchen.

'We were shouting our heads off at this stage. I remember seeing his face getting redder and redder as if he was about to explode and that's when I noticed the knife on the worktop. He must have seen where I was looking because he turned and saw it too. And this is where it gets a bit hazy because I truly can't remember if I thought to pick it up in defence or just to get it away from him. And he must have feared I was going to use it against him because he grabbed it.'

Cate glanced up at Charles. He'd turned quite white.

'I wish I'd never noticed it.'

'Did he attack you?'

'Yes. But I think I might have attacked him too. I can't remember now. I can't remember!' She put her head in her hands, trying to block out the knife flash, the pain and the blood.

'But there's one thing I do remember. At some point, he must have left the house. Maybe the sight of the blood scared him. I don't know. I was on the floor, my hands over my head when I heard a little cry. It was Eliza. She was standing in the door of the kitchen in her nightdress. She saw everything. Me on the floor with my head bleeding and the knife lying beside me.'

'God, Cate! I'm so sorry.'

'I've tried to be grateful for that night since. After all, it's a miracle he didn't kill me and it gave me the strength to leave him because I knew that – one day – he really would kill me.'

'And that's when you applied for this job?' Charles asked.

Cate nodded.

'Cate – what happened that night – why didn't you call the police?'

She shook her head. 'I couldn't. And, to be fair, there was far more blood than there should have been. Head wounds are like that, apparently.'

Charles gave a grave sort of laugh. 'That is the oddest sentence I've ever heard,' he told her. '*To be fair?* Cate – your husband attacked you with a bread knife. The police should have been involved.'

She shook her head. 'It wasn't really an attack. It was more of an odd kind of fight. I was fighting him as much as he was fighting me.'

'You were defending yourself against a mad man as far as I can see it. He should have been arrested.'

'Yeah? And then what?' Cate cried. 'They might have held him for a while and he might have told them some story about how I flew at him with the knife. Then he'd have been released and on his way back home to me. The police wouldn't be there then, would they?' She shook her head. 'I knew that night that there was only one way to stop it all and that was to leave.'

'And is that when Eliza stopped talking?'

'Yes. She just kind of froze inside herself. I did my best to reach her, but I think she was protecting herself in the only way she knew how.' Cate could feel tears rising now. 'I felt like I'd failed her,' she told Charles. 'I'd failed to protect my only child and she felt that she had to protect herself by withdrawing from everything including me.'

Charles shook his head. 'She didn't withdraw from you.'

'Charles! She doesn't *talk* to me!'

'But she does!' he told her, reaching across to hold her hand. 'She talks to you by being close to you. She talks to you with those big blue eyes of hers and the way she smiles. Even when she frowns! She's talking to you then too.' He gave a half laugh.

'And all the notes she writes,' Cate said.

'And all the notes,' Charles said, nodding. 'And she'll come round, Cate. In time, she'll come round. I'm sure of it.'

'You are?'

'Yes!' Charles said emphatically and then he frowned. 'Why? Aren't you?'

Cate could feel her eyes misting over with tears again. 'I worry,' she whispered. 'She's been silent for so long now. What if she's lost the will to speak? What if I never hear my child ever again?'

'But you have! Remember when Rigs made her laugh?'

Cate nodded.

'You've got to hang on to that because, one day, she'll want to follow that laughter with words.'

Cate reached into her pocket for a tissue and dabbed her eyes and blew her nose.

'Listen,' Charles said a moment later, 'I've got an idea. How about Eliza comes with me later today?'

Cate looked up. 'Where are you going?'

'To see my mother.'

Cate frowned. It was the first she'd heard mention of Charles's mother. 'She lives nearby?'

Charles paused before answering. 'She's in a care home. She has dementia. She – erm – doesn't talk a lot.'

'I'm so sorry,' she said, blowing her nose again and hoping that her face wasn't the blotchy red it usually went whenever she cried.

'Some days are worse than others. But...'

'What?' Cate asked when he stopped.

'I don't know – I was wondering what Eliza might be like around somebody else who doesn't always talk. Maybe that would encourage her to say something. My mother might enjoy the experience too. What do you think?'

Cate thought about this for a moment. 'That's an interesting idea.'

'Yeah?'

'Yes.'

'So you're okay if I take her with me?'

Cate nodded. 'I think it would do her good to see somewhere different and have a new experience.'

'And it'll give you a chance to have some space. Take a bit of time for yourself, okay?'

She smiled. It was kind of Charles to think of that.

CHAPTER SIXTEEN

Eliza seemed strangely excited when Charles mentioned the care home idea to her, which was unexpected because he'd half expected her to decline his offer because of her shyness.

'Now, don't be scared,' Cate told Eliza as she got ready to leave with Charles, even though she herself was feeling a little anxious about letting her daughter go out without her.

Eliza quickly scribbled a note.

I'm not scared!

'Well, good,' Cate said, looking up at Charles and smiling. 'You take good care of her now.'

'Of course,' Charles told her. 'We'll be a couple of hours at least. Maybe longer if we go into Bridport for some cake afterwards. How about that, Eliza?'

Eliza nodded, a big grin on her face, and Cate watched as the two of them left Hollow House together. It felt odd seeing her daughter going off with somebody else and Cate realised that it was an experience she'd never had before. Other than taking her to school, Cate had never left Eliza with anyone before. For one thing, her husband hadn't allowed it and doing what he'd told her to do had bred a kind of fear in Cate and she'd protected Eliza a little more than was probably healthy.

And how strange it was that she now felt comfortable to let Eliza go with Charles. She remembered how abrupt and cool he'd been with them when they'd first arrived and how he hadn't wanted a child in the house at all. Now, here he was, happy to have Eliza's silent companionship.

Cate walked through to the kitchen.

'It's just you and me, Rigs,' she told the little terrier. He was in his basket, licking a paw and, after making a cup of tea, Cate left him to it, walking through to the living room where she sat in a patch of sunlight. She took a deep, settling breath. Her eyes still felt sore from her earlier tears, but a wonderful calm had come over her at having told Charles the truth about her past. She felt peaceful and pure – free from the burden of carrying her dark secret around. She was glad that Charles knew everything now and that he'd responded with such kindness and understanding. And she couldn't help wondering if, one day, he'd trust her with his own past too. Would he share what had happened to him and his family? And would she be able to help him a little just as he had helped her today?

Cate took another deep breath. What a strange day it had been. First, her altercation with Allie, then her revelation to Charles, and now this quiet moment in the house. It felt odd to be sitting here in the middle of the day on her own with no immediate pressure to do anything. But hadn't Charles told her to take some time out? And who was she to disobey her boss's orders? So she took a sip of her tea and watched the late autumn sun's progress across the garden.

As Charles entered the care home, he glanced down at Eliza who seemed to be taking it all in.

'Ah, you have a companion today, Mr Thorner?' the lady on reception said as he signed himself and Eliza in.

'Yes, I thought it might do my mother some good to meet somebody new,' Charles said, although he wasn't at all sure about that notion. In fact, it could backfire horribly. Her condition often dictated that any change in routine might upset her. He could only hope for the best.

'Go on through – she's in her room.'

'Thank you.'

They walked down the corridor together and paused outside his mother's room. Charles rested his hand on Eliza's shoulder, noticing for the first time that she was carrying a book with her.

'Now, remember what I said? She sometimes doesn't talk much and she's often asleep, but – every now and then – she gets confused and cross, and you mustn't be scared if she does because it's just the way the illness makes her, and it's got nothing to do with either you or me or anyone else. Understand?'

Eliza nodded.

'Good. Let's go in, then.' He knocked on the door before opening it. 'Mum? I've got someone who wants to meet you.' Keeping his hand on Eliza's shoulder, he encouraged her to take a seat next to his mother's chair. As usual, Anna Thorner was staring out of the window, but turned as Eliza sat down next to her and frowned.

'I don't know her,' she said.

'This is Eliza, Mum.'

His mother frowned and stared out of the window again.

This, Charles thought, was not one of his better ideas. Now, he was stuck in a room with two people who didn't talk.

'I'm going to get a cup of tea. Would you like one, Mum?'

His mother didn't reply.

'I'll get you one anyway. Eliza – can I get you a squash?'

She nodded.

'I won't be long, okay?'

Charles made his way down the corridor to the communal kitchen which guests were encouraged to use. There, he made two cups of tea and poured a glass of orange squash for Eliza. He found a tray and paused for a moment, wondering what he was going to say and do once he was back with Eliza and his mother. Some people were good at this kind of thing – he'd seen them. There was a young woman who visited her grandfather at the home and she had all the patience in the world. Nothing ever seemed to faze her. Even when Frank was being at his trickiest – and he could be incredibly bad-tempered some days – his granddaughter would go on smiling, waiting for him to calm down, talking to him softly as he found his way back out of the fog of confusion. Charles so admired that. He wished he could be easier around his mother and have that innate confidence. But he didn't and he couldn't go on beating himself up week after week. He could only do what he could and, today, that seemed to be making the tea.

Cate wasn't sure how long she'd been sitting on the sofa when she heard the doorbell. Perhaps it was a delivery, she thought, as she made her way to the door. But it wasn't a delivery. It was Allie.

'Cate!' she cried as soon as the door was open.

'Allie – what are you doing here?'

'I couldn't work – not after what happened between us!'

Cate stood stiffly in the doorway feeling awkward and not knowing what to say.

'Can I come in?' Allie asked. 'Please?'

Cate hesitated and then nodded, waiting for Allie as she stepped gingerly into the hallway before closing the door.

She walked into the dining room and whistled as she placed a bag on one of the chairs. 'And this is *since* you've tidied around?'

'It's all important stuff,' Cate said in defence of Charles. 'Allie – what do you want?'

Allie turned around, looking embarrassed.

'I came to say I'm sorry.'

Cate didn't respond. She still felt horribly wounded by their earlier encounter.

'Please say something,' Allie went on, taking a step closer. 'Oh, my god! You've been crying, haven't you?'

Cate's hands instinctively flew to her face. 'It's not because of you,' she confessed.

'Isn't it?'

'I told Charles.'

'About how mean I was to you?'

'No. I told him about... about my past.'

Allie gasped. 'You did?'

'I thought it was time he knew the truth.'

Allie nodded. 'What did he say?'

'He swore quite a lot actually.'

'Did he?'

'I was quite shocked!' Cate said and then she stopped, suddenly feeling awkward in front of her friend again.

'Cate? You do forgive me, don't you? I feel just awful about what happened. I haven't been able to think about anything else. I said some stuff – some really bad stuff – and I shouldn't have said it. I think I was just in a bad place and I was really afraid of everything that was happening to me and I kind of projected that onto you. And I shouldn't have.' Allie was chewing her lip and Cate now noticed how pale she looked.

'I shouldn't have stormed off like that.'

'You had every right to,' Allie said. 'I would have if I'd been you.'

Cate shook her head. 'We should have – I don't know – given each other time to...'

'Calm the hell down?'

Cate smiled. 'Something like that.'

Allie pulled a sad face. 'I'm so sorry, Cate.'

'Come here,' Cate said and they hugged one another closely.

'I never want to fight with you again,' Allie said.

'Then let's not!'

'I brought you something,' Allie said, suddenly remembering the bag she'd placed on one of the chairs.

'You didn't need to do that.'

Allie opened the bag and brought out a paper bag from inside it and handed it to Cate.

'It's a millionaire's square,' Allie told her. 'It was the last one from my favourite bakery. If I'm ever feeling down, this is guaranteed to make me feel better. This and a walk on the beach to burn the calories off afterwards otherwise I won't feel better at all.'

Cate laughed. 'It looks wonderful, but I think I might have to half it so I don't feel too guilty. Want to share?'

Allie beamed her a smile. 'I was hoping you might say that!'

Charles realised that he couldn't hide out in the kitchen forever and finally made his way back to his mother's room. She was still sitting in her chair gazing out of the window and Eliza was sitting in her chair reading her book.

'All right in here?' he asked, placing the tray of drinks on a little table. 'Been chattering away, have you?' He smiled at his own joke and then felt a little mean. It wasn't their fault that they didn't talk, was it?

He took his cup of tea and sat down on the edge of the bed. His mother didn't move and certainly didn't acknowledge he was there. Nothing odd there, he thought, but her face seemed softer than when he'd left the room, and he watched as she slowly smiled.

And then she turned to face him and nodded towards Eliza.

'She reads beautifully, Charles.' Anna said.

Charles nearly spilt his tea in his lap at the declaration. He stared at his mother in disbelief and then looked at Eliza who was sitting reading her book. In silence as she always did. She hadn't glanced up when his mother spoke. There was nothing to suggest that she'd been reading aloud and he hadn't heard anything on the way back to the room.

So was his mother telling the truth? Had Eliza been reading to her? Or was it just one of her moments of confusion? Perhaps she didn't mean Eliza at all. Perhaps she'd imagined somebody else had been reading to her from another time and place entirely. He wouldn't be a bit surprised.

'Eliza?' he asked.

She looked up from her book and Charles examined her face, sweet and silent. And he couldn't ask her. He wasn't quite sure why. Perhaps he was scared to know the truth. It was such a wonderful thing to imagine having happened and he wanted to hold onto that for a little longer.

Or at least until he told Cate.

Cate and Allie were in the kitchen having just polished off the millionaire's square.

'I know we said we didn't want to fight again but, if this is what you bring me after we do, perhaps we should rethink that decision,' Cate said with a grin.

Allie blushed. 'I'm so sorry. I don't know what came over me. I think I went a little crazy.'

'It's okay. You don't need to keep apologising.'

'It's *not* okay. I really didn't mean to upset you or worry you about – well, you know what.'

Cate sighed. 'You certainly made me anxious – that's for sure.'

'You shouldn't be worried, Cate. You've been smart and you've made a good life for you and Eliza here. Nobody's going to take that away from you.'

'I wish I could be absolutely sure of that.'

Allie sighed. 'Surely, if he wanted you and Eliza back, he would have turned up by now. He'd have found a way to find you.'

'Oh, god! Don't even *talk* about it.'

'Sorry.'

There was a pause.

'You know, I have nightmares about him turning up here?' Cate revealed and then she shook her head. 'Sorry – I wasn't going to talk about it, was I?'

'It's hard not to talk about something when it's on your mind all the time,' Allie pointed out.

'But he isn't. I've managed to leave most of him behind. You know I love it here? Truly love it! I have a job that makes me feel valued and a comfortable place to call home and a boss that...' She stopped and smiled to herself.

'A boss that what?'

'Is it too presumptuous to think of him as a friend?'

Allie smiled. 'I wouldn't have thought so. *Is* he? Is he friendly now?'

'Friendly enough for me to confide in him and to feel safe around him. And to let him take my daughter out with him.'

'You mean Eliza's not upstairs?'

Cate grinned. 'She's out with Charles.'

'Wow! This *is* a new development.'

'I think he's really bonding with her.'

'Since the tuition began?'

'Yes,' Cate said, 'And possibly even before. To think he initially didn't even want her in the house.'

'And is she – you know – talking yet?'

Cate felt her smile fading. 'I'm afraid not, but she's making all sorts of other progress. She's got her own room up in the attic now. Did I tell you about it?'

Allie shook her head.

Cate filled her friend in on the adventure of the attic.

'Gosh, I'm really happy for you both,' Allie told her.

'None of it would have happened if it hadn't been for you,' Cate reminded her.

'I only told you about the job for purely selfish reasons,' Allie admitted with a wink. 'I wanted my old friend back in my life.'

That managed to restore Cate's smile.

'So,' she began, 'how are you feeling about Craig now? Have you...?' She stopped, not quite knowing how to phrase what she wanted to say.

'Do you mean, have I calmed down?' Allie said.

'No!' Cate jumped in. 'Well, *maybe* just a little.'

'It's okay,' Allie assured her. 'I know I overreacted, and I've been thinking about it and I know it's just me being horribly insecure when it comes to anything involving Jack.'

'So, what are you going to do?'

'I'm going to try and be more relaxed, around Craig and around Jack too. I think I might have been a little bit overprotective over the years. Do you think that's a fair assessment?'

'Oh, Allie. That's really not for me to say.'

'I know you've only just met him,' Allie said. 'It's unfair of me to ask you that.'

Cate smiled encouragingly. 'But being a little bit more relaxed can only help, can't it?'

'Yes, I suppose.' Allie sighed and then stood up. 'I really should get going.'

Cate walked with her to the front door and the two of them embraced.

'Let me know how it all goes, won't you?' Cate said.

'You too.'

An hour after Allie left, Cate heard Charles's Land Rover pulling up in the driveway and, a moment later, the front door opened. Rigs got there first, greeting Charles and Eliza with a succession of small, excited barks.

'How did it go?' Cate asked as she joined them all in the hall.

'Good,' Charles said. 'We went into Bridport after seeing Mum and had cake.'

Cate examined him. 'Is everything okay?' she asked him.

'Yeah,' he said in a vague sort of way that gave Cate the distinct impression that everything was certainly not okay. She looked at her daughter.

'Eliza? Why don't you run through to the kitchen and give Rigs a treat?' Eliza nodded and trotted off with the dog in tow and Cate turned her attention to Charles once again. 'So?'

He beckoned her towards the living room and they walked through together, sitting down on the sofa a moment later.

'What's the matter?' Cate asked him, seeing him frown.

He shook his head, the strangest of expressions on his face.

'Charles, you're worrying me.'

'No – no, Cate – please don't be worried. It's just, well, I'm not sure how to tell you this.'

'Just tell me, please!'

'Something strange happened at the care home. At least, I think it did. I can't quite be sure because I wasn't there, you see.'

'No, I don't see.'

His face broke into a smile now, which disturbed Cate even more than when he'd been frowning.

'I think Eliza might have said something.'

'What do you mean, *said something*? When? To whom?'

'To my mother. Perhaps she didn't exactly speak. But I think she might have been reading to her.'

'You think Eliza was reading to your mother?'

Charles shrugged. 'I don't know! I went out of the room to get drinks and, when I came back, Mum told me that Eliza reads well. Now, Mum might just have said that. She might have made it up. I really don't know.'

'But why would she do that?'

'Because that's what her condition does to her.'

'She said that Eliza was reading to her?'

'Yes. She said she reads beautifully!'

'And did you ask Eliza about it?'

'No. I didn't want to freak her out. I wasn't sure what to do, to be honest.'

'And it didn't happen again while you were in the room with them both?'

'No, she was just reading silently to herself. I actually thought about leaving again and hanging around in the hallway to see if I could catch her, but that just didn't feel right.'

Cate sat there quietly, taking it all in and wishing with all her heart that she had been there to witness whatever might have happened at the care home.

'Do you think I should ask Eliza if anything happened?' Cate asked Charles.

'It's up to you. What do you think would be the best?'

'I really don't know,' Cate said honestly. 'I know we shouldn't draw attention to whenever she speaks. We shouldn't make a big fuss about it, but that's so hard, isn't it? I mean, I want to go to her right now and ask her what happened.' She shook her head, doing her best to contain her excitement. 'Leave it with me,' she told Charles. 'I'm not quite sure what I'm going to do, but thank you so much for telling me.'

He smiled and Cate noticed that he was still wearing that same dazzled expression. It was truly as if he was as thrilled and as baffled as Cate was.

Cate spent the rest of that day carefully tiptoeing around Eliza, never once mentioning the care home or what may or may not have taken place in the reading department. It wasn't easy. More than anything, Cate wanted to sit down with her daughter and talk gently to her, encouraging her to confide what had really happened.

Finally, it was time for bed and Cate walked upstairs with Eliza, supervising her bath time and brushing her fair hair once it was dry. They climbed the stairs up into the loft and Eliza settled into bed, the glow of her bedside lamp comforting in the long dark space of the room. Cate glanced across at Dennis the dinosaur, wondering if Eliza might have been reading aloud to him as well. In fact, it might just be possible that Cate was the only person in Dorset whom Eliza *hadn't* been reading to.

She took a deep breath. She was becoming agitated and that wasn't a good energy to have around Eliza.

'Shall we have a bedtime story?' Cate asked her now.

Eliza nodded and Cate picked a book from the bedside table, smiling as she saw some of Jamie's dinosaur and fossil books there mixed in with a few of the ones she'd brought from home. Cate picked an old favourite – a story about a ballerina. The prose was exquisite and the illustrations divine. Even if Eliza ever decided she had finished with the book, Cate wasn't sure she could part with it. That book, that story, had seen them through some pretty rough times together, and it was always a joy to sink into its comfortable pages.

Cate read for a while, sinking into the luxurious world of the story until she felt pretty tired herself. She laid the book down in her lap and then an idea occurred to her.

'Do you want to read for a bit?' she asked hesitantly, watching as Eliza's fingers reached out to clasp the book. Cate waited, barely daring to breathe, but nothing happened. Eliza took the book and read to herself, her eyes moving from left to right across the page. Cate sighed inwardly, trying not to show her disappointment.

She sat there for a few minutes longer and then she reached across to kiss her daughter's cheek.

'Time for lights out,' she said. Eliza's eyes grew wide. 'Don't worry – the landing light will stay on and the door will be ajar.'

Cate tucked Eliza in.

'Good night, sweetie,' she said as she descended the stairs a moment later.

She'd just made it to her bedroom door when Charles's head popped round his own.

'All okay?' he asked.

'Yes,' she whispered back, crossing the space between them. 'I – I encouraged her to read aloud.'

'And?'

'She just read silently to herself.'

Charles nodded. 'It'll happen.'

'Will it?' Cate suddenly felt engulfed by fear once again. 'I sometimes think I'll never hear that sweet voice again.'

'You will. Just give her time.'

'What makes you so sure?'

Charles looked pensive for a moment. 'Because I really believe my mother was telling the truth today. There was something different – in her eyes.'

'Was there?'

Charles nodded. 'I'm sure of it, yes. The more I think about it.'

Cate attempted a weak smile as she clung on to the promise of Eliza healing in the future.

'I miss my girl so much.'

'I know you do,' Charles said gently and it was all Cate could do to stop the tears from forming. 'She'll come back to you. I know she will.'

CHAPTER SEVENTEEN

It was still strange for Allie to look into her living room in the evening and see not only Jack there, but Craig too. Jack, who spent a good proportion of his life in his bedroom, looked completely out of place in the cottage's cosy living room, and Craig didn't look totally natural in there either. He was used to the great outdoors and seemed somehow trapped whenever he was inside. But Allie was slowly getting used to seeing them both together like that – sitting, talking, exchanging views. Could it be that she was really beginning to relax with the idea of Craig in their lives? Perhaps her outburst in front of Cate and their subsequent chat had done her some good. She'd been carrying around all her insecurities and pent-up emotions and had needed to release them, and now she was enjoying the ensuing calm. Yes, she thought, she was going to be calm and rational about this.

She'd truly surprised herself by how much she liked hearing Jack and Craig's voices together each evening and she endeavoured to give them plenty of space and would often leave them to themselves in the front room while she worked quietly in the kitchen. She liked listening to their laughter as she busied herself with a new recipe she was trying to perfect. On other evenings, however, she would join them and they would swap stories together, catching up on the years with surprising ease.

One evening when she'd left them to it, Craig came into the kitchen.

'Everything okay?' she asked him as she rolled out a piece of pastry for an apple pie she was making with some windfalls from a neighbour's garden.

'Yeah, good,' he said, but she could tell that there was something in his voice which hinted that all was not quite perfect. He had something to say, didn't he? Was he leaving?

Allie brushed her hands down the front of her apron and turned to face him.

'What is it?' she asked, not wanting to be kept in the dark a moment longer than necessary.

'Nothing,' he said, 'it's just I've been thinking.'

'Oh?'

He shuffled from one foot to the other. A sign that never boded well.

'I've been telling Jack about some of my travels and he's shown a real interest in the South American ones. You know – all those ancient civilisations and volcanoes and jungles and stuff.'

'Oh, yes?' Allie tried to keep her voice bright and easy even though she could feel her breath stopping somewhere inside her chest.

'He's a bright kid – he was asking all the right questions,' Craig paused and Allie nodded, trying desperately not to jump to conclusions. He'd only been talking about his adventures with their son but, when Craig stopped talking, Allie knew he was building towards something. It was only a small lull in the conversation, but she still had time to imagine all sorts of horrors during that lull.

'He wants to go with me.'

And there it was. Allie swallowed hard.

'Is that what he said?' Her voice came out as a squeak.

'Yeah. It was totally his idea.'

She paused, trying not to panic and waiting for Craig to say more.

'I think it would be a pretty good idea, don't you?' Craig went on.

'What do you mean?'

'For him to come with me. You know, to have an adventure together. Father and son, maybe during the next summer holiday.'

Allie could feel tears stinging her eyes. This was exactly what she had been dreading. She'd only just managed to get a lid on her emotions, and begun to relax having Craig around, but this had always been in the back of her mind. The fear that he would take Jack away from her. It'd been bad enough Craig taking Jack into Dorchester for the day. She really didn't think she could cope with him taking their son out of the country. And how long was he talking about? 'Craig...' Her voice faded.

'Listen, before you say anything, I know how you feel.'

'*Do* you?' Allie couldn't disguise the sarcasm in her voice.

Craig nodded. 'He's a special kid and it's just been the two of you for a long time. I get that. I really do. But he's growing up fast, Allie. I think he needs a father in his life now and I'd really like him to see a bit of the world.'

'But South America? God, Craig!' Allie cried, finding her voice at last. 'Be sensible and at least make it the South of France or somewhere safer!'

He shook his head. 'That wouldn't be an adventure, would it?'

'It would. He's never been.'

'He's never been to South Yorkshire either, but I'm not going to take him there, am I?'

'Why does it even need to be an adventure? Why can't you just have a normal sort of holiday with him?'

'Because I'm not a normal guy. I don't do normal sorts of things. You know that!'

Allie knew only too well. When he'd dreamed of Brazil for a holiday, she was hoping more for Brighton.

'It's just that I've watched *way* too many documentaries about dangerous places. South America's dangerous, Craig.'

'Only if you don't know what you're doing, and I do.'

'But you can get into all sorts of trouble in those places,' Allie told him. 'Kidnapping, shootings, drugs. And that's before any of the natural disasters. Those places are always having earthquakes and hurricanes and volcanic eruptions, aren't they? And the spiders are the size of dinner plates and there are snakes that can kill you!'

'Anything else?' he asked, his voice full of sarcasm.

'I'm sure I'll think of something.'

'I'm sure you will.'

'Don't be like that,' she said. 'I'm just trying to protect my son.'

'So you want to keep him here, do you? You want to smother him and make sure he never sets foot out of Dorset. Out of bloody Lyme Bay!'

'I didn't say that!'

'I think you did.'

'He's too young for somewhere like South America. It's absurd. I'm not even going to have this conversation.'

She turned away from him and started to fiddle with her baking, only her hands felt all hot and sticky now.

'I think you'd better leave,' she told him without turning round.

'Oh, yeah – because that's how you get your way, isn't it? Not by talking things through and considering what another person wants, but by throwing them out!'

'That is not true!' Allie said, turning to face him now.

'So you're *not* throwing me out?' Craig's expression was fixed and firm.

'I think it's getting late, that's all, and we're baiting each other now. Nobody's going to say anything tonight to fix this, are they?'

Craig frowned and then he slowly nodded. 'Don't think you've got your way, though. I mean if I leave now.'

'You *are* leaving now, Craig.'

'Hey, I don't know why you're getting so mad at me,' Craig said. 'It was Jack's suggestion!'

They stared at each other for the longest moment and then he turned to go just as Jack came out of the living room.

'Hey, Dad – did you tell Mum your cool idea yet?'

Charles was constantly surprised by Eliza's willingness to learn. She was increasingly spending more time in his workshop, reading through her textbooks as he got on with his work. He liked her silent companionship and was surprised by how well he'd adapted to having somebody in his sacred space with him. Jamie had used to spend time in there, of course, but he was a part of him. The idea of having a stranger in his space was still a new one for Charles, and it had only been a few short weeks since the idea had been unthinkable to him, and yet here he was now, quite happy with Eliza sitting close to him.

He turned to look at her now, her head bent as she read one

of the books he'd given her about Dorset geology. It was quite advanced, but he believed she could cope with it.

'How are you getting on?' he asked after they'd both been working for half an hour or so.

Eliza nodded and gave a little smile. Charles approached her and, seeing where she'd got to in the book, he sat down beside her.

'So you've been reading about our amazing coastline?'

She nodded.

'Do you know the name of the highest point along the south coast? It's right here in Dorset, you know.'

She reached for her pencil and pad and wrote something.

Golden Cap.

'That's the one,' he said with a smile. 'Maybe we could climb it one day. The views from the top are wonderful. You probably saw Golden Cap when we were on the beach together at Charmouth. Remember seeing it in the distance?'

She shook her head.

'Well, I know your eyes were very firmly fixed on the ground in search of fossils, weren't they?'

She smiled.

'So, Eliza, do you know the name given to the limestone and shale layers around our part of the coast – where lots of the good fossils are found? Remember that?'

Eliza looked thoughtful for a moment and then her eyes widened.

'Blue Lias!'

'That's right,' Charles said and then he blinked, realising what had happened. Eliza hadn't written the words down – she'd *spoken* them, and they'd popped out of her mouth so naturally that he'd just taken it as normal. But it wasn't normal, was it? He took a moment to absorb it, remembering Cate telling him that they had to act normally if and when it ever happened. But the fact was, this was the first time he'd ever heard her speak.

'Okay if I leave you to it for a bit?' Charles said, getting up. Eliza nodded. 'I've just got to... check on something.' The truth was, he couldn't wait a single second to tell Cate what had happened. Whether Eliza realised that or not, he wasn't sure, but he did his best to appear calm, fiddling with a few things on his workbench and checking through some papers that really didn't need checking before he left the workshop.

He walked through to the dining room and living room, but Cate wasn't there. She wasn't in the kitchen either. She must be upstairs, he thought, taking the steps two at a time.

'Cate?'

She walked out onto the landing, a bunch of bath towels in her arms headed for the washing machine.

'Put those down for a minute,' Charles told her.

Cate did as she was told, putting the towels down on the floor. 'Is everything okay?'

He smiled because he couldn't help it. He realised he was smiling a lot more these days and it felt good, really good.

'It's Eliza. She spoke.'

'What?'

'Just now as we were looking at one of the books we've been studying together.'

'What did she say?' Cate asked.

'Now, don't get excited. It wasn't a whole sentence or anything.'

'Okay. Well what did she say?'

Charles paused before answering. 'Blue Lias.'

'Pardon?'

Charles smiled. 'Blue Lias. It's a kind of clay formed in the early Jurassic period.'

Cate frowned. '*That's* what she said? She hasn't said hello or good morning or good night for months and yet she's talking about dirt?'

'In all fairness, I did ask her a question about it. And she said it right too. I mean, it's a pretty odd name by any standards so it's impressive that she pronounced it right and everything seeing as she's not spoken for a while.'

Cate shook her head. 'What's going on, Charles? She's laughing with Rigs, she's apparently reading to your mother and now she's talking with you! Why isn't she communicating with me like that?'

'I'm not sure.'

'Do you think she blames me for what happened to us?'

'I don't know,' Charles said honestly. 'But – well – perhaps you're inevitably linked to that dark time in her life.'

Cate stared at him, looking totally helpless. 'And how do I fix that?'

Charles sighed. 'I wish I knew, but it seems to be that she feels less pressure around others. What do you think?'

'I don't know what to think. All I know is I'm her mother. Surely she should be confiding in me, not shutting me out like this! I can't bear it!'

Charles raked a hand through his hair, wondering how he could make the situation easier for her, but not seeing an obvious solution.

'Don't make too much out of it,' he said, instantly feeling like a fool for uttering such a useless platitude.

'How can I not?'

'Eliza speaking – well – it's a step in the right direction, isn't it? You should be happy instead of anxious.'

Cate sighed. 'Yes, of course it is and of course I'm happy,' she replied and Charles could see that she was doing her best to remain calm and positive.

'Listen,' he said, 'why don't you do some work in the office while I'm tutoring Eliza later? You can leave the door open and see if it happens again.'

'You mean spy on my daughter?'

'Well, if you want to look at it like that.'

Cate nodded, and he guessed that she was torn between hating the idea and leaping upon it.

'Okay. Let's do it.'

They agreed to stagger going into the workshop. Cate went in first with a cup of tea, trying to look as casual as possible.

'Hi sweetie,' she said. 'All okay?'

Eliza nodded.

'I've just got some work to do in the office, but we'll tackle some history together later, all right?'

Eliza smiled and returned to her book and Cate pushed the office door behind her so that it wasn't quite closed. She peered through the gap. Eliza didn't seem to have noticed that there was anything unusual in her mother's behaviour and for that she was grateful.

A few minutes later, Charles entered the workshop.

'How about we continue with that book?' he suggested to Eliza. 'I could ask you some more questions if you like – make up our own quiz. What do you think?'

Eliza nodded and Charles looked pleased, Cate thought, and what a good idea of his it was. Surely, a quick fire round of questions would encourage quick fire answers from Eliza. In the form of speech.

She saw him glance towards the office door and then he began.

Cate had been hovering close to the door, but she took a step back now. It felt wrong to be spying on Eliza in this way and maybe it wouldn't work at all because Eliza knew her mother was only a few feet away. And perhaps this venture would be equally ill-fated because Cate's intentions weren't quite above board.

She saw Charles pick up the book Eliza had been reading.

'Let me see,' he said. 'Okay, here's the first question for you. Ready?'

Cate saw Eliza nodding and smiled, watching as Eliza picked up her pencil and wrote down the answer to the first question. She saw an expression of disappointment flit across Charles's face and her heart ached. It wasn't just her who wanted to hear Eliza speak. She realised, perhaps for the first time, that Charles was desperate to hear her voice too.

He fired another question at Eliza. Then another. And another. He was so wonderfully patient with her, taking her strange way of communicating totally in his stride and waiting as she wrote each of her answers down.

Cate waited. She couldn't get any work done, not while there was the merest hint of a chance that her daughter might actually speak, but she felt so guilty eaves dropping like this.

Several more questions came and, to each one, Eliza wrote her answers.

'I think we've done enough for the day, don't you?' he finally said. 'Why don't you take a break and I'll go through your answers?'

Cate watched as Eliza closed the book in front of her and left the workshop – no doubt going to the kitchen to see Rigs.

Charles turned towards her and she opened the door.

'I'm sorry,' he said. 'I thought a quiz might do the trick.'

'It's not your fault. You did your best.'

'I was so hopeful it would happen again,' he said, 'and it will.'

She smiled at him and tried, with all her heart, to remain as hopeful as Charles.

❀ ❀ ❀ ❀ ❀

Allie was fuming after Craig had left which had put Jack in an instant mood.

'It's not fair!' he'd cried. 'You always blame Dad and it's not his fault.'

'Oh, *how* isn't it his fault that he lied and said that you want to go to South America with him?'

'I *do* want to go with him!'

'He said you suggested it, Jack!'

'So what? Who cares who suggested it? I don't see why that's such a big deal.'

'He's planting ideas in your head and then lying to me so I don't get mad at him. It's not right and it's not fair.'

'But I want to go. I want to spend time with him. You said that was a good idea.'

'Yes, but you don't need to fly across the world to some bug-infested jungle to do it.'

Jack sighed dramatically. 'Dad said I needed to get out more and see different places. He said it isn't healthy to be cooped up here all my life.'

'Jack, you're twelve. You've got your whole life to explore the world. Now's the time to work hard at school,' Allie told him. 'Anyway, since when have you felt *cooped up*? If anything, it's *you* that locks yourself away in your room. And I thought you were happy there.'

'I was, Mum. I am. But I want to see places. I don't want to be stuck in Dorset my whole life.'

Allie sighed. He was sounding like a carbon copy of Craig now. She should have been monitoring things more closely. She shouldn't have let them have all that time alone together. And yet, she knew she couldn't chaperone her son. That wouldn't be right for him or fair on Craig.

Before she could say anything else, Jack had stomped upstairs with a fair amount of attitude thundering in his feet and in the way he slammed his bedroom door a moment later.

Allie closed her eyes, trying to remain calm. This was going to work itself out. She wasn't sure how yet, but it would. She just needed to stay calm.

Feeling utterly drained by it all, she walked upstairs and, as she passed Jack's room, she remembered a time when she'd wanted to travel. She'd never had such ambitious dreams as Craig, but she had nursed a romantic notion about buying a little vehicle and tootling around the UK. That was the kind of safe, fun adventure that appealed to her.

Heading to her bedroom, she opened the wardrobe door. There was a shelf at the top where she kept a few hats and scarves and she pulled out the large photo album that lived there and placed it on the bed, opening it up and smiling at the young Allie who greeted her. Not many people kept albums like this anymore, she thought, and what a great shame that was. Everything was digital. But did anything beat physically flipping through the pages of an album? Allie thought not and she'd kept up the tradition of the album, filling them with photos of Jack as he'd grown up.

This one, though, was of her journey through her teenage years up until the time she'd become pregnant with Jack. There were photos of her at school, her hair almost down to her waist. There were photos of parties, summer holidays, family celebrations and pets she'd loved and lost over the years. It was a wonderful jumble of memories that not only included photos but concert tickets too and funny little bits of paper with notes she'd written in a long ago classroom, a couple of pressed flowers that had lost their colour, and a horseshoe charm off a bracelet that had broken years before. There were even some photos of Cate, and Allie grinned as she saw the happy, bright face of her friend, remembering how shocked she'd been when she'd seen how pale and fragile Cate looked when she'd first arrived in Dorset. That was changing though, wasn't it? Now that she was safe and had time and space to heal.

Allie vowed to share her album with Cate at the earliest opportunity. She was pretty sure that Eliza would love to see what her mother had looked like all those years ago.

But these weren't the photos that had made her get the album out. There was one in particular she was hunting for and, flipping over one more page, she found it. The mere sight of it made her smile and a rush of long-forgotten dreams engulfed her as she gazed at it.

Dilly. The Volkswagen Camper Van. She'd belonged to Linda, an older cousin of Allie's, who'd arrived one day and parked the noisy old seventies vehicle in their driveway. Allie had fallen madly in love, swearing she'd have one herself one day. Linda had taken her out in Dilly and they'd driven across the flat landscape of the Fens towards the coast, where they'd opened the door and sat on Dilly's long seat as they'd drunk hot tea from a flask. Allie had been in heaven, thinking it the height of sophistication.

She looked longingly at the photo in the album. Dilly was baby blue with large daisies and the odd rainbow painted along her flanks. She was a babe on wheels and Allie had longed to have her own. It had been one of her dreams to drive around the coastline of Britain – from Lyme to Liverpool, from Hemsby to the Humber. But dreams changed with circumstances, didn't they? She'd found herself a single mother, and buying a clapped-out old Volkswagen – because that's all she would have been able to afford – no longer seemed like a priority. How would she have travelled with a baby in tow? Didn't babies need security and stability? That's what Allie had believed back then.

But he's not a baby anymore, she thought to herself now, and he wants to travel. Would it be right to stop him from doing that? He was so obviously his father's son and it would be wrong of her to suppress that need in him.

Closing the photo album, Allie got up from the bed and picked up her laptop, logging into her bank account a moment later and checking the balance. No, she thought. It was a crazy idea. She was having the most ridiculous knee-jerk reaction to Craig's crazy idea. And yet...

She looked at her balance again. Would it be enough? There was a part of her – a very big part – that told her that this was her safety net money or funds for Jack's future or if she was ever in an unthinkable position and couldn't work. That money was the sum total of everything she'd saved from her first job as a babysitter aged fourteen. And it could sit there making her feel all warm and secure for a day that might never arrive, or she could plunder it and have some fun.

She chewed her lip, trying to gauge the pros and judge the cons, and telling herself she shouldn't really make such a weighty decision after being emotionally riled and so she logged off and closed her laptop.

CHAPTER EIGHTEEN

The nights were slowly drawing in with Rigs's afternoon walk taking place ever closer to lunchtime and the curtains of Hollow House being drawn earlier. Cate, who'd only ever known central heating her whole life, was getting pretty good at making a fire now, and was really enjoying the simple pleasure of sitting beside it in the evening with a book, glancing up every so often to stare into the orange flames. It was still a novelty for her to feel so relaxed in the evenings and to be able to sit in the living room with Eliza and enjoy the sensation of time passing without feeling anxious that she had to be doing something to please or appease somebody else.

Sometimes, as she sat watching the patterns in the flames and listening to the gentle shift of the wood, her mind would drift unwillingly back to evenings in the past when she'd move nervously around the front room after a day of cleaning the house, desperately trying to make sure that everything was in its place because she'd be in trouble if it wasn't.

It was strange to her that a man who could tell if a vase wasn't perfectly centred on a shelf or be outraged if there was a smidgeon of dust on a table, didn't seem to mind if he started smashing things up in rage, leaving glass shards everywhere. Cate had never understood that. But could another human being ever really be understood? Her marriage had made her wonder that. Her husband had had so many faces. There'd been the face that had made her fall in love with him – the charmer, the apparently sweet-natured guy who'd bought her flowers and told her she was beautiful and that he wanted her to be the mother of his children. Then there was the professional man – the one his boss and colleagues relied upon. He'd always been so popular at work. She'd often hear him on his phone, laughing with someone from the office and making arrangements to socialise with them. Cate had always been secretly glad whenever he did because it meant fewer hours she'd have to spend with him. There'd also been the father and, in all fairness, she couldn't fault him completely in that role because he genuinely seemed to care for his Elizabeth. He would often buy her gifts and make a fuss of her, but the little girl innately felt fearful of him. Cate could see it and her father could too. Sometimes, he chose to ignore it, but other times, he'd get upset and shout at her.

'What the hell's wrong with you anyway? I've just spent good money on a gift and you won't even look me in the eye!'

Cate was perplexed that he couldn't see it might have something to do with the fact he'd belted the girl's mother the night before. No gift – however expensive – was going to undo that damage.

Then there'd been the role of husband. Cate closed her eyes as she remembered. Other than Eliza, Cate believed that she was the only one who saw that cruel streak in him. She was the only one to witness the intense rages he could fly into, the violence and the remorse. She'd once thought to ask his mother about it as they sometimes visited her in Norfolk, but Cate was never left alone with her. It was as if he knew something would be revealed if the two women started to confide in each other. Cate felt she might be able to talk to her mother-in-law because she always showed concern for her.

'You're pale, my dear,' she'd say. 'My son not taking proper care of you?'

How many times had Cate wanted to scream out loud, 'No! Look at these bruises!' But she'd catch a glance from her husband and would give a nervous laugh instead.

There were times when he was gentler with her, giving her little compliments and bringing a bunch of flowers home. It was as if he knew she was on a precipice and that too much cruelty might push her away completely. So this strange dance of abuse and tenderness had continued for many years, with Cate trying to convince herself that he could change and that things would get better one day.

Well, that's what she believed until she could lie to herself no more.

Opening her eyes, she gazed into the fire again. Rigs was laying on the rug in front of it and Eliza was sketching beside him, her pens laid out in front of her on the floor. The only person who was missing was Charles. More often than not, he spent his evenings in his workshop. Cate had to smile at that. He would often try to deny it, but he was a true workaholic. Tonight, however, Cate decided to do something about it so, putting her book down on the sofa, she got up.

'I'm going to find Charles,' she told Eliza. Rigs looked up from the rug by the fire, but wasn't going to give up his place there.

Cate walked through to the workshop. She could hear Charles at work and tapped lightly on the door.

'Charles?'

'Come in.'

Cate opened the door and walked inside. It felt cold after the cosy living room and she felt bad that Charles was still working while she'd been relaxing by the fire.

'Everything all right?' he asked, glancing up quickly from what looked like a pile of rubble.

'Yes!' Cate said, noting that he always seemed concerned about her. Perhaps he thought she was one of those people who only seemed to attract problems. 'I was just letting you know that we've got a lovely fire going in the living room and we were wondering if you were ever going to down tools and join us.'

He looked up properly now and Cate could see that his eyes looked red and sore.

'You should join us,' she said, and then wondered if using the word *should* was entirely appropriate. She was, after all, still his employee and, although they were living together, she had no right to tell him what he should and shouldn't do.

'I can't,' he said, almost automatically.

'Why not?'

'I want to get this finished.'

'Is there a deadline?'

'There's always a deadline.'

'On a two-hundred-million-year-old fossil? Surely an extra few hours won't matter?'

He smiled at that. 'No, you're right.'

Cate relaxed. She'd pushed and she'd been anxious about doing so, but it seemed to have worked for he put his tools down, washed his hands and followed her out of the workshop, switching the lights off for the night.

'Can I get you a cup of tea or anything else?' Cate offered as they entered the living room a moment later.

Charles shook his head, smiling at Eliza. 'No, thank you,' he said. Rigs looked up, thumped his tail and got on with his little sleep.

Cate watched Charles for a moment as he sat beside her and then she picked up her book.

'This feels strange,' he said a few minutes later.

'What does?' Cate asked.

'This. Just sitting. I can't remember when I last took an evening off.'

'Well, you should do more of that. It isn't healthy to work so hard.'

He frowned as if not understanding her. 'But I love my work.'

'I know you do. But you can't work all the time.'

'It doesn't feel like work.'

'But it still is and you need to rest every so often. Rest reinvigorates you.'

Charles gave a snort. 'I don't need reinvigorating.'

'Your red eyes are begging to differ.'

'My eyes aren't red,' Charles declared, causing Eliza to look up from her home on the carpet and giving a look which clearly told him he was wrong.

'That's not overwork – that's just the strong winds from earlier today.'

'You need to rest more,' Cate insisted.

Charles sighed and Cate watched as his eyes slowly closed. Perhaps that was his quiet way of letting her know she was right. Cate picked up her book again.

'What are you reading?' Charles asked after a few minutes.

'*Remarkable Creatures*,' Cate said. 'It's a novel by Tracy Chevalier about Mary Anning.'

'Ah, our local heroine again!'

'Yes. It's quite eye-opening.'

'I read it a few years ago. It really gives a feel for the time, doesn't it? What life in Lyme must have been like in the nineteenth century.'

'And reminds me that I'm glad I'm a twenty-first century woman,' Cate said, thinking of how hard it had been for Mary Anning to make a living in Victorian times even when she was the very best in her field.

Charles sighed contentedly. 'You know, this feels okay.'

Cate smiled. 'See! I told you it's good to rest.'

'Sophie and I never really just sat without us doing something.'

'What do you mean?' Cate asked.

'I mean, I was usually reading and she was always fiddling with that phone of hers. She was one of those people who seem umbilically attached to their phones. I don't know,' Charles said, shaking his head. 'She was always on one of those social media sites moaning about something or laughing at silly videos. I'm not really sure I see the point of all that.' He turned to face Cate. 'Now I think of it, I'm not sure I've ever seen you on your phone.'

'I'm not even sure where it is,' Cate confessed with a laugh. 'And, even if I knew, it wouldn't be on. I only use it to contact Allie and look stuff up on Google from time to time.'

'That's good. That's how it should be,' Charles declared. 'I don't like how they're taking over and turning people into monosyllabic robots who aren't aware of the real world around them. You know, there's a young fossil hunter who seems permanently attached to his. He'll have his hammer in one hand and his phone in the other. You can't work like that. He's going to have an accident one day and I bet he misses a ton of stuff from not concentrating properly.'

'Is he photographing things for social media? That's popular now. Allie does it for her shop. She's got quite a following.'

'I don't know what he's doing.'

'Well, I've started taking photos of your stock for the website and shop. Perhaps we should think about having a presence on one of those social media sites too other than Facebook.'

Charles gave a derisive snort. 'I don't think so.'

'Why not? It could increase traffic to your website and shop if it's done right. Allie takes the most beautiful photos of her shop and says it's worked wonders for orders of her jewellery.'

Charles seemed to mull this over for a moment. 'Let me think about it.'

'Okay,' Cate said, her mind already whirling at the possibilities.

They lapsed into a comfortable silence again, the sound of the fire crackling, the snores of Rigs and the gentle scratching of Eliza's pens in her notebook acting as a calming soundtrack.

'I remember when Sophie first saw this house,' Charles began after a few minutes. 'She loved the fireplaces and insisted we always had wood for a fire, only we rarely made time to just sit here together. Isn't that crazy?'

Cate nodded. 'It is!'

'Did you have a fire at your...?' he paused.

'No. Well, not a useable one,' Cate said, wondering if Charles had been going to use the word "home" but had then thought better of it.

'We had a fireplace, but it was never used. I did...' Cate stopped and glanced at Eliza, but she didn't seem to be paying any attention to what they were saying. 'I did mention it once, but he said it would be too messy. Not that he would have had anything to do with tidying it up.'

'He liked things kept clean?' Charles asked in a low voice.

Cate nodded. 'There'd be trouble if things were ever out of place,' she whispered and Charles seemed to understand her meaning.

Cate stared into the fire, willing herself not to think of anything else other than the room she was in now and the company she was keeping, but all too aware that the past could drag her under at a moment's notice. But here she was, sitting comfortably and companionably with Charles, her daughter and Rigs and life was good. She felt so at ease with this man now that she could talk to him about her past, and that felt comforting. She'd removed a barrier between them and that had made all the difference.

They sat for a little longer. At one point, Cate got up to throw another log on the fire and, a little later, Charles did the same. Cate's eyes were beginning to tire and the words on the page before her became blurry. Eliza looked tired too. She'd long since put down her pens and was sitting looking into the fire, a dreamy expression on her face.

Then, quite suddenly, Rigs raised his head and gave a low, slow growl.

'What's that?' Charles asked.

'Did you hear something?' Cate asked, closing her book now as she strained to hear. There was definitely a noise from outside.

Charles stood up and went to the window, drawing the curtains back. This immediately got Rigs's attention and he was up and barking.

'Quiet Rigs,' Charles said, peering out into the darkness.

'What is it?' Cate asked, feeling fearful, as if their safe and cosy haven had been invaded.

'It's a car,' Charles told her.

'Do you recognise it?'

'No, I don't think so. But it's too dark to tell.'

Cate got up from the sofa but felt reluctant to go to the window. She could feel that her heartbeat had accelerated, which was silly really. It was just a car. An ordinary car.

'It's leaving,' Charles said and he drew the curtains against the night, making the room feel protected once more.

'Who do you think it was?' Cate asked.

'I don't know. Maybe they got the wrong house. That happens sometimes. People take a wrong turn and end up getting lost in these little country lanes.'

Cate glanced in the direction of the window, trying not to feel anxious.

'Cup of tea?' Charles suggested. Cate shook her head.

'I think I'll call it a night,' Cate said.

Charles's face seemed to fall. 'There's still life in the fire,' he said, nodding towards it.

Cate smiled, looking at the bright flames. 'Yes, just not in me. Eliza? Time to get ready for bed.'

Eliza got up from the carpet and wobbled a little.

'You're half asleep already!' Cate said with a laugh. 'Night, Charles.'

'Good night you two,' he said.

'Make sure you don't go back in that workshop,' Cate warned.

He waved a hand at her as if dismissing her notion as ridiculous, but she didn't altogether trust him not to return to his work the minute she was upstairs.

After Eliza had undressed and washed and was tucked up in bed, Cate had a sudden misgiving about leaving her. The loft seemed, that night, to be a very long way from her own room and she really didn't want to leave her daughter up there on her own.

'Eliza? Would you like to come down to my room tonight?' she asked her.

Eliza looked confused by this request and shook her head.

'Well, how about if I stay up here with you tonight?'

Eliza nodded and Cate immediately felt better.

She didn't take long to sort herself out in her own bedroom

and then return to the loft. Eliza had drifted into a deep sleep and wasn't disturbed when Cate got into bed next to her.

Letting out a sigh of relief to be next to her daughter once more, Cate closed her eyes. Only sleep wouldn't come. She wasn't sure how long she lay awake. Rain sounded heavy and close on the slanted loft roof above her and, for one dreadful moment, she thought she heard the sound of tyres on the driveway outside again. Her eyes blinked open and her whole body tensed, but she soon realised that it was hail.

She closed her eyes again, half-aware of the great papier-mâché head of Dennis the dinosaur staring at her in the darkness. She could only hope that he was guarding them, she thought, as she finally felt herself drifting off to sleep.

CHAPTER NINETEEN

The rain and the hail had mercifully stopped by the next morning and Cate saw that the day looked freshly washed, with a glimmer of late November sunshine doing its best to brighten the mood and banish all memories of the wet night before.

After Eliza had finished her morning lessons and they'd enjoyed a quick lunch together, Cate decided to make the most of the sunshine because winter was fast approaching and it was hard to tell how many more days like this would come.

Whistling for Rigs, who was quite used to accompanying them for a walk now, Cate slipped his lead on and the three of them left the house together. Charles had gone into Dorchester on business and had decided not to take the dog with him and Cate was glad of that. Somehow, she felt a little safer with the dog walking alongside them. Not that she'd ever felt unsafe walking in the village, but she couldn't quite shake the feeling of unease she'd felt the night before.

Cate needed the sea. She wanted to stand on the beach and look out into the vastness of the waves, to inhale the sharp saltiness and feel its breath in her hair. That way, she felt sure she could clear her mind of the fears of the night before.

They took the direct route through the village rather than walking down the holloway. There was something about the way the trees met over the middle and blocked out the light that she couldn't bear today, even if most of the trees' leaves had been lost. So they took the road.

With the rain and high winds of the night before, this was the perfect day to scour the beach for fossils, but she wasn't interested in that. Today was a day for staring and Cate focused her gaze out to sea. How had she lived without the sea in her life for so long? It was such a great comfort, she thought as she stared into the pale grey waves. It had a hypnotic effect that soothed and washed away any thoughts from her mind which was exactly what she'd been hoping for. She'd woken up in Eliza's bed in the pale dawn and had still felt some of the fear of the night before. The car. The unseen driver. She hadn't dared to acknowledge it to Charles, but perhaps he had guessed.

Cate stared at the rolling waves. They were menacingly large today, but she found watching them curiously comforting despite their power. She had hold of Eliza's hand and looked down at her daughter's face. What was going through that mind of hers? Was she wondering what they were doing here on such a wild day? If only Eliza would let her know what she was thinking. Even if it was just a solitary sentence. Or even a phrase. One word would do. That wasn't being too greedy, was it?

Suddenly, there were tears in Cate's eyes as she felt a stab of isolation at being so close to Eliza and yet still shut out. She felt so helpless and wished she could reach into her daughter's mind and pull her thoughts out of her. There was a part of her that wanted to shake those young shoulders until the words were forced to spill out. But, looking down at Eliza again, she knew she couldn't do that. All she could do was wait. Patiently and lovingly.

The air was saturated with spray and Cate could taste the saltiness of it even when they turned away from the sea and faced the cliffs. And that's when she remembered that it was this very beach where the accident had happened – where Charles had lost his son. She could clearly see where the recent stormy weather had worked on the cliff.

They marched further down the beach, careful to stay clear of the danger. Cate felt her daughter's tiny fingers bunched up in her own gloved hands and she then realised how cold it was. But she continued to walk, head down, against the wind. She needed to outwalk her fear and she wasn't leaving the beach until she did. The wind seemed to be picking up and it was hard work walking into it. She glanced down at Eliza. Her face looked white and pinched and Cate took pity on her.

'Shall we go back?' she asked her.

Eliza nodded.

When Charles got home that evening, Cate was in the kitchen.

'Hey,' he said as he walked into the room. 'Had a good day?'

'It was okay. We went for a walk.'

'Where?'

She hesitated before answering. 'To the beach,' she told him, deciding to be honest.

He nodded, but didn't say anything.

'How about you?'

'Just saw one of my collectors. I've been working on a piece for him for some time now and I wanted to deliver it in person.'

'Was he happy with it?'

'Well, he paid me in full.'

Cate smiled. 'Good.'

Charles looked as if he was about to leave the room, but stopped. 'You haven't had any strange incidents today, have you?'

'What do you mean?'

'No – erm – random cars turning up?'

'No,' Cate said, memories of the night before assaulting her again even though she'd done her best to rid herself of them during the day.

'It was probably nothing,' he told her.

'I imagine so,' Cate said, trying to quash the panic that was threatening to rise again. 'Just a wrong turn, right?'

'Yes.' Charles gave a hesitant smile. 'I'm going to spend a bit of time–'

'In your workshop?'

'How did you guess?' he said with a laugh.

'Want me to bring you in a cup of tea?'

'Thanks.'

Cate nodded and watched as he left and then she turned to put the kettle on. There was a part of her that wanted to confide in him. But she didn't want to play the victim. For one thing, she didn't feel it was right to when he was still suffering his own loss. How could she burden him with some unfounded fear? And so she kept it locked away, telling herself over and over that her imagination was getting carried away and the likelihood of that car turning up in the driveway having anything to do with her was very remote indeed.

Allie left a few days between her and Craig's South American spat before she texted him. By that time, she'd cooled down. And she had a plan she believed was worth sharing.

Come over tonight for dinner. 7pm.

Jack was thrilled to see his father again and they were soon talking about more of Craig's adventures. Allie listened, hearing some of the stories herself for the first time like the trip Craig had made to the Atlas Mountains and broken his wrist falling off a camel, and the day he got to see his first tiger in the wild in Sumatra.

After dinner, Jack sat on the floor of the living room, gazing up at his father as he told his stories, the occasional 'Wow' falling from his lips. And Allie had to admit that Craig had led a pretty 'wow' sort of a life, certainly to a young school boy who'd only ever left Dorset to visit East Devon.

'Craig? Can I have a word?' Allie said after several more tales from the far corners of the world.

Craig looked up, his smile vanishing in an instant and she felt sorry for him because he probably thought she was going to throw him out again.

'We won't be long, Jack,' she assured her son. 'There's just something I want to tell your father.'

Allie and Craig walked through to the kitchen together and she quietly closed the door behind them both.

'Don't tell me I can't even *talk* about my adventures to Jack now.'

'I wasn't going to.'

'Well good.'

'I was going to suggest that we start talking about going on an adventure together.'

He frowned. 'Who? You and me?'

'No, silly! Well, yes, you and me, but Jack too. The three of us. As a family.'

'You want to come to South America with us?' Craig said, sounding confused.

'No!' Allie cried. 'That's the last thing I want. I've been

thinking of something else. Something a little closer to home that we might all be able to enjoy together.'

'Like where? Bognor Regis? Weston-super-Mare?' His tone was ever so slightly sarcastic.

'Craig – you have to work with me on this. South America is not going to happen. It's so wildly outside my comfort zone that it's a total non-starter, so you'd better just get that out of your head, okay?'

He continued to frown, but wisely said nothing.

'Come and see this and don't make any snap judgements, okay?' Allie gestured to the kitchen table where an A4 piece of paper lay.

'What's this?' he said, unfolding it.

'It's a campervan.'

'I can see that.'

'I thought we could–'

Craig suddenly started laughing. In fact, he did more than laugh; he tipped his head right back and roared.

'You want us to hire a Volkswagen camper van.'

'Not exactly.'

'What do you mean?'

'I mean, I don't want to hire one. I want to buy one.' She chewed her lip. 'Actually, I already have. That one you're holding there.'

Craig looked at her as if she'd gone quite mad. 'Seriously? You've bought a campervan?'

Allie nodded. 'It's arriving next week.'

'Really? You're not joking?'

'I'm not joking.'

'But aren't they a bit – pokey?'

'I imagine they are.'

'And you wouldn't mind shacking up in one with me and Jack?'

Allie shrugged. 'I figured we could take a couple of tents too to give us more room.'

'I've got a couple of tents,' Craig told her.

'I know.'

Craig smiled. 'How long have you been thinking about this for?'

'Since you threatened to take my son into the jungle.'

Craig nodded. 'Well, I like your resourcefulness.'

'So, are you up for it?'

'What exactly are you proposing, Allie?'

She smiled then because he was still looking at her as if she'd completely lost her mind.

'I'm proposing that we take a little trip around the UK. We can head along the coast into Devon and Cornwall and then up into Somerset and – well – I don't really want to plan it in detail because I didn't think you'd like that.'

Craig nodded.

'Well, say something!' Allie cried, becoming anxious now.

'How old is this thing?'

'It's from the mid-seventies.'

'And you're confident driving something this big?'

Allie swallowed hard. 'I will be.'

Craig grinned.

'Well, you can drive it too. I won't want to hog all the driving,' Allie said.

'And you're proposing that we all spend the summer holiday together, driving around the UK?'

'Yes. We can do anything. We can go surfing in Cornwall, hiking across Exmoor. There's no end of adventures you can have in the UK. You really don't need to leave the country.'

'And what about your work?'

'I'm getting some cover for the shop and maybe I'll even rent out this place too,' Allie told him.

'You've really thought this through, haven't you?'

'Yes, I have.'

He smiled again. 'And it's roadworthy this van?'

'I'm led to believe so. It just needs a bit of refurbishment, but there's plenty of time before the summer, isn't there? And maybe you and Jack could lend a hand too. It could be a fun project for us all.'

Craig looked at the printed picture of the yellow and white VW campervan again.

'You know what?' he said at last. 'This could be a lot of fun.'

'You think so?'

'I do.'

Allie smiled, a mixture of excitement and relief making her feel slightly giddy.

'Can I tell Jack?'

Craig nodded and then Allie did something she hadn't planned doing. She flung herself across the room and hugged Craig.

'Thank you!' she cried as she felt his arms closing around her. 'Thank you!'

December arrived with a flurry of frosts, turning the once green fields to white sparkling wonders and making the golden cottages of the village look as if they belonged on a biscuit tin. It was a joy to walk out among it all. To hear your feet crunching the crisped leaves and to see the branches of the trees edged with tiny crystals.

It was remarkably sunny too. The storms of November seemed but a distant memory. Until one day when they returned. Cate and Eliza gave their walks up and Rigs didn't even want to poke around the garden and stayed curled up in his basket in the kitchen. Charles, who'd spent the last few days working at Black Ven on the coast, was now in his workshop, aware of the severe weather warning that had been issued. Everyone, it seemed, knew the sanity of staying indoors at such a time.

Eliza was splitting her time, working with Cate in the kitchen and then joining Charles in his workshop when Cate had to get on with her chores. It was a routine that seemed to be working well and that they'd fallen into quite naturally together.

One early evening as Cate was dusting the banisters, Eliza caught her eye as she was coming downstairs.

'Everything okay?' she asked her daughter.

Eliza shook her head.

'What is it, sweetie?'

Eliza pointed towards Charles's workshop.

'Charles?'

Eliza nodded and pulled out her pad and pencil.

He's sad, Cate read a moment later.

'What about?'

He's not talking to me. He stopped.

Cate chewed her lip. That didn't sound right.

'Why don't you go and sit in the kitchen with Rigs?'

Cate wasn't sure what to expect as she approached the workshop. The door had been left ajar by Eliza and Cate tapped on it now.

'Charles? Can I come in?'

There was no answer so she popped her head round the door.

Charles was standing with his back to her staring out of the small window which looked out over the back garden.

'Charles? Are you okay?'

He didn't respond and so she approached him, reaching a hand out to touch his arm gently. And then she saw his face.

Cate had never seen Charles with such a sorrowful expression before. She'd seen him when he was cross. She'd seen him when he was reticent. But she'd never seen him upset like this and it wracked her to her very soul.

'Come and sit down,' she told him, gently placing a hand on his elbow and guiding him from the workshop and into the living room. His face was ashen and his eyes looked bloodshot as if he'd been crying. She sat next to him, giving him a little bit of space while being close enough in case he needed her.

'Charles? Are you okay? Do you need me to get you anything?'

Slowly, he shook his head. 'I'm okay. I mean...' he stopped.

'What?' Cate pressed, anxious now.

'It's two years today,' he said in a low voice.

'Your son?' Cate said softly.

He nodded. 'I didn't think it would still hurt as much as it does. I thought that rawness would have left me, but it hasn't. And I don't think it ever will. And this bloody weather doesn't help.'

Cate saw him glancing out of the window at the storm, realising that he was remembering the storm of two years ago. She watched him closely, feeling a great swelling of compassion in her heart and she desperately wanted to reach out and help him in any way she could.

'Do you want to talk about it?' she asked him. 'It might help. Like when I told you what happened to me. I didn't think I ever wanted to tell anybody about that, but telling you...' she paused, 'well, I think it helped me. It got some of those feelings I'd been carrying around *out* of me. Does that make sense?'

Charles didn't respond at first, but then he nodded.

'I've never spoken about it. There wasn't really anyone I

could talk to. Sophie left so quickly and I couldn't have told her the truth anyway.' He paused again and Cate sat patiently.

Finally, he spoke again. 'It had been stormy all week,' he began. 'You've had a taster of what it can be like here. Very wet and very windy. Just the sort of conditions us fossil hunters revel in. Anyway, the sky cleared one morning and I got up before it was light. Sophie was on to me right away because of the weather. It became something of a battle between us. But, I won that morning. She was sleepy and murmured something about me knowing what I was doing and I took that as a yes. So I went to wake Jamie. You'd have thought it was Christmas Day. He was out of bed in an instant.' Charles smiled at the memory.

'We got washed and dressed and had a quick breakfast. All as quietly as we could so we wouldn't disturb Sophie in case she changed her mind. Jamie knew exactly how his mother felt about him coming with me so it was no bother keeping him quiet. It became a game, really, with us tiptoeing about like bad actors.'

He paused again. Perhaps he was seeing it all in his mind's eye.

'There wasn't anybody else out on the beach that day,' he continued. 'They were all far too sensible. I was showing off a bit – telling Jamie how clever we were and that we deserved to find something really special because we'd made the effort. He got it into his head that that was the day we were going to find The Big One, and I remember laughing.'

'"Don't laugh, Daddy",' he told me. '"This is serious."'

Charles smiled at the memory.

'He sounds like a very earnest young man,' Cate said.

'Oh, he was,' Charles told her. 'I sometimes think he was more obsessed with The Big One than I was. Anyway, we started by walking along the beach. The tide was on its way out so we had plenty of time. Jamie started his hunt straightaway, peering down at the sand, but I was looking at the cliffs to see what had shifted in the storm. You get to know the cliffs along the coast really well – their contours and angles – and it's easy to see if a piece is missing, if it's fallen in the night.' He stopped and Cate heard him sigh and he slowly shook his head. 'It all happened so fast,' he told her. 'One minute, he was standing right next to me and I swear I only took my eyes off him for a second.'

Charles covered his face with his hands for a moment.

'A second is all it can take with a child, isn't it?' Cate whispered, placing her hand on his arm.

'When I turned around, he was at the base of the cliff and I yelled at him to get away, but the wind was too strong by then and he didn't hear me. I ran towards him, but I wasn't fast enough. I'll never forget that dreadful sound of the cliff collapsing. It was almost as bad as the sight of it. Suddenly, I couldn't see Jamie. God!' He closed his eyes again. 'I couldn't find him at first. And there was nobody there to help me. I wished with all my heart we hadn't been the only ones on the beach that day. I'd been celebrating that earlier, but it wasn't so clever, was it? And by the time help came, Jamie was dead.'

He stopped talking and a pain spread across his face the like of which Cate had never seen before.

'Oh, Charles! I'm so sorry,' Cate said, tears now streaking her cheeks as she tried to imagine the desperation he must have felt that day – the panic and the helplessness.

'I didn't want to go home,' he went on. 'I wanted to stay there at the beach. I think I was kind of hoping the cliff might take me next. I couldn't leave that dreadful spot even when they took Jamie. I kind of became rooted there. I think somebody helped me up. I can't remember who it was now. I was aware of these voices talking to me, but I couldn't seem to hear them.'

'You were in shock,' Cate said.

'And I can't remember exactly what happened after that. Someone drove me home, I think. I had to leave my car down at the beach. Sophie was in the kitchen and I think she knew something was wrong as soon as she saw me. I remember trying to tell her what had happened, but she kept insisting that Jamie was upstairs in bed. She went a little crazy, I think.'

He shook his head. 'I can't bear to think of that scene now. 'I was trying to keep calm, but it was impossible because Sophie was hysterical and so I did the only thing I could to calm her down.'

'What did you do?'

'I told a lie.'

Cate frowned, not quite understanding him. 'What did you say?'

He sighed, blinking hard as more tears threatened. 'There isn't much you can say in a situation like that. But there is something. And so I told Sophie the best thing I could. The only thing you can say really to someone who wasn't there. I told her Jamie had died instantly. That he knew no pain. He didn't have time to be frightened. He didn't suffer.'

Cate felt the breath in her body freeze. 'And that wasn't true?'

Charles shook his head. 'No, it wasn't.'

'Oh, Charles!'

He took a deep breath, his eyes bright with tears. 'When the cliff came down, Jamie was completely trapped. I found where he was, but he was lying on his back, knocked over by the weight of the earth. I could see his face staring up into the sky. It was amazing that he hadn't been totally buried. I scrambled to get to him and dug with my hands, but the earth was so thick and wet and heavy and I could see Jamie fading fast. So I stopped digging and knelt beside him. I kept telling him it would be okay and that I was right there beside him. I didn't know what else to say. What *do* you say when a life is slipping away in front of you?'

Charles stopped and covered his face with his hands again.

'Jamie looked so frightened. His eyes were open, but he couldn't seem to speak so I kept talking, telling him the same things over and over. That I was there. That he'd be all right. I hate myself for that. I hate that I was lying to him in his last moments with me.'

'You were doing your best as a father, Charles,' Cate assured him. 'You were comforting him.'

'Was I? How can I know that? I'm not even sure he could hear me.'

'You were there beside him. That would have been a comfort.'

Charles's hands dropped to his lap and Cate saw just how red his eyes looked.

'I'm not sure how long he was like that for. Probably ten, fifteen minutes. And I don't know how much pain he was in. But I couldn't tell Sophie that, could I? I couldn't let her know that he suffered like that and so I told her that he died instantly and that he wouldn't have known anything about it. But he did know. I saw the fear in his eyes.'

Cate picked up Charles's hands and squeezed them tightly in hers, willing her comfort into him and hoping she could ease his pain if only just a little.

'I should never have taken Jamie that day,' he told her. 'Not *ever*. I should have protected him. That's a father's job, isn't it?'

'It wasn't your fault, Charles!'

'But it was! I knew the conditions were dangerous and I took him there all the same, even when Sophie told me not to over and over again.'

'But Jamie wanted to go, didn't he? He wanted to be with you more than anything.'

Charles took a moment as if considering this for the first time. Finally, he nodded. 'Jamie loved it there. Just like me. He seemed to be in his element on the beach with the wind in his hair and his nails full of dirt.'

'I bet he was. And I bet he wouldn't want to see you like this now. He'd want you to be out there – looking for The Big One – and remembering how much that made him happy.'

Charles gave a sort of half laugh at the thought. 'You think so?' he asked.

'Yes! Absolutely!'

'I haven't been back to that beach since,' Charles confided.

'Even though you think The Big One's there?'

He shrugged. 'It could be there. Could be anywhere, really.'

'Maybe in time,' she suggested.

'I don't think so,' he said.

They sat in silence for a few moments, the weight of Charles's revelation settling into the room.

Cate got up from the sofa and went to draw the curtains.

'You look tired,' she told him as she turned round to face him again. 'You should go to bed.'

He frowned. 'What time is it?'

'Does it matter?'

He sighed. 'I guess not. It just doesn't seem right to go so early in the evening.'

'Charles – you're exhausted – I can't think of anything *more* right.' She watched as he stood up. 'I'm going to make you a hot chocolate, okay? I'll bring it up to you.'

He gave a light smile. 'Cate?'

'Yes?'

'Thanks.'

'It's okay. I was going to make one for me and Eliza anyway.'

'No! I mean, thanks for listening.'

They held each other's gaze for a moment. 'Thank you for trusting me with the truth.'

He smiled at her sadly. 'You're the only one,' he told her.

Cate watched as he went upstairs and she moved through to the kitchen and heated up a pan of almond milk for the hot chocolates and put a little into the mugs, adding the cocoa and sugar to make a paste. She poured the warm milk into the three mugs a few minutes later with Eliza watching her from the kitchen table.

'I'm taking this one up for Charles,' she told Eliza. It was then that Cate noticed that Rigs wasn't in his basket. 'Where's Rigs?'

Eliza shook her head before taking a sip of her hot chocolate.

Cate went upstairs and made her way to Charles's bedroom. The door was ajar and the bedside lamp was on. He was in bed and he wasn't alone. Rigs was there too. It was as if the little dog had known that his owner needed him.

'I've brought you–' Cate stopped. Charles was fast asleep. She watched him for a moment and didn't have the heart to disturb him and so she left him to sleep, hoping that it would be deep, restoring and dreamless.

CHAPTER TWENTY

Charles was up early the next morning. Cate was still lying in bed when she heard the front door open and close and the sound of his Land Rover pulling away. She was kind of relieved in a way – more for him than for her because she was worried how things would be between them after such a confession. Perhaps a little bit of time apart would allow things to settle.

After a morning of history and an afternoon of science, Cate and Eliza left Hollow House for the short walk to Allie's. Allie had texted her saying she'd shut the shop early as it was quiet and her heater had packed up so she was working from home and would love some company. Cate was actually quite happy to leave the house. The storm of the day before had lessened and, although there was still a strong wind, the sun was doing its best to cheer everything up.

'Hey!' Allie said as she opened the door of her cottage, hugging Cate in a warm embrace and then examining her face. 'Thanks for coming. Are you all right? You look a bit...'

Cate motioned to Eliza as they entered.

'Eliza? How would you like to let Carrot out of her hutch and give her a cuddle?' Allie said.

Eliza beamed her a smile and ran through the house and out into the back garden.

'Now, come on through,' Allie said, going to the kitchen and putting the kettle on. Tea was needed.

'So, what's happened?' Allie asked once the tea was made and they were sitting at the kitchen table together.

'Charles told me.'

'Told you what?'

'About what happened that day.' Cate watched as Allie swallowed hard.

'The day his son died?'

Cate could feel the instant swelling of tears in her eyes. She wasn't sure if she could tell Allie. But she took a deep breath and repeated a little of what Charles had revealed to her the day before, keeping back his darkest confession as she felt he'd not want that shared.

When she came to the end of her narrative, Allie stared at Cate in undisguised horror.

'But that's awful,' she said and Cate nodded. 'No wonder he hasn't got over it .'

'I don't think you ever can, can you?' Cate said. She'd deliberated whether or not to tell her friend about Charles's revelation, but knew she could trust her not to tell anyone else. Indeed, she could see the tears swimming in Allie's eyes, and knew that her pure heart would protect Charles's privacy.

'I can't even imagine what he must have gone through,' she said, bringing the tea to the table.

Cate nodded. 'It's too painful to even try.'

'Jamie was so young.'

Cate sighed and sipped her tea. 'I sometimes think I can hear him in the house. I know these old houses are full of creaks and squeaks, but I sometimes think I can hear someone there. Is that crazy?'

Allie shook her head. 'I don't think it is. I kind of believe in spirits and I wouldn't be surprised if he's still there. It is his home after all.'

Cate gave a little smile and then remembered back to the time she'd gone into Jamie's room and taken his books. She hadn't felt that there'd been anything wrong in doing that so perhaps Jamie had been present that day, giving her his blessing. It was a comfort to think of him being there, watching over them all, and she couldn't help wondering what he made of two strangers living in his home. Maybe he was glad that his father had some company at last.

'How was Charles this morning?' Allie asked.

'I haven't seen him yet. He went out early. Maybe he wanted to avoid me after last night.' Cate frowned. Maybe he'd regret telling her all he had and it would hang awkwardly between them. Maybe he'd find a way to distance himself from her now or – even worse – let her go. Cate felt her heart tugging at the thought.

'That poor man,' Allie said. Charles must have felt so powerless.'

They sat in silence for a moment, their dark thoughts too much to speak of. Finally Allie got up, nodding to the tea cups.

'Yes please,' Cate said, checking out of the window and seeing Eliza happily cuddling Carrot.

They waited while the kettle reboiled and Allie made the tea. Only then did it seem okay to move the conversation on.

'Have you seen Craig recently?' Cate asked.

Allie nodded. 'Actually, I have. I invited him round the other night because I had a proposition for him.'

'Oh?' Cate said, raising her eyebrows.

Allie sighed. 'Not *that* sort of proposition!'

'What then?'

'Just wait here a mo.'

Cate watched as Allie left the kitchen. She came back a moment later with her laptop which she placed on the table, her fingers dancing over the keyboard until a picture came up.

'What's this?' Cate asked.

'A VW campervan.'

'I can see that.'

'I've bought it.'

Cate gasped. 'You've bought *that*?'

'Don't sound so horrified!'

'I'm not – I mean, I didn't mean to sound... it's just, well, *old*!'

'It needs a bit of love and attention, I know.'

'Why did you buy it?'

'To save my family,' Allie said, suddenly looking serious. 'Craig wanted to take Jack to South America and I couldn't bear the thought of that. I kept thinking of all the things that could go wrong and it was driving me insane, so I thought I'd try and – well – take control of the situation.' She paused. 'Without being a control freak! I don't want to stop Craig having a relationship with Jack, but I wanted it conducted somewhere slightly safer than the jungles of Brazil!'

'What did Jack say?'

'He laughed when I showed it to him, but he's really come round to the idea. He thinks it's quite cool, now. You know – doing up an old vehicle and reducing his carbon footprint by not flying. I could tell he was a bit disappointed not to be going to South America, though.'

Cate smiled. 'Plenty of time for that when he's older, right?'

'Exactly! Mind you,' Allie continued, 'Jack's promised me that we'll do lots of adventurous things on this holiday and he's already found a zip wire over a quarry in Wales and a caving experience in Yorkshire!'

'That sounds like a small price to pay,' Cate told her.

Allie smiled. 'I guess so.'

Cate laughed. 'I think it's a brilliant idea.'

'You do?'

'Got room for two more?'

'Oh, Cate – I wish we did!'

'I'm kidding! Although I'm going to be very envious when you take off round the country.'

Allie's eyes suddenly lit up. 'Hey – maybe we could have some jaunts in it first. To warm her up.'

Cate nodded enthusiastically. 'I'd love that!'

'This is so cool!' Allie said. 'We can drive along the coast into Devon or go up into Exmoor.'

'Or maybe see Cheddar Gorge if that isn't too far. I've always wanted to see it.'

'The world will be our oyster,' Allie declared. 'Or at least the south of England will. Just while I get the hang of driving her.'

Cate sighed. 'It doesn't seem right to feel this happy when Charles is still suffering so much.'

Allie reached across the table and squeezed Cate's hand. 'We all have to live our lives, Cate, and you've already had more than your share of sorrow. Don't feel guilty when you have the chance to enjoy life.'

Cate smiled, knowing Allie was right.

She left Allie's with a huge smile on her face. It was good to see her friend so happy and her happiness had been infectious, lifting Cate's mood.

It was still windy as she and Eliza walked the short distance through the village back to Hollow House. The road and pavement were full of muddy puddles and the bare branches of the trees rocked and swayed overhead. It wasn't the sort of day to be out any longer than you had to and Cate was glad to get back home. Perhaps they'd light a fire that evening and get cosy like the other night. It would be nice if they could make that part of their routine over the winter months. It could certainly benefit Charles, she thought.

They hadn't been in long when Cate heard Charles's Land Rover pulling up outside. For a moment, she felt anxious about seeing him again, but she took a deep breath and waited for him to come in.

'Oh, hello, Cate,' he said, looking surprised to see her standing in the hallway.

'Hello,' she said. 'Been busy?'

He gave the faintest of smiles. 'I had to get out.'

She nodded in understanding. 'You okay?'

He took his coat and boots off and unwound his scarf, hanging that up just as Rigs came charging through from the kitchen.

'Hey, boy,' Charles said, bending down to tickle him behind his ears. He then stood back up and faced Cate.

'Last night...' he paused.

'You don't regret telling me, do you?' Cate jumped in, unable to stop herself.

He frowned. 'No,' he said, but Cate couldn't quite tell from his expression if he meant it or not.

'I really appreciate you sharing that with me,' she said gently. 'Oh, god – that sounds so condescending, doesn't it? I didn't mean it to come out quite like that. But – what can I say without sounding clichéd?'

'You don't need to say anything,' Charles told her. 'I'm not really sure there is anything to say anyway.'

'I just wanted to let you know that I'm here. If you ever need to talk.'

He looked slightly awkward and Cate noticed how pale he looked. 'Thanks,' he said simply and she watched as he disappeared into his workshop. He didn't come out for the rest of the evening.

The weather continued to deteriorate. The lane outside Hollow House turned into a river and Cate dreaded to think what the holloway would be like now. When she'd taken some of Charles's packages to the post office, she'd heard two villagers talking about one car that had got stuck up there recently.

'He wasn't from round here,' one of them said knowingly, and Cate couldn't help feeling a little sorry for the man who'd made the same mistake as she had when she'd first arrived.

It was proving less enticing going out for a walk and Cate and Eliza hadn't visited the beach in a few days. Rigs was making do with quick walks down the lane and back and nipping out into the garden when he needed to, but Eliza was obviously beginning to feel a bit confined in the house all day. Cate had noticed how she'd been spending more time in the garden. She'd even begun keeping a nature diary, drawing things she found like leaf skeletons and pine cones. She was becoming a real country girl, Cate thought with a smile.

So Cate was no longer surprised if she couldn't find Eliza in the house. She'd often take Rigs out and they'd poke around the piles of autumn leaves together on a mini adventure while Cate would do her best to keep her eye on them while she was going about her chores.

Late one afternoon, as the dark was creeping across the sky and the shadows were lengthening, Cate opened the front door to call them both back inside, surprised that they hadn't returned already.

Rigs was standing by the hedge which divided part of the garden from the lane. But he wasn't just standing there. He seemed to be scenting the air.

'Rigs?' she called.

Rigs ignored her but, as she approached, she heard him let out a long, low growl.

'What is it, Rigs?' Cate asked, looking around as if she might spot somebody coming up the driveway. But there was nobody there. Still Rigs growled.

'What is it, boy?'

Eliza appeared by her side.

'What's wrong with Rigs?' Cate asked, not really expecting Eliza to know. Eliza shrugged. 'Come on – let's get inside. It's freezing out here.'

Charles was just coming out of his workshop when they entered the hallway.

'Rigs was growling at the hedge,' Cate told him. 'Is that normal?'

'Probably a squirrel,' he said.

Cate frowned. She hadn't seen any squirrels while she'd been outside, but she admitted she didn't have the nose of a dog who might very well be able to sniff these things out before seeing them.

The next day, Cate went into the kitchen expecting to find Eliza finishing her morning's work, but she wasn't there. Maybe Eliza had completed the questions and had gone through to Charles's workshop early, Cate thought, leaving the kitchen.

'Charles?' she called as she knocked and entered.

'What is it?' he asked, looking up from his workbench where a long thin prehistoric bone lay.

'Have you seen Eliza? I thought she might be in here with you.'

'Has she gone out in the garden?'

'Not that I'm aware of.'

Charles frowned.

'Eliza?' Cate called, walking back through to the kitchen where Rigs was sitting up in his basket, his head cocked to one side. 'Have you seen her, Rigs? Where's Eliza?'

The little dog leapt out of his basket, ran across the room and down the hallway towards the front door. It was odd that Eliza hadn't taken the little dog with her, Cate thought.

'He thinks she's outside,' Charles said as they went towards the front door.

Cate opened it and the little dog charged across the lawn barking.

'Let me check her room,' Charles said, quickly disappearing upstairs. Cate waited by the front door, anxious for his return.

'She's not there,' Charles said a moment later. 'I checked her bedroom and yours.'

'We've got to find her,' Cate cried as she and Charles pulled on their coats and boots, closed the front door, and joined Rigs outside. 'Find Eliza, Rigs!' Fear was beginning to rise in Cate's chest now. Eliza wasn't the sort to just wander off. She was sensible and she knew that her mother was a worrier. She was very good at never giving Cate cause to worry unnecessarily. But she'd become a little bit obsessed with her nature diary and might have popped into the garden on a whim to collect some leaves or twigs to sketch.

'Eliza?' Cate called, her voice instantly carried off by the high winds.

The two of them skirted the house with Rigs running on ahead of them, but there was no sign of Eliza.

'Where can she be?' Cate asked, hearing the panic in her voice.

'Don't worry – she'll be somewhere. Keep looking.'

Cate did just that, peering into the bushes and hedges

around the garden, expecting to find her daughter huddled somewhere, but she was nowhere.

'Charles? Have you found her?' Cate cried as she came round to the front of the house again and saw him standing at the end of the driveway staring into the lane.

'Whose car's that?' he asked as she approached him.

Cate followed his gaze.

'Oh, God no!' she cried. 'It's his car.'

'Whose?'

'*His!* Eliza's father.'

Charles cursed and Cate could feel her body flood with fear as they ran towards the mud-splattered car. It looked just like hers had after she'd got it stuck at the entrance to the hollow lane, but there was nobody inside.

And then something occurred to her. It had been him, hadn't it? It had been *his* car the women in the post office had been talking about. It had been *him* she'd felt sympathy for. And now he might have Eliza.

It was then that Rigs shot out into the lane barking.

'Rigs!' Charles shouted as his little dog ran off.

'He's heading to the hollow lane!' Cate cried.

The two of them set off on foot, running down the road which was slick with rain.

'You think she's there?' Charles called as they ran. 'With her father?'

'I don't know! It's his car though.'

They entered the hollow lane which was thick and slippery with mud after the torrential rains of the last few days. Cate was glad she'd pulled her boots on, but she was now worrying what Eliza might be wearing. Did she have her winter coat on or had she quickly nipped outside without it? Cate couldn't remember seeing it in the hall.

'Where is she?' Cate cried as they went further up the lane, the wind tossing the bare branches above them.

'I can't see them,' Charles said. 'Are you sure they went this way?'

Rigs, who was running ahead of them stopped. Had he lost Eliza's scent or was he just bored of chasing something he couldn't see?

'Wait – Eliza knows there's a track to the beach,' Cate suddenly said. 'Do you think that's where they've gone?'

Charles frowned. 'I don't know.'

'She loves the beach. Maybe she ran over the fields thinking she'd be safe there.'

As soon as the words were out of her mouth, she knew that the local beach was the last place Charles would want to go and the very last place he'd associate with being safe because that's where Jamie had died.

'Let's go back,' Charles said.

'What?'

'We'll take the car to the beach. It'll be quicker than going across the fields.'

Cate nodded, glad for his foresight.

Whistling for Rigs, Charles led the way back and the three of them climbed into the Land Rover a few minutes later.

Cate was doing her best to keep calm, but it was hard. She was worried for Eliza's safety, but also anxious about what her husband would do next. How long had he been in their village watching and waiting before he made his move? Cate felt cold with fear at the thought of it.

'What if he's got her? What's he going to do?'

'We'll get her back, Cate.'

'But he might have taken her already.'

'His car's still in the lane, remember?'

'But he might have help? He might have just grabbed her and gone hours ago!'

'You know she hasn't been gone for hours. Just calm down. We'll be there in a moment.'

Charles screeched the Land Rover to a stop in the beach car park and the three of them jumped out, Rigs barking in excitement at this unexpected adventure.

The wind was strong and it was raining now too. The rollers were coming in fast. It would soon be high tide.

'These are the worst conditions, Cate!' Charles yelled above the wind. 'It's not safe here.'

'We've got to find her!'

'I know. Be careful, okay?'

Cate nodded, but how could she think of putting her own safety first when Eliza was in danger? If her daughter was at the foot of a vulnerable cliff then there was no way Cate wouldn't run towards it.

They ran to the beach together and Cate couldn't help wondering if Charles was thinking about that other day two years ago. The weather had been similar and Cate's panic swelled as she thought of the dreadful possibility that history might be about to repeat itself. She glanced at Charles who was just behind her. Was he thinking the same thing?

They'd just made it to the shore when Cate looked up at the cliffs and screamed. There at the top was Eliza. She was so close to the edge, but her back was to it.

Cate was frantic. 'Charles!'

He was by her side in an instant and cursed when he saw the danger Eliza was in.

Rigs started barking and then took off, heading up the path to the left which connected the beach below to the cliff above.

'Rigs!' Charles called after the dog. 'Damn it!'

And then Cate saw him. Her husband. He was standing

close to Eliza at the top of the cliff. What on earth were they doing up there? Eliza knew how dangerous it was, but maybe in her fear of getting away from her father, she'd taken the wrong path and, instead of coming out on the beach, had found herself on the top of the cliff. Both Cate and Charles had gone out of their way to make sure she knew the dangers of the coast, but logic and knowledge are soon forgotten when panic sets in and Eliza wasn't looking at the edge of the cliffs. She was staring at her father as he approached her, his hands in the air as if he was trying to tell her that he wouldn't hurt her.

'Charles! We've got to do something!' Cate cried, grabbing his arm.

'If we catch her attention, she might panic.'

'What do we do?'

Charles shook his head. He was looking up and down the beach as if he might find an answer there and, all the time, Eliza was moving ever closer to the edge.

'Eliza!' Cate shouted. The little girl turned around and saw her mother and, for one dreadful moment, started moving towards the edge of the cliff.

'NO! NO!' Cate and Charles yelled at once. They both started flapping their arms, directing her away from the cliff edge, but that meant going towards her father. Cate had never felt a fear like it. Was it even possible that her daughter would rather risk falling off a cliff than being near that man?

Cate watched in horror as Eliza kept walking beside the cliff edge, trying to keep away from her father who was still approaching her. What the hell did he think he was doing? Couldn't he see the danger they were both in?

Suddenly, Eliza darted to the left, her speed startling Cate whose hands flew to her mouth in fear. There was nothing she could do from down on the beach. She could only watch helplessly as her daughter ran along the cliff top.

And that's when they heard it. That dreadful rumble.

Cate felt herself being pushed by Charles.

'RUN!' he yelled above the noise.

'Eliza!' Cate cried, tears of panic stinging her eyes as the whole cliff face seemed to implode, folding in on itself as it fell from its great height, tumbling, crashing and spilling onto the beach below in a thousand thundering thuds. It was like nothing Cate had ever experienced before. The air seemed full of danger and darkness. Instinct made her cover her head and close her eyes, but she wanted to look and to search for Eliza.

'Keep down!' Charles told her and she realised that she was on all fours on the beach.

'Eliza!' she said again, helplessly.

'We'll find her. Just wait. You're no good to her if you get caught up in this.'

But Cate was on her feet now. Parts of the cliff were still falling onto the beach and she could hear Charles shouting behind her, but she couldn't stop. She had to find Eliza.

Please, please, please, Cate chanted over and over, her mind desperately trying to make a bargain with the universe. She'd do anything, sacrifice anything, as long as her daughter was all right.

The air seemed full of earth and chaos and the sky was darkening rapidly. Cate was frantic. She felt like she was in the middle of a waking nightmare and she didn't know what to do.

'ELIZA!' she cried into the wind.

Then she saw her. That *was* her, wasn't it? The child running along the beach towards her with a little dog by her side.

Please, please, please, Cate chanted again. *Let that be my daughter. Let that be my baby girl.*

'Mummy!'

The one word resonated across the beach. It *was* Eliza. And she'd spoken!

'Eliza!' Cate called, running towards her and hugging her so close to her body that the breath was crushed out of both of them.

'Are you okay?'

Eliza nodded, Rigs barking wildly as he jumped around Eliza's legs.

'You're not hurt?'

She shook her head.

No more words. That was fine for now. Cate was just feeling so blessed that Eliza was there to say anything at all.

'How did you get down from the cliff?'

Eliza pointed to the long path that led from the cliff down to the beach. It was a long way to run, but it was definitely better than the alternative.

'Cate!' Charles was behind them. 'Oh, my god!'

'She's okay,' Cate quickly told him. 'Shaken, but no damage done.'

'Eliza!' he said, gasping for breath after running across the beach. 'We were so worried.'

Cate saw his eyes scanning the child, looking for signs of trauma or injury.

'She's okay, Charles.'

'Yes, yes!' he said, nodding, his face flooding with relief.

'But what about him?' Cate said, glancing around as if he might appear at any moment. Had he moved away from the cliff edge in time as Eliza had or was he somewhere underneath the heavy clay and the rocks?

Charles concentrated his gaze on the base of the cliffs. 'Over there!' he suddenly said, pointing.

And that's when Cate saw him. He'd been up on the cliffs a couple of minutes ago, but he was now at the foot of them and she could only see half of his body. It didn't look good.

'Eliza – stay here where it's safe, sweetie,' she told her, and then she walked across the beach to where her husband lay. Charles was by her side, his arm around her shoulder and then he knelt down on the beach amongst the thick dark clay that had fallen from the cliff.

'He's not breathing!' Charles said.

Cate looked down into the ashen, blood-streaked face of her husband as he stared, sightless, up at the sky, wondering how to respond to that piece of news. And then she realised that she felt absolutely nothing for him.

There was somebody else on the beach now and Cate saw them running towards them, their phone pressed up against their face. Things were a bit of a blur after that. More and more people were crowding the beach. Cate registered the blue lights of an ambulance in the car park and saw a stretcher, but all she could do was move a safe distance from her husband, and hold Eliza close to her as if she never meant to let her go.

Finally, when the rescuers had managed to get his body onto the stretcher, Eliza left Cate's side. She approached the base of the broken cliff.

'Eliza!' Cate called after her in fear, catching up with her quickly. What was she doing? Did she want to see her father before he was taken away forever?

'What is it?' Cate asked as Eliza pointed.

But it wasn't her father Eliza was pointing at, but rather the large protrusion of bone hanging out of the crumbled cliff. It took a moment for Cate's eyes to focus, but she finally realised what Eliza was telling her.

'Charles!' she called.

Charles, who'd been talking to one of the paramedics, came over to her. 'You okay?'

'Show him, Eliza.'

Eliza pointed again and Charles stared at the cliff.

'Is that... is that what I think it is?' he said, squinting and staring, his mouth open wide.

'I'm not sure,' Cate said, an unexpected laugh escaping her.

'Eliza!' he cried. 'You've found it!'

'What?' Cate cried. 'What's she found?'

Charles was grinning from ear to ear now. 'The Big One. She's found *The Big One!*'

CHAPTER TWENTY-ONE

Charles couldn't quite believe what was happening. They'd found The Big One: the beast he and Jamie had often spoken of. It existed. It *really* existed. Charles had always suspected that it was still there, hidden in the cliffs, but it was kind of a myth along the Jurassic Coast – a fun tale told over a few pints in the pub. Where was it and who would find it?

Charles grinned as he thought of the answer now as he stood in his workshop with Eliza. A young girl of eight years old had been the one to discover it. In the true spirit of Mary Anning, Eliza Rivers' name would go down in history, and she'd be the envy of many a fossil hunter who'd been scouring the beach and the surrounding area for years, unable to find the creature entombed in the cliff for two hundred million years.

It had been there all along – the ichthyosaur. An extinct marine reptile, a kind of sea dragon, that could grow to eight metres or more, and one of the greatest ever predators of the sea. Similar in shape to a modern dolphin with two large pairs of paddles, it really was something to behold and, from the size of the head they'd found which measured a good three metres,

Charles estimated that this particular beast was around twelve metres long. Nothing of this size or magnitude had ever been discovered in England before, although there had been speculation down the years as to its existence with pieces of bone belonging to a massive beast found every so often.

The local newspapers and a TV crew had been on the site pretty fast after the cliff fall, and the national press would follow. But Charles and his friends who'd come out to help recover the specimen weren't easily distracted by such a fuss. They had work to do, and quickly too, timing things with the tides so that they arrived as soon as there was room enough to work safely on the beach, and leaving when the tide came roaring back in, making work dangerous. The limestone slabs and soft lias clay that had fallen onto the beach were difficult to work with and the cold weather made conditions uncomfortable as well as dangerous, but the team worked on, recovering what they could before the tougher work of discovering what had been left behind in the cliffs began.

Permission had been sought to dig into the cliff and an area of the beach had been secured to keep members of the public safe. But the truth was that the rest of the work was best left until the spring when the conditions were better. Charles knew he had enough to be working with in the meantime and had cleared his workshop's central table to make space for the slabs that were delivered there, piecing them together like the best sort of jigsaw puzzle ever.

It was hard to keep his head at such a time. This was the stuff of which careers were made. He tried not to get too excited, but it was impossible really. It was his biggest project ever and, what was even better was that he got to share the process with Eliza. She was fascinated by it all and he watched as she traced her fingers along the great ribs and vertebrae that had been found.

Charles couldn't help thinking of Jamie as he gazed at the fossilised bones now. His son would have loved to have seen all this. It had been their dream to find the creature together. Indeed, if it hadn't been for the landslip that had taken Jamie's life, then the one that had killed Eliza's father, the ichthyosaur would never have been discovered.

Tide and time, Charles thought. They revealed everything eventually.

Can I help clean it? Eliza wrote in her notebook, showing Charles a moment later and bringing him back to the present.

'I'd be miffed if you didn't,' Charles said. 'But you do know it'll take hundreds, even thousands of hours?'

Eliza nodded, seemingly unfazed by this.

'Okay then,' he said. 'We can tell your mum that your input will be the equivalent of at least six years of homework, okay?'

Eliza smiled and nodded, and the two of them got to work.

It was a week after the cliff had collapsed on the beach and Cate was sitting in Allie's kitchen, a mug of tea in her hands.

'I still can't believe what happened with your husband,' Allie said, shaking her head before sipping her tea. 'What on earth possessed him?'

Cate took a deep breath. 'Eliza told me – well she wrote down what happened. She said that she was in the garden. She'd seen a squirrel from the window and wanted to get closer. And he just appeared.'

'God, poor girl! She must have been terrified!'

'She was. And she ran. She said she remembered the hollow lane and thought she'd be safe there because he couldn't follow in his car.'

'Why didn't she run back to the house?'

'She said he got between her and the door. It was as if he was herding her out into the lane.'

'That's horrible!' Allie said.

'We now know he'd been stalking us for a while, hiding in the hollow lane near the house and watching us for days.'

'That's so creepy.'

'Rigs knew too,' Cate said. 'The dear little boy had been trying to tell us'

'I'm just glad you're all okay. When I think of what might have happened.'

'Don't!' Cate said. 'I'm still having nightmares.'

'Are you?'

Cate nodded.

'Well, I'm not surprised,' Allie said. 'I'd be having them too, I'm sure.'

'Sometimes, I wake in the middle of the night and it's as if I'm back on the beach and I can still smell the wet earth falling from the sky.'

Allie shivered theatrically.

'I'm beginning to understand – just a little – of what Charles went through now,' Cate told her friend and Allie nodded.

'And this ex of yours,' Allie went on, 'he died right there on the beach?'

Cate nodded. 'I still can't believe he's gone.'

'But that's a good thing, isn't it? He tried to abduct Eliza.'

'Well, technically, she was his daughter.'

'But all the abuse, Cate...'

'I know!' Cate closed her eyes. 'I had to tell the police everything. It was horrible living through all those moments again. But I don't want to think about all that now.'

Allie gave her friend a hug.

'How did he find you?' she asked at length.

'The police said he hired a private investigator and they used some dodgy means to track my car.'

'Oh, god!'

'And I thought I'd been so careful.'

'Yeah, well you were dealing with a psychopath. You can never be as careful as you need to be. Anyway, he's gone and you don't need to worry about him anymore, okay?'

'Okay.'

'So,' Allie said, 'what's happening with this dinosaur thing?'

Cate smiled, glad of the change of subject. 'Actually, it's not a dinosaur at all. It's a marine reptile.'

'Yeah, yeah!' Allie said with a grin. 'You're an expert now, are you?'

Cate laughed. 'It's an ichthyosaur, but we're calling it the Elizasaur because Eliza saw it first.'

'Oh, very good!' Allie said.

'Actually, Charles has mentioned it could be named after her if it's proved to be a new species, which he strongly believes it is. Honestly, nothing like this has ever been found before.'

'Cate – that's so exciting!'

'I know! But it's early days yet. Charles and some of his friends still have to remove sections of it from the cliff. It's going to be a long process, but you should see him in his workshop with the bits he's managed to save so far. He's like a big kid. Eliza's helping too. I think she might have a future in all this palaeontology stuff. I can see she's as addicted to it as Charles is and he's giving her full credit for this find which is very kind of him. Even though she did spot it first, she wouldn't have been able to move it all on her own or prepare it or anything.'

'Oh, that's mere details!' Allie told her. 'It's spotting it that's the important thing.'

Cate grinned. 'Exactly!'

'They're going to make a great team, aren't they?'

'Yes, they really are.'

'And... has she spoken yet?' Allie dared to ask.

'No. Not since calling "Mummy" on the beach. I'm hoping this whole episode hasn't put her back, but I fear it might have. She's been through so much.'

'Oh, Cate!' Allie said, a sympathetic smile on her face. 'Still, this ex of yours – he was good for something at least. I mean, if it hadn't been for him, that ichthyosaur might never have been discovered.'

Cate mused on this. 'I suppose you're right,' she said, not having thought of it in that way before. 'It's about time something positive came from his actions.'

Allie nodded. 'And now you, Eliza and Charles can get on with your lives together.'

Cate started at that.

'What?' Allie said.

'You made us sound like a...' Cate couldn't quite finish her sentence.

'Like a what?'

'Never mind,' Cate said. But a very particular word kept circling her mind.

Family.

CHAPTER TWENTY-TWO

'Gosh, I'm really quite nervous,' Cate said, fiddling with her hair as she glanced in the hallway mirror at Hollow House.

'You've got nothing to be nervous about.'

'Charles – I'm about to meet your mother for the first time!'

He sighed, taking her hands in his in an attempt to calm her and, most likely, himself. 'She probably won't even look at you,' he told her. 'And you mustn't be disappointed if that happens. She often doesn't even recognise me.'

'That must be so hard.'

'It isn't easy,' he confessed as he grabbed his coat and put it on. 'Right, are we ready?'

'Eliza?' Cate called, watching as her daughter emerged from the workshop a moment later.

'Have you been tinkering with those bones again?' Cate asked.

Eliza nodded.

'Charles – is that allowed when you're not supervising?'

He shrugged. 'She knows what she's doing.'

Cate smiled, surging with pride.

'You know what they call you in the village?' Cate asked Charles.

'What do you mean?'

'I mean your nickname.'

He frowned. 'I have a nickname?'

'You really don't know about it?'

'No! *Tell* me!'

Cate laughed. 'Mr Fossil.'

'What?'

'They call you Mr Fossil.'

'Since when?'

'I don't know. Since forever probably.'

'You're making it up.'

'Why would I make it up?'

He shook his head. 'I suppose it'll be even worse now with this new find.'

'The whole world will soon know your name,' Cate told him as the three of them left the house together.

Cate sat in the front of the Land Rover next to Charles, her fingers tying themselves in knots in her lap right up until the moment they arrived at the care home.

'Okay?' Charles asked as he cut the engine.

Cate nodded. 'Yes.'

The Christmas decorations had just gone up at Beeches and there was an enormous tree in the entrance hall, sparkling with silver, gold and green decorations, reminding Cate just how close the big day was now. Charles had already agreed that she and Eliza could decorate Hollow House and they were going to choose a tree together. She'd even persuaded him to remove his fossil collection from the dining room table so that they could eat there on Christmas Day. She'd laughed at his startled expression when she'd first suggested it, but he'd finally agreed.

And now here she was about to meet his mother. Anna Thorner.

'This way,' Charles said to Cate, leading the way through reception and saying hello to the woman on the desk as he signed them all in. Cate felt his hand in the small of her back and was grateful for his reassurance.

'Is this the room?' Cate asked as Charles stopped outside a door that stood ajar.

Before he could answer, Eliza entered and, to Cate's surprise, walked straight up to Charles's mother who was sitting in a chair beside a window and hugged her.

Cate and Charles followed her inside.

'Hello, Mum,' he said. 'You remember Eliza, don't you?'

His mother beamed him a smile and nodded. She was having a good day.

'And I'd like to introduce you to Cate,' he went on.

'Hello, Mrs Thorner,' Cate said, moving forward.

Mrs Thorner gazed into her face and then looked up at her son.

'Is this your new family, Charles?' she asked him.

Cate gasped at her use of the word, and Charles was so surprised by her question that he didn't answer at all. But he didn't need to because somebody else answered for him.

'Yes,' Eliza said, a huge smile on her face as she looked from Charles's mother to Charles and then to her own mother whose eyes were full of tears of joy. 'We're a family.'

THE END

ACKNOWLEDGEMENTS

Huge thanks to Chris and Tracey for sharing their fossil journey with me and for being on hand to answer all my questions while I was writing this book. And thank you to Ted the terrier who inspired Rigs!

Thanks to Chris Andrew at the Lyme Regis Museum for showing us some special treasures before the school party arrived!

Big thanks to Marc Jones at the Natural History Museum in London.

Thanks also to Holly Lyne.

To Catriona for her care and attention, and to Design for Writers for their wonderful cover.

And, as ever, thank you to my husband Roy for being the very best of fossil hunting partners.

I found a number of books and publications both useful and enjoyable during the research and writing of my novel: Christopher McGowan's *The Dragon Seekers*, Robert Macfarlane's *Holloway*, Richard Edmonds's *Fossils*, Chris Moore's *Attenborough and the Great Sea Dragon*, and Tracy Chevalier's novel *Remarkable Creatures*.

ALSO BY VICTORIA CONNELLY

Christmas at the Castle

Christmas at the Cottage

The Wrong Ghost

The Christmas Collection Volume One

The Christmas Collection Volume Two

A Summer to Remember

Wish You Were Here

The Runaway Actress

Molly's Millions

Flights of Angels

Irresistible You

Three Graces

It's Magic (A compilation volume)

A Weekend with Mr Darcy

The Perfect Hero (Dreaming of Mr Darcy)

Mr Darcy Forever

Christmas With Mr Darcy

Happy Birthday Mr Darcy

At Home with Mr Darcy

Escape to Mulberry Cottage (non-fiction)

A Year at Mulberry Cottage (non-fiction)

Summer at Mulberry Cottage (non-fiction)

Finding Old Thatch (non-fiction)

The Garden at Old Thatch (non-fiction)

Secret Pyramid (children's adventure)

The Audacious Auditions of Jimmy Catesby (children's adventure)

ABOUT THE AUTHOR

Victoria Connelly is the bestselling author of *The Rose Girls* and *The Beauty of Broken Things*.

With over a million sales, her books have been translated into many languages. The first, *Flights of Angels*, was made into a film in Germany. Victoria flew to Berlin to see it being made and even played a cameo role in it.

A Weekend with Mr Darcy, the first in her popular Austen Addicts series about fans of Jane Austen has sold over 100,000 copies. She is also the author of several romantic comedies including *The Runaway Actress* which was nominated for the

Romantic Novelists' Association's Best Romantic Comedy of the Year.

Victoria was brought up in Norfolk, England before moving to Yorkshire where she got married in a medieval castle. After 11 years in London, she moved to rural Suffolk where she lives in a pink thatched cottage with her artist husband, a springer spaniel and her ex-battery hens.

To hear about future releases and receive a **free ebook** sign up for her newsletter at www.victoriaconnelly.com.

VICTORIA CONNELLY

The

BEAUTY
of
BROKEN
THINGS

The Beauty of Broken Things

United by tragedy, can two broken souls make each other whole?

After the tragic loss of his wife, Helen, Luke Hansard is desperate to keep her memory alive. In an effort to stay close to her, he reaches out to an online friend Helen often mentioned: a reclusive photographer with a curious interest in beautiful but broken objects. But first he must find her—and she doesn't want to be found.

Orla Kendrick lives alone in the ruins of a remote Suffolk castle, hiding from the haunting past that has left her physically and emotionally scarred. In her fortress, she can keep a safe distance from prying eyes, surrounded by her broken treasures and insulated from the world outside.

When Luke tracks Orla down, he is determined to help her in the way Helen wanted to: by encouraging her out of her isolation and back into the world. But Orla has never seen her refuge as a prison and, when painful secrets and dangerous threats begin to resurface, Luke's good deed is turned on its head.

As they work through their grief for Helen in very different ways, will these two broken souls be able to heal?

Printed in Great Britain
by Amazon

23799150R00162